# THE 50 BEST
# (AND WORST)
# BUSINESS DEALS
# OF ALL TIME

By
Michael Craig

## CAREER
## PRESS

Franklin Lakes, NJ

THE 50 BEST (AND WORST) BUSINESS DEALS OF ALL TIME
Cover design by Design Solutions
Printed in the U.S.A. by Book-mart Press

To order this title, please call toll-free 1-800-CAREER-1 (NJ and Canada:
201-848-0310) to order using VISA or MasterCard, or for further information
on books from Career Press.

CAREER
PRESS

The Career Press, Inc.
3 Tice Road, PO Box 687, Franklin Lakes, NJ 07417
www.careerpress.com

## Library of Congress Cataloging-in-Publication Data

Craig, Michael.
    The 50 best (and worst) business deals of all time / by Michael Craig.
        p.      cm.
    Includes index.
    ISBN 1-56414-478-X (paper)
    1. Negotiation in business—United States—Case studies. I. Title: Fifty best (and worst)
business deals of all time. II. Title.

    HD58.6 .C73    2000
    658.4'052—dc21

                                                                    00-037899

# *ACKNOWLEDGMENTS*

This book would not have been possible without the resources of the Internet, particularly the excellent archives of the leading business publications and newspapers. Although LEXIS/NEXIS is a great resource, I look forward to the time when those archives are available for free from their sources.

Franklin Dohanyos, the world's greatest publicist, who was generous enough to introduce me to his editor.

Michael Lewis, the editor in question, who was willing to take a chance on an unpublished writer.

Jodi Brandon and Kristen Mohn, able editors at Career Press who turned a raw manuscript into a finished product.

My 13 years as a securities lawyer provided me with the foundation for this book—exposure to the significant business transactions during that period, and the tools to evaluate them. Nevertheless, I could not have compiled this list of transactions without the input of many people, who reminded me of deals about which I had forgotten, or educated me on deals about which I never knew. My dad, Robert Craig, reminded me about the disastrous LBO of Revco. My brother, Barton Craig, encouraged me to devote some space to the three great real estate transactions in American history, as well as the most famous baseball trade of all time. Richard Sheiner reminded me of the circumstances under which Microsoft entered the operating-system business, and that the HFS-CUC merger into Cendant was not only a great fraud, but a bad business deal as well.

My mom, Myrna Messenger, was the first person to encourage me to write a book, when I was 12 years old. Thanks, and sorry it took me 29 years to finish one.

My greatest gratitude goes to my wife, Jo Anne, and my children, Barry, Ellie, and Valerie. They were unconditionally understanding of the commitment necessary to produce this work. Jo Anne, in addition, is expert at talking me out of bad or idiosyncratic writing.

# CONTENTS

# INTRODUCTION

I have always been fascinated by big business deals—the money, the strategy, the risks, the personalities. Before I became a participant in some of these deals, I assumed that, at this high level, there was little opportunity for taking advantage. When big companies and very rich individuals engage in big-money deals, everyone is smart and experienced. Everyone has countless lawyers, bankers, and accountants advising every move. How could the process not be extremely rational?

I was in for a rude awakening. My introduction to deal making came during a contested takeover of Roper, an appliance maker, in the late 1980s. Whirlpool and Roper had a friendly deal, but General Electric (GE) made a higher, hostile bid. I was representing some shareholders challenging Roper's agreement to be taken over by Whirlpool.

The parties fought like cats and dogs. GE sued Whirlpool and Roper in Delaware Chancery Court (as had my firm, as well as several others), claiming violations of Delaware corporate law, and in federal court, claiming violations of federal securities law. Whirlpool and Roper turned around and sued GE, claiming its attempted takeover violated federal securities law as well. There was also a separate federal antitrust suit, but I don't remember who sued who.

Expedited discovery was ongoing in all the actions, so I attended the deposition of Whirlpool's CEO on a Sunday morning in March at a Chicago law firm's office. When I arrived early at the nearly deserted building, I was escorted to the largest conference room I had ever seen; the table must have seated 50. By 9 a.m., every seat was full, and additional chairs were brought in for the overflow. During one of the GE attorneys' introductions on the record, a fight broke out, necessitating a half-hour delay.

When we resumed, the GE attorney made it through his introduction and was about to ask his first question when a new disagreement arose. GE had both securities and antitrust attorneys present, and both planned to ask questions. This was contrary to Delaware's practice of only one attorney per side asking questions—an arcane rule that had no application to this kind of case—and the Whirlpool lawyer was not going to let the witness answer questions unless GE agreed that one lawyer would ask all the questions.

First, they argued on the record. Then, they screamed at each other off the record. Each side called its Delaware counsel and the entire chorus of attorneys had a conference call with the Delaware chancellor, at his home. Only one attorney would ask questions.

This necessitated a two-hour break. Out of spite, GE's attorneys were going to write out every single question to be asked by the one attorney. They were going to make Whirlpool—and everyone else in that room—pay for delaying the deposition by delaying it even more themselves.

When we finally resumed, it was nearly noon. Progress was amazingly slow. Every question met an objection, along with various threats to pull the witness from the deposition and call judges around the country at home for emergency rulings. This made all of us very cranky, a condition not helped by the fact that it was unseasonably warm in the conference room and there was no one in the building to turn off the heat or turn on the air conditioner.

For lunch, one of the GE lawyers had ordered a wedding-sized deli tray. We didn't make a dent in the thing.

To this day, I believe that tray helped end the hostilities. No one came to remove it when we resumed for the afternoon session. As the questions, answers, objections, and threats piled up during the afternoon, that tray took on an animal-like presence. As the afternoon sun beat down on that deli tray, the overheated room filled with a smell not experienced in Chicago since they shut down the slaughterhouses.

The deli tray wore down the resolve of the GE, Whirlpool, and Roper attorneys. By 3 p.m., Whirlpool's attorney seemed to run out of gas. By 4 p.m., GE's attorney (literally) lost his stomach for asking argumentative questions. As we all staggered out of that room, the lead attorneys practically apologized for making us endure the ordeal.

A few days later, GE and Whirlpool agreed to carve up Roper. GE would get the company, Whirlpool would get the brand name, and shareholders would get a sweetened offer. Everybody won, but I could hardly call the process "rational."

I learned, in a dozen years as a securities attorney, that the outcome is rarely the result of a rational, mechanical process. There is plenty of room for the best operators to maneuver, even in those conference rooms crowded with white-shoe bankers and Ivy League–educated lawyers (and rotting corned beef).

Still, as chaotic as the process seemed, certain people—and certain methods—usually won out. The investment partnerships organized by leveraged buyout pioneers Kohlberg Kravis Roberts & Co. (KKR) always seemed to earn phenomenal returns. Gordon Cain was regarded as a master of chemical-company buyouts; he made a billion dollars for himself, his employees, and his partners in one year as a result of buying up a bunch of chemical plants in 1987.

In the same way, certain strategies were destined to lose. Merv Griffin entered into what looked like an insane deal to buy Resorts International. He sold its jewel, the unfinished Taj Mahal, but kept all the debt. That enterprise went bankrupt in a year. Likewise, it seemed like William Farley was asking for trouble when he took over West Point Pepperell, which was already leveraged up to the eyeballs as a result of Pepperell having recently completed a hostile takeover. That deal turned into a disaster as well.

Patterns began to emerge, refined by extensive research. The result? Ten rules that should provide the basics of a deal maker's handbook. Neither the rules nor the 50 deals profiled as examples are exhaustive. There are certainly other factors that can influence the success or failure of a business deal, and it would be impossible for any qualified group to agree on the 50 best and worst deals (or even on the criteria for measuring them).

I can, however, say this with certainty: These rules describe the best way to conduct business transactions, and you would be hard pressed to find many better (or worse) deals than the ones profiled in this book.

## *The Ten Rules*

1. Focus on your strengths.
2. Take advantage of your adversary's weakness.
3. Find value where others don't see it.
4. Don't get caught up in the wanting.
5. Innovate.
6. Take care of the little people.
7. Be a pest.
8. Do your homework.
9. Predict the future and seize it.
10. Don't negotiate with your betters.

Although each of the 50 deals profiled demonstrates at least one of the 10 rules, several deals illustrate more than one rule. For example, taking advantage of your adversary's weaknesses (Rule 2/Chapter 2) is an important factor in many of the deals profiled throughout the book. Many of the deals in Chapter 2 focus on the bonanzas obtained when a buyer encounters a "desperate seller." Desperate sellers pop up in deals elsewhere in the book. Leon Black found himself the beneficiary of government largesse when the California Department of Insurance offered to sell him the massive junk bond portfolio of ex-Drexel Burnham Lambert client Executive Life. To score political points by bringing the Executive Life rehabilitation to a quick conclusion, Commissioner Garamendi let Black's group get away with an obvious lowball offer. This echoed the situation from a few years earlier when Ronald Perelman, dealing with an embarrassed federal government, was able to wring billions in guarantees and tax benefits to take five S&Ls off its hands in its effort to sweep the S&L crisis under the table. (See Chapter 10 for profiles of these deals.)

# CHAPTER 1

# RULE 1: Focus on your strengths

$    LTV's acquisition of Jones & Laughlin Steel (1968)

$    Priscilla Presley's control of the Elvis Presley Estate (1982)

$    IBM's acquisition of Rolm (1984)

$    Kohlberg Kravis Roberts & Co.'s acquisition of Beatrice (1986)

$    Management LBO of Revco (1986)

$    Nelson Peltz and Peter May's sale of Triangle Industries to Pechiney (1988)

$    AT&T's takeover of NCR (1991)

$    Kohlberg Kravis Roberts & Co.'s restructuring of Flagstar (1992)

$    Novell's acquisition of WordPerfect (1994)

If there is any rule in deal making that is nearly universal in its application, it is that you should focus on what you do best. Although it is possible to go into a negotiation with inferior abilities and plans and still come out on top, that would have to be the exception. Far more often, the winner of the deal stuck more closely with a well-thought-out plan. Nearly always, the loser of the deal was seeking something that was better left alone. Where there is a clear winner and loser, the loser usually strayed into an unfamiliar area, reducing the probability of success.

Look at the hundreds of millions Priscilla Presley made for the Elvis Presley Estate. Priscilla has proven herself an unbelievably shrewd businesswoman, and has gotten terrific advice, but when she became an executor of her late ex-husband's estate in 1979, all she was trying to do was assure some level of financial security for her daughter and preserve some of Elvis' legacy. She could have cashed out of Graceland, cut a deal with the IRS, and invested the remaining money so Lisa Marie could live comfortably. Instead, she invested the remaining cash from the estate to turn Graceland into a tourist attraction. She knew Elvis' appeal and, with her advisors, learned to exploit it.

For financiers, the best deals are the ones where they control the most variables. As deals get bigger, it becomes impossible to control it all, so a level of comfort may be all the deal maker has to evaluate the likelihood of success. Leveraged buyout firm Kohlberg Kravis Roberts & Co. (KKR) has a time-tested method of performing a leveraged buyout (LBO). It does not guarantee success, but it usually works. When the firm can stick to the plan, as it did with Beatrice, the money literally comes racing in. KKR also used its formula successfully in LBOs of Safeway (see Chapter 3) and Duracell (see Chapter 6).

KKR is the most successful organization devoted entirely to doing deals in the last 25 years, if not ever. Still, it has had some failures. Although its formula for doing deals has changed over time and from deal to deal, when it significantly deviates from the things it does best—finding good management, providing financial incentives to get it to perform, cutting overhead, identifying and negotiating favorable asset sales—the likelihood it will make a mistake increases significantly. When the company paid $300 million to obtain control of the recapitalization of Flagstar (parent company of Denny's and other restaurants), it was on unfamiliar ground and lost its entire investment in a bankruptcy.

Gordon Cain, though less famous than KKR, similarly developed a game plan for petrochemical buyouts, borrowing from his long career at DuPont. After leading two successful employee buyouts of former DuPont chemical divisions, Cain, at age 75, engineered the creation of Cain Chemical out of seven commodity chemical businesses. His experience and well-tested strategies proved valuable: He correctly recognized that he was catching the cheap end of the pricing cycle, and he quickly made changes he knew would work. Cain, his financial partners, and his employees made approximately a billion dollars in one year. (See Chapter 6 for a profile of this deal.)

Nelson Peltz and Peter May, in building Triangle Industries on a mountain of debt, were considered little more than Michael Milken's pawns in the mid-1980s. They knew how to run the packaging business, though, and turned out to be builders rather than bust-up artists. They pieced together a formidable company, which Pechiney bought for a premium price in 1988. Peltz's and May's stock, which was purchased for almost nothing (except for borrowed money, which the acquirer became responsible for), became worth $850 million.

Leon Black was a major player in junk bond–financed takeovers with Drexel Burnham Lambert during the 1980s. After Drexel collapsed in 1990, Black emerged as a leading "vulture capitalist," using his knowledge of junk bonds and the companies issuing them to buy the bonds at attractive prices. His best deal was his purchase, on behalf of Credit Lyonnais, of the massive junk-bond portfolio of former Drexel client Executive Life Insurance Co. (See Chapter 10 for a profile of this deal.)

Unfortunately, the simple advice to stick with what you know is usually proven in the negative in big deals. Conglomerates are susceptible to this problem; if you make a habit of buying companies in a variety of businesses, you can easily venture into an area of ignorance. This killed off the Conglomerate Era of the 1960s, when LTV bought Jones & Laughlin Steel. CEO James Ling, in Congressional antitrust hearings attacking the purchase, bragged that he knew nothing about the steel industry. LTV nearly went bankrupt and, after Ling's dismissal, the company focused on its steel operations, eventually sliding into bankruptcy in 1986.

Consider the strange dance of industrial giants AT&T and IBM. So concerned was each that the other would encroach on its territory that each attempted a preemptive strike on the other's business. IBM bought Rolm, a maker of telephone systems for business. AT&T bought NCR, a computer maker. Both acquisitions involved culture clashes, failure to integrate operations, and difficulty competing with companies much better than the ones they acquired. Both companies slinked away from these forays with huge losses. In AT&T's case, it already had a computer-making subsidiary, but it was such a loser that the NCR takeover was viewed by some as AT&T's attempt to pay to have NCR take it off AT&T's hands.

Novell, the maker of network operating systems, tried to expand into application software by purchasing WordPerfect, a deal that ended so badly that it cost the company its leadership in network operating systems. Novell overpaid for a troubled company that it had no expertise to fix. It lost a bundle when it was forced to resell WordPerfect a couple years later, but the damage had been done: Novell not only failed to scare Microsoft out of its lead in application software, but Microsoft used the time (not to mention

Novell's diversion of resources) to challenge Novell with Windows NT. Many software companies had their epitaphs written by Bill Gates, but most of them at least went kicking and screaming to their deaths; Novell, though not dead, seemed to leap out the window on its own volition as a result of this deal.

Managing weakness is an important business attribute, especially for deal makers. It is difficult to admit failure, take an earnings hit, fold the tents, and go home, but it is occasionally necessary. Too often, as AT&T did, companies dealt a losing hand foolishly raise the stakes. This exact problem put Revco in bankruptcy. Its CEO had done a successful job, but when the chain of drug stores had a few problems, he became obsessed with someone trying to take Revco over. That led to bad acquisitions, angry dissident shareholders, and a botched leveraged buyout.

Focusing on what you do well and avoiding areas of weakness seem like obvious ideas. Nevertheless, in high-stakes deal making, only the best operators can stick with their plans—and even then, they occasionally stumble—and many excellent companies, such as AT&T, can venture into areas of weakness.

# LTV's acquisition of Jones & Laughlin Steel (1968)

Ling-Temco-Vought (LTV, though it did not officially adopt that designation until 1972) was one of the high-fliers during the Conglomerate Era of business deals in the late 1960s. Along with companies such as Textron, Litton, Gulf + Western, and ITT, LTV became involved in an endless series of purchases, sales, and financings that befuddled analysts and were generally seen as brilliant by an adoring bull market. For LTV, it was one deal too many when the 1968 purchase of Jones & Laughlin Steel for $465 million brought the whole structure crashing down. It led not only to LTV's crashing stock price and founder James Ling's ouster, but also to a long, slow decline that ended in bankruptcy 18 years later.

James Ling founded Ling Electric in 1947, with $2,000 in capital and his sales and electrical abilities. The company flourished, and by 1955, Ling was selling shares to the public out of a booth at the Texas State Fair. He soon recognized that his public status gave him access to three forms of currency to expand: cash (now more available as bank loans because his stock, with its liquidity, could secure it), stock (which could be issued in exchange for assets), and debt (now available through access to public debt markets).

Ling soon acquired the other components of LTV, as well as many other companies. When a falloff in military procurements in the early 1960s hurt the Chance-Vought operation, harming company-wide results (with regard to earnings and revenue), Ling vowed never to be too reliant on any one business. To protect his company's stock price, he also began to engage in constant recapitalizations, involving a dizzying array of spin-offs, holding companies, partial stock sales, debt offerings, warrants, and exchange offers. Some cleaned up the balance sheet, which ballooned with debt as a result of the myriad of acquisitions, and others appeared to increase value because they simply confused shareholders and analysts so much that they were willing to assume that Ling's genius would make the deals work.

By the mid-1960s, Ling began acquiring other conglomerates. One profitable acquisition was Wilson & Co. in 1966. Wilson was a leading meat packer, and also had sporting goods, pet food, and pharmaceuticals operations. Wall Street referred to the company as "Goofballs, Golfballs, and Meatballs." Accompanying the transaction was the now-familiar round of divestitures, leasebacks, stock offerings, and debt financings. In 1968, LTV also acquired Greatamerica, which owned insurance companies, Braniff Airlines, and National Car Rental.

The stock market loved LTV and James Ling. LTV's stock went from $10 to $170 per share during the 1960s. Ling was featured on numerous magazine covers. It was not uncommon to joke about conglomerates soon owning everything, and many financial people predicted that at some future time, the stock market would consist solely of large, diversified companies.

Whether LTV's 1968 acquisition of Jones & Laughlin Steel (J & L) caused this vision to fall apart, or merely coincided with the demise of that vision, is unclear. It is clear, however, that Ling ignored numerous warning signs and proceeded, despite many good reasons for passing on this deal.

J & L was clearly undervalued, but that was all it had going for it. It was part of an industry Ling admitted he knew nothing about. It did not have assets that could be sold or spun off to assist in financing. It was a big user of capital and had a large unionized labor force. (Along with LTV's later concentration on the steel industry, it was the multibillion dollar under-funding of pension obligations that pushed the company into bankruptcy in 1986.) As a cash offer—$465 million to buy 63 percent—it put a terminal strain on LTV's already huge debt. Finally, it provided a target for the government to take an anticonglomerate stand.

Although there was little basis, the new Nixon administration challenged the purchase on antitrust grounds. The challenge gave Ling an out, which he should have taken. He was having trouble selling assets and issuing stock and debt necessary to complete the purchase. Still, he pushed on, later settling with the government by selling Braniff and Okonite (a copper and wire company) and promising to do no big deals for 10 years.

By 1970, the acquisition had wrecked the company. It announced a 1969 loss of $38 million (compared with 1968 profits of $29 million). Its stock price dropped back down to $10 per share. The debt issued in connection with these final moves traded at 15 to 25 cents on the dollar. In May 1970, at the request of the board of directors, Ling resigned.

Under CEO Paul Thayer from 1970 to 1982, LTV restructured and enjoyed some temporary success. It divested itself of nearly all its assets *except* steel, and acquired additional steel companies. Thayer's successor bought Republic Steel in 1984, and LTV, still burdened by high debt, stuck with billions in underfunded pension liabilities, filed for bankruptcy in 1986.

## What Went Wrong

James Ling and LTV succeeded because they continually acquired companies susceptible to asset sales, spin-offs, and other financial maneuvers. The purchase of Jones & Laughlin Steel plunged the company into the problematic and cyclical steel business, about which it knew nothing. The acquisition also provided Ling with no opportunity to exercise the financial legerdemain Wall Street had come to expect and reward.

# Priscilla Presley's control of the Elvis Presley Estate (1982)

Elvis Presley was arguably the most popular entertainer of the twentieth century, and billions had been spent on his records, movies, concerts, and merchandise even at the time of his death. Still, he left an estate of only $4.9 million. Worse, the estate appeared to have little means of growing and was getting eaten up by expenses.

By the time of Elvis' death in 1977, he was waylaid financially by bad business deals and bad spending habits. Elvis sold a billion albums in his life, but had a poor royalty deal. His manager, "Colonel" Tom Parker, negotiated a good deal in 1957, but rarely had it increased as record prices increased over the next 20 years. In addition, Parker received 50 percent, and Elvis also had an agent who received 10 percent.

For all the management fees Elvis was paying, he should have been shielded from an incredibly stupid deal in 1973. Hard up for money, Elvis directed Parker to sell the 700 master recordings he had made during his career (which included the rights to future royalties as well as the ability to use the masters to make future compilations). RCA bought them for the rock-bottom price of $5.4 million. After paying Parker ($2.7 million) and the IRS ($1.3 million), Elvis received less than $1.5 million for what were arguably the most valuable recordings in music history. With the huge increase in demand for Elvis recordings immediately after his death, the estate probably lost out, even after deducting for Parker, between $10 and $15 million in royalties in 1977. Twenty-five years later, Elvis was *still* earning more per year for RCA than any other artist.

Then there were Elvis' spending habits, which necessitated the sale of the master recordings. Elvis owned at least five lavish residences, four airplanes, and scores of expensive automobiles. He was generous to a fault, buying hundreds of cars as gifts, giving away untold sums to family, friends, and hangers-on.

In those days of higher tax rates, Elvis never received—or never listened to—tax advice. He always paid the top rate, never took advantage of legal tax shelters then available, and did things such as donating $50,000 to local churches every Christmas and not claiming the deductions.

Elvis could get away with these extravagances during his life because his answer when the money ran out was so simple: Get more. He was good for $1 million per movie (even when the movies were lousy), $250,000 for a recording session, and more than $100,000 for a concert. In his later years, as his dangerous lifestyle began to catch up with him, he still toured extensively because he needed the money.

His estate of $4.9 million, however, could not call on Elvis to make more money any of those ways. (At least, it didn't realize it could.) Vernon

Presley, Elvis' father, was the executor for two years, until his death in 1979. Priscilla Presley, Elvis' ex-wife and mother of Lisa Marie Presley (the will's beneficiary), became executor, along with Memphis accountant Joseph Hanks and a representative of a Memphis bank.

Under Elvis' will, the estate was to be held in trust for Lisa Marie until she turned 25 (in 1993). Priscilla was shocked to find out, however, that the estate was being depleted and might not last that long. Elvis' Memphis home, Graceland, had been shuttered but ran up expenses of $500,000 per year, mostly for security and insurance. (All those loyal fans wandering around outside the gates were an expensive nuisance.) Yearly income from Elvis' post-1973 royalties and some merchandising (after Tom Parker's 50 percent was deducted) was $1 million in the year after Presley's death, but only half that amount by 1981. Worst of all, the federal government had recalculated the value of the estate, taking into account the money made since Elvis' death, figuring it at $22.5 million, and slapped on a $10 million inheritance tax.

Beginning in 1979, Priscilla educated herself on ways to save the estate. Working with Jack Soden, the junior partner of Priscilla's financial advisor (who had just died in an airplane crash), she worked out a strategy. Rather than sell Graceland to cut losses and pay the IRS, they would invest the remaining cash in the estate (about $560,000) and open Graceland to the public as a tourist attraction. To manage this and other nascent businesses, they created Elvis Presley Enterprises, Inc. (EPE). They spent nearly a year visiting residences on display throughout the United States such as the Hearst Castle and Monticello.

Graceland was an immediate hit with the public when it opened in July 1982 (a month before the five-year anniversary of Elvis's death). It took just 38 days for Priscilla and Soden to recoup the estate's investment. Now with some breathing room, the pair, along with the other executors and a small team of advisors, mapped out a comprehensive strategy. First, they would salvage what they could from Elvis' music catalogue. Second, they would do something about Parker and his confiscatory contract. Third, they would use some of the money to fight merchandisers who were capitalizing on Elvis' name and image without paying the estate. They would also expand into the merchandising business themselves. Fourth, they would continue improving and capitalizing on Graceland.

Parker had wisely insisted that songwriters trying to get Elvis to record their songs give Elvis a songwriter credit, but he had been careless about registering and obtaining royalties for the music publishing rights to the songs. EPE began asserting those rights, and now generates a stream of income from them. Nothing could be done, unfortunately, with the rights to the pre-1973 performances themselves, though the estate litigated the matter with RCA and won, at least, $1 million in royalties withheld from post-1973 music.

The disputes with Parker were resolved in 1983. A guardian *ad litem* (a court-appointed representative, in this case because Lisa Marie was a minor) protecting Lisa Marie's interests concluded that Parker, since Elvis' death, "violated his duty both to Elvis and the estate," taking actions that were "excessive, imprudent...and beyond all reasonable bounds of industry standards." At the probate court's direction, Parker was sued. He settled, agreeing to sever all ties with the estate.

EPE then hired lawyers and lobbyists to stake its claims to Elvis' likeness and name. When a federal court ruled against EPE on the issue of whether there is an intellectual property right to a dead person's image, EPE convinced the state of Tennessee to pass a law similar to California's establishing such a right. The law has been upheld in court, and the estate remains vigorous in controlling Elvis' likeness, approving all merchandising (and getting a cut). EPE has filed more than 100 lawsuits on the issue.

Finally, Priscilla Presley and Soden have carefully mined the public's interest in Elvis through Graceland. In its first year, it attracted 300,000 visitors. That number rose to 500,000 in 1988, and it increases a little every year. In 1999, 750,000 people visited. Graceland brings in more than $20 million annually. Prices have gradually risen, and the quality and quantity of the attractions have improved. A visitor can now tour not only the mansion but a museum of Elvis' cars, his tour bus, and two of his airplanes. Surrounding land has been purchased, and Graceland now contains a visitors' center, complete with merchandise. EPE even paid Colonel Parker an estimated $10 million for his collection of Elvis' memorabilia, including some of Priscilla's love letters to Elvis. Working on the model developed and refined by Disney, the estate is always on the lookout for new ways to extend the Elvis brand name: A shopping-mall tour of Elvis memorabilia with several permanent sites brings in $5 million per year; hotels, restaurants, night clubs, theme parks, and expansion outside the United States are all under consideration.

Everything is being done with care. Although, for example, it is easy to imagine an Elvis-themed restaurant, or even an entire hotel resort, thriving in Las Vegas, the estate is proceeding slowly, first with a restaurant in

Memphis. According to Jack Soden, "You might ask why we're not there already. If Elvis fails in Las Vegas, he would not fail quietly."

*Forbes* estimated in 1999 that Elvis' 1998 earnings were $35 million. (Dead Elvis began out-earning live Elvis's best earning year in 1988.) With that kind of cash flow, estimates of Lisa Marie Presley's net worth of between $250 and $600 million are not unreasonable.

## What Went Right

From the idea that those people hanging around the gates of Graceland might pay for the privilege of peeking inside, an empire was born. Priscilla Presley and her advisors have always known the value of Elvis as a brand name, and have always maximized that value with limited financial risk.

# IBM's acquisition of Rolm (1984)

Starting in the mid-1970s, IBM spent heavily to diversify beyond computers into telecommunications. The company was trying to counter some (largely unsuccessful) moves AT&T was making into the computer business. The final, and most expensive, move by IBM was the acquisition of Rolm in 1984. In three transactions in 1983 and 1984, IBM purchased the company for about $1.6 billion.

IBM entered the relationship with a history of failures in the telecommunications equipment business. It developed a private branch exchange (PBX) system for businesses in Europe, but it was such a failure that IBM never sold it in the United States. It lost hundreds of millions in a joint-venture investment called Satellite Business Systems. It traded its share in that business to MCI for 16-percent ownership in MCI, but MCI languished and IBM sold out long before that company became one of the great business successes of the last two decades. In 1982, it attempted a joint venture with equipment maker Mitel, but Mitel was unable to develop the product in time. In 1983, IBM bought 15 percent of Rolm, a leading PBX company, for $228 million. It later increased its stake to 23 percent.

Rolm was, at the time, what could be called a typical Silicon Valley success story. Led by a charismatic CEO, M. Kenneth Oshman, Rolm's employees worked hard in an entrepreneurial fashion, were compensated accordingly, and enjoyed perks including an employee swimming pool and Friday beer bashes. In less than 10 years, it developed into the third largest seller of PBX systems.

In late 1984, IBM bought the rest of Rolm for $1.3 billion. While most analysts and reporters focused on the potential clash of corporate cultures, largely ignored was the fact that Rolm's business was falling apart. Rolm's core PBX product was eight years old and was losing market share because of its age. Worse, competition in the field was burgeoning, and Rolm's competitors—AT&T, the Baby Bells—were selling products at a loss to increase market share. In 1984, Rolm reported a quarterly loss and, in the year before the acquisition, saw sales rise more than 30 percent but earnings rise only 6 percent. IBM saw these problems up close as a 23-percent owner of Rolm. Its 17-month relationship with Rolm had not been productive, despite an attempt to develop products together.

People were concerned that Rolm would lose its free-spirited ethic when acquired by button-down IBM. When IBM's top executives attended a Rolm party and IBM CEO Jack Akers, the embodiment of IBM's conservatism, had a beer with some Rolm employees, people assumed the two corporate cultures had begun to mesh. It was a very naive way of thinking. In the first year as an IBM subsidiary, Rolm lost about $100 million and market share. Within the next few years, IBM's hands-off policy regarding its acquisition changed. It introduced Rolm employees to its corporate bureaucracy. It sent its own salespeople on calls with Rolm's sales force. CEO Oshman left, and many other executives and sales people left after him. When Rolm regained market share, it was only as a result of drastic price-cutting. The losses rose to approximately $300 million per year.

In 1988, after losing an estimated $1 billion in less than four years of operating Rolm, IBM sold most of Rolm (all but a portion of its marketing) to Siemens for $1.15 billion. It sold the rest to Siemens in 1992. IBM seemed to give up its attempts to combine computers and telephones to compete with AT&T.

Ironically, AT&T's attempt to combine computers and telephones, culminating in the acquisition of NCR (a deal profiled later in this chapter), proceeded in an almost identical fashion: years of trying to enter the other giant's markets without success, purchase of a company in that field with a strong culture, destruction of that culture, withdrawal amid failure, and humiliation. The good news, if there was any, is that IBM lost *only* $1 to $1.5 billion on its folly; AT&T lost at least four times as much.

## What Went Wrong

IBM was so anxious to expand into the telephone business that it ignored Rolm's weaknesses. It also neglected Rolm's corporate culture, which was important to Rolm's success.

# Kohlberg Kravis Roberts & Co.'s acquisition of Beatrice (1986)

Not every Kohlberg Kravis Roberts & Co. (KKR) deal was a bonanza. Several required restructurings, and one of its large deals, Jim Walters Industries, ended in bankruptcy court as a high-profile failure. Its restructuring of Flagstar also ended in bankruptcy. (See a profile of this deal later in this chapter.) In addition, KKR did not get every last dollar out of all its good deals. But even with problems, there is no substitute for a good business plan and smart people to implement it. In KKR's 1986 buyout of Beatrice, the largest LBO ever at the time, many things went wrong, but the company stuck with its plan and made itself and its investors nearly $2 billion in four years.

Until KKR came along, Beatrice itself was a study of a series of good deals gone bad. By the mid-1970s, Beatrice was a model of a successful food conglomerate. CEO James Dutt, however, reversed nearly a century of smart deals and smart operations. Corporate overhead became bloated with superfluous advertising (the infamous "We're Beatrice" campaign), abuse of assets ($70 million to fund two auto racing teams when the company had little connection to racing), a revolving-door executive suite, and ill-advised acquisitions. The latter reached a head when Dutt had Beatrice pay a premium price to outbid management's attempt to buy Esmark Corp., in retaliation for Esmark CEO Donald Kelly's attempt to acquire Beatrice the year before.

Beatrice stock had for several years been a laggard in the early 1980s bull market. Dutt was finally kicked out in a boardroom coup in August 1985. KKR stepped in and made an offer of $45 per share. Acting without the prior cooperation of management, KKR was in unfamiliar territory with its unsolicited bid. It tapped Kelly and his staff of deposed officers from Esmark. Beatrice responded favorably to the proposal. After soliciting competing bids and negotiating with KKR, Beatrice agreed to be acquired in February 1986.

KKR agreed to pay $40 in cash and $10 in stock per Beatrice share, or $6.2 billion. KKR also had to assume $2 billion in prior indebtedness. The complex financial structure was difficult to carry off, but it took KKR less than two months to put it into place:

▸ $400 million in equity capital from fund investors (KKR did not have fund commitments available in advance and had to solicit them on the fly) and $7.1 million from Kelly and management;

▸ $800 million in preferred stock;

▸ $3.3 billion in bank debt;

▸ $2.5 billion in junk bonds, sold by Drexel Burnham Lambert; and

▸ $1 billion in debt that did not need to be refinanced.

The banks required that Beatrice, to operate with only 5-percent cash equity, sell $1.5 billion in assets in the first 18 months. Kelly began attacking this task with relish. Less than a month after taking over as CEO, he sold Avis to Wesray for $250 million. (Although he and KKR later both reversed course on divestitures, KKR counseled Kelly to slow down and hold out for more money. They were probably right, as Wesray made a fortune on the transaction; see Chapter 5 for a profile of that deal.) He also cut $100 million from Beatrice's bloated overhead in a matter of months.

This started a string of asset sales that lasted four years, until Beatrice was completely liquidated in 1990. The Beatrice assets were sold off as 11 mid- to large-sized companies, five of which were structured as management buyouts. By the end of 1986, Kelly had sold Coca-Cola Bottling for $1 billion, International Playtex (to management) for $1.25 billion, and three other businesses, raising a total of $3.5 billion, which allowed KKR to pay down virtually all the bank debt.

Relations between KKR and Kelly fell apart in 1987 and 1988. Donald Kelly had the idea of reconstructing an Esmark-type conglomerate, taking advantage of his deal-making abilities and rapport with some of the retail industry's top operating managers. Although KKR entertained some thoughts of holding and growing the remaining Beatrice businesses, it was easier and less risky to sell out piecemeal, particularly with the booming stock market driving up the prices for these assets. Each side seemed to get its wish when KKR spun off a conglomerate of 15 Beatrice divisions, including Samsonite luggage, Culligan water treatment, and Stiffel lamps, plus a number of specialty food companies. The new company was called E-II Holdings, and KKR received 41 million shares and $800 million in debt. Kelly became CEO of E-II but continued on with Beatrice. With several other asset sales in 1987, KKR had divested itself of $6.5 billion in assets and still held Tropicana, Beatrice/Hunt-Wesson, Swift-Eckrich, and Beatrice Cheese.

Kelly's dreams of further conquests were dashed in May 1988—but profitably so—when his attempt to acquire American Brands led to the target turning around and acquiring E-II, less than a year after it went public. KKR received $650 million for its shares.

While Kelly was busy at E-II, KKR sold one of his favorite divisions, Tropicana, for $1.2 billion in early 1988, more than double KKR's estimate of its value. When Kelly returned to his position at Beatrice after the sale of E-II, he fought with KKR over whether to sell or hold the remainder. KKR won out, expecting the food businesses to bring in as much as $6 billion.

Kelly may have been right about that one. In 1988, 100 companies examined the books of the remaining businesses, but all refused to buy. Three different investment banks were hired to sell the remaining divisions, without success. Finally, in June 1990, after some small sales over the previous two years, KKR sold its remaining assets to ConAgra for $1.34 billion, plus the assumption of $1.8 billion in debt. That group of assets, though owned by KKR/Beatrice, also had its own debt, made up of pre-LBO operating debt, post-LBO operating debt, and possibly debt from the LBO. In addition to paying the cash, ConAgra agreed to be responsible for that debt.

Over four years, KKR had to do a lot of fighting and a lot of negotiating to complete the acquisition and liquidation of Beatrice. Clearly, it made some mistakes. In the end, however, the $400 million equity stake turned out to be worth $2.2 billion, which is a terrific four-year return, especially with all the risks and the occasional errors.

Even though this was KKR's biggest business deal (up until that time), it demonstrated that its method of operation, developed in much smaller acquisitions, could work with large companies. In fact, even with some problems with asset sales and fights with Beatrice's management, KKR scored a phenomenal return.

## What Went Right

KKR followed the formula that generally led to its success. In acquiring Beatrice, it was able to engage quality, motivated management, cut expenses, and sell assets at premium prices. Even though all the variables did not work perfectly—it ended up fighting with its chosen CEO, and the food business was sold for only half the expected amount—KKR had a familiar plan and executed it brilliantly.

# Management LBO of Revco (1986)

Do not take aggressive actions from a position of weakness. Although there are certainly some business successes that developed from aggressive, acquisitive, last-ditch efforts, there are far more failures.

Revco Drug Stores, which was taken private in a December 1986 leveraged buyout, managed to land in bankruptcy only 19 months later. There were many causes for this failure, a failure magnified by its status as the first LBO to file for bankruptcy, all related to a series of ever greater and more desperate risks taken by a company that should have been reducing its risk exposure.

By the early 1980s, Revco was a successful company by every possible measure. Much credit for that success belonged to its founder and CEO, Sidney Dworkin. Dworkin had taken a small chain of Detroit drug stores, built it to 2,000 stores in 29 states, and added a vitamin company and other assets. Earnings increased for 20 straight years.

In the three years before the LBO, however, Dworkin was tested by some serious problems in Revco's business, and his responses, culminating in the LBO, were terrible. And they were compounded by poor planning and execution by his subordinates and successors.

In 1983, Revco's vitamin subsidiary was implicated in the deaths of 38 infants, causing Revco's stock to plummet. Rather than focusing its responses to assuring consumers of the safety of its product, or even getting out of the business, Dworkin masterminded an evasive maneuver, putting a substantial amount of stock in friendly hands to thwart a hostile takeover. Rather than merely finding an investor to pay for stock, which would have enriched Revco, Dworkin arranged to buy a company owned by two friends for $113 million in stock.

The company, discount store Odd Lot Trading, caused problems for Revco from the outset. Within two weeks, the former owners, who still ran the company for Revco and now owned 12 percent of the parent company's shares, alleged that Dworkin's son Elliot, a company executive, had bought—and overpaid for—unneeded merchandise for Odd Lot.

The fiasco escalated Revco's problems. In 1985, it paid $98 million cash to buy back the stock from the Odd Lot owners, increasing debt (resulting in a lowering of Revco's credit rating). Of course, that stock was no longer in friendly hands. The boardroom furor dashed Dworkin's hope that his sons would succeed him in running the company. Finally, without its old management, Odd Lot became a big money loser. That same year, it suffered a $35 million loss from unsold video game cartridges. This was a particularly bad time for Revco to take its eye off the ball. Competing chains were discounting prices, picking up market share, and cutting profit margins. Earnings for 1985 fell 58 percent.

Dworkin, who never owned more than 3 percent of the company himself, responded to these new problems by further entrenching himself. He took the company private, with the help of LBO promoter Glenn Golenberg, equity investor Transcontinental Services Group, underwriter and financial advisor Salomon Brothers, and company management. The original offer was $33 in cash and $3 in securities per share. When shareholders approved the deal in December 1986, the price had risen to $38 per share in cash, or $1.4 billion, including preexisting debt assumed under the new structure.

The buyout never had a chance of succeeding. Salomon's projections accompanying the deal assumed a 92 percent improvement in profit margins. Just four days after the deal closed, Revco's treasurer said, "I am very concerned about cash flow since the sales for the past six weeks have been poor resulting in approximately $30 million less cash flow. It will be very difficult to make up this loss of funds. In fact, we have no excess cash going forward."

These revelations led the bankruptcy trustee to conclude that Revco was so poorly capitalized from the LBO's conception that fraudulent conveyance claims could be brought against the advisors and principals. Salomon paid $30 million to settle class claims brought by bondholders. A 1992 study by Robert Bruner and Kenneth Eades determined that Revco had only a 5- to 30-percent chance of making interest payments for three years.

At the end of March 1987, just three months after the LBO, Sidney Dworkin was fired. By May, the new chief financial officer concluded that the company was already in serious danger of default.

A further series of missteps followed, as management grew more desperate. Inventory had been piling up, so new merchandise schedules were deferred. This went too far, however, and it left the company inadequately supplied for the 1987 Christmas season. As results worsened, banks began cutting the short-term financing that Revco relied on to finance its inventory. This, in turn, led to a decision to stock up primarily on higher margin items, such as appliances. These turned out to be slow movers, though, and the strategy alienated customers, who were not finding the high-traffic items (such as pharmaceuticals) that brought them into the stores. Sales fell further.

On July 28, 1988, Revco filed for bankruptcy. Subsequently, Salomon had to pay in settlements more than it received in fees for the buyout. (In addition to the $30 million it paid bondholders, it paid Revco $9.5 million and agreed to assign to it any securities received in the bankruptcy reorganization.) Salomon's initial foray into the junk bond business ended in disaster and humiliation. Glenn Golenberg had to settle insider-trading charges for tipping numerous people on the deal, which led to fines and returned profits of $1.68 million.

In order to get Sidney Dworkin to leave just months after he put up money to buy Revco (even though the company soon went bankrupt, making his equity worthless), part of the price of peace was returning his financial contribution to the LBO. He also obtained the small discount chain, Buy It For Less, which he ran with his sons.

Although Revco recovered from bankruptcy in 1992 and subsequently returned to profitability, the biggest losers were the investors of $700 million in unsecured "junk" debt. Other than the proceeds from their class-action settlement with Salomon, they received virtually nothing in the reorganization.

## What Went Wrong

Once Revco was facing a crisis in 1983, it did everything wrong. When its stock price tumbled, its CEO became preoccupied with being taken over. As a defensive measure, Revco acquired a subsidiary in a business with which it was unfamiliar. When that business further dragged down Revco's fortunes, CEO Sidney Dworkin performed an LBO, despite abundant evidence that the deal was financially unfeasible.

# Nelson Peltz and Peter May's sale of Triangle Industries to Pechiney (1988)

Nelson Peltz and Peter May, as deal makers, have never really been given their due because they were viewed, in the 1980s, as creatures of Michael Milken's invention. It never helped that they were conspicuous about their wealth, or that their first post-Milken deal, a takeover of British property company Mountleigh, was a mess. Peltz and May have made some savvy moves since then, however, and someone deserves credit for the duo's five-year building and sale of Triangle Industries.

Nelson Peltz was born to a wealthy New York family in the food business. In 1972, Peter May joined the business and he and Peltz eventually became partners. In 1983, they acquired Triangle Industries, a vending-machine company. According to the popular story, this is when they got the attention of Michael Milken, who was looking for entrepreneurs beholden to him as both buyers and sellers of junk bonds.

In 1985, the infamous Victor Posner was unable to find financing to complete a takeover of National Can. Posner was reviled on Wall Street because of his heavy-handed management techniques and his habit of bleeding companies with self-serving deals. He had been an early client of Milken, but he had turned into a liability as Drexel Burnham Lambert became better known and its services were more in demand. Milken provided the junk-bond financing for Peltz and May to buy National Can, a company six times the size of Triangle. The price was $465 million, nearly all debt.

In 1986, Triangle purchased National's rival, American Can, in another deal financed by Milken. This time, the cost was $510 million, again nearly all in the form of unsecured debt. Rather than follow the expected route and bust up the company, Peltz and May embarked on a capital-intensive (that is, junk-bond financed) campaign to build the new assets, named American National Can, into a preeminent packaging company. They updated factories and acquired additional assets in the plastics and glass industries. Peltz commented that "never have so few owed so much to so many." By 1988, American National Can controlled nearly 30 percent of the metal container market in the United States. Operating profits were strong but obscured by $1.5 billion in debt.

All the while, Triangle was a public company—albeit one with a mountain of debt—in which ordinary investors could become a part if they had the stomach for risk. Peltz and May paid about $50 million for their stake in Triangle, nearly all in borrowed money. Four days after the October 19, 1987, stock market crash, Peltz and May, through their takeover vehicle, CJI, offered to purchase another 56 percent of Triangle stock for $35 per share, or $1 billion. In a highly complex arrangement, shareholders would receive $25 in cash and $10 in junior preferred stock that paid no cash dividends for each share of Triangle. Thanks to a subsequent merger with Triangle, which would also be the name of the surviving entity, the additional stock cost CJI nothing, as the new Triangle would assume all the debt. The deal was completed in February 1988. It raised Peltz and May's ownership to 65 percent and Triangle's debt to more than $2.5 billion.

Nine months later, Pechiney, the French-subsidized aluminum company, offered nearly $4 billion for Triangle, assuming $2.6 billion in debt and paying $1.3 billion for the outstanding stock, or $56 per share. Peltz and May, who used virtually none of their own money for their ownership, made $850 million.

The shareholders who disregarded the recommendations of the board of directors and its advisors nine months earlier made out far better than those who did. They got an extra $20 per share, all in cash. Some of the tendering shareholders filed a class action, which settled a couple years later for $75 million, half of which was paid by Pechiney.

Labeling Peltz and May as nothing more than Milken's pawns does not give them enough credit. Certainly, without Milken's sponsorship, they could not have built Triangle into the powerhouse that attracted Pechiney to pay so dearly. But Milken provided only the money; Peltz and May built the business into a highly attractive one, even with all the debt. When they sold, Drexel did not act as an advisor. Although the timing of the CJI merger was suspicious, Peltz and May paid for that (and got Pechiney to pick up half the tab) and still made $800 million in five years.

After the ill-fated takeover of Mountleigh, Peltz and May returned to the U.S. and, ironically, bought out some of Victor Posner's interests in 1993, including Royal Crown Cola and Arby's. In 1997, they bought Snapple from Quaker Oats for $300 million, a fraction of the price Quaker had paid just three years earlier. (See Chapter 4 for a profile of that deal.) By all accounts, they have been successful in acquiring and managing these assets.

## What Went Right

Peltz and May were regarded as pawns or bust-up artists, but they had skills and knew how to use them. They could operate comfortably under the pressure of enormous debt, and they knew how to build the mundane container business.

# AT&T's takeover of NCR (1991)

As with many bad business deals, AT&T's failure in its takeover of NCR was the culmination of a series of bad business decisions. AT&T viewed the 1984 divestiture of the Regional Bell Operating Companies as the price it paid to enter non-regulated businesses and saw its chief opportunities in the computer business. It never happened. By 1990, AT&T had lost about $2 billion pursuing the computer business.

Rather than walk away, or sell its computer business to someone else—anything that would have cut its losses—AT&T bought a computer business and put those executives in charge of its failing effort. Thus AT&T began a particularly clumsy embrace of NCR Corp. In December 1990, after two years of talks produced no agreement, AT&T announced to the public that it had offered $90 per share, or $6 billion, for NCR. The stock had recently been trading at $56 per share. A lawyer hired to defend NCR from the takeover said, perhaps presciently, "A marriage of the companies makes no business sense."

It took six months of hostilities for AT&T to acquire NCR. Each company sued the other. They waged a proxy fight, complete with negative ads in *The Wall Street Journal* and in the *New York Times*, and AT&T won seats on NCR's board of directors. NCR created a defensive employee stock ownership plan (ESOP), which would borrow money and buy a large block of NCR stock to be held for the employees. A federal court disallowed the ESOP. AT&T launched a hostile tender offer and obtained tenders for a majority of NCR's stock, but did not purchase the shares because of NCR's poison pill. Finally, in May 1991, AT&T agreed to pay $110 per share, or $7.4 billion, to acquire NCR.

Within two years, following some disappointing results from NCR, AT&T changed its mind about giving NCR its independence and letting it run the show. AT&T picked an outsider to succeed NCR's CEO and took away NCR's brand name. (In the five years after the AT&T takeover, NCR had five CEOs.) As of the beginning of 1994, NCR became known as AT&T Global Information Services. The new CEO was charged with shaking up NCR's culture and trimming its workforce by 15 percent.

In another two years, during 1995, AT&T announced hundreds of millions of dollars of losses at the division, layoffs of 20 percent of the workforce, and an intention to walk away from the computer business, through a spin-off of the business to AT&T shareholders.

Between 1992 and 1996, AT&T Global Information Services lost nearly $4 billion on its computer operations. The initial market capitalization in December 1995 of the newly independent entity (rechristened NCR) was $4 billion, nearly $3.5 billion less than the market value of the company when AT&T acquired it. Adding the $7.4 billion purchase price to the $3.3 billion AT&T spent on NCR, the loss on the investment totaled $6.8 billion.

Incidentally, as a consequence of the takeover, AT&T sold the 19 percent of Sun Microsystems that it owned. It acquired the stake for $517 million during the late 1980s and sold it for about $700 million by the end of 1991. In August 2000, 19 percent of Sun was worth nearly $35 billion.

> ### What Went Wrong
>
> AT&T bought NCR as a means of unloading its own losing computer business. Having already demonstrated its inability to operate a computer business, it should not have bought another one.

# Kohlberg Kravis Roberts & Co.'s restructuring of Flagstar (1992)

When it comes to large deals, no one has the record of Kohlberg Kravis Roberts & Co. (KKR). But even the smartest, most careful deal makers, however, make mistakes. KKR's involvement in the restructuring of Flagstar in 1992 was one of those mistakes. Flagstar's biggest asset, the Denny's restaurant chain, has, unfortunately, been a magnet for bad news over the last several years.

This saga began four years prior to KKR's involvement, when another takeover outfit, Coniston Partners, bought TW Services. (TW changed its name to Flagstar in 1993.)

In June 1989, after a seven-month fight, TW agreed to be taken over by Coniston for $34 per share, or $1.7 billion. In addition, Coniston had to assume $1.1 billion in TW debt, most of which had been borne to acquire Denny's in 1985 for $850 million. (In addition to Denny's, TW owned or was a franchisee of El Pollo Loco, Winchell's Donuts, Hardee's, and Quincey's. It also owned a food catering business and some nursing homes.)

Coniston did not have the resources to weather the downturn in the junk-bond market at the end of 1989 as Drexel Burnham Lambert went out of business. A year later, it was still trying to pay off the last $400 million of a bridge loan, it was paying up to 17 percent interest on its acquisition debt, and it had to double (to $440 million) the amount of equity contributed to the deal. Because Coniston was unable to structure the deal to its liking, it had difficulty making asset sales and had to cut its ownership to 50 percent. Donaldson Lufkin & Jenrette (DLJ), which provided the financing, received 15 percent of the company.

Coniston eventually lost its equity investment. In 1992, Coniston had to admit that it did not have the financial wherewithal to rescue TW from the financial bind its takeover had caused.

TW would take down an additional savvy investor, however. In 1992, KKR agreed to purchase $300 million in equity (20 million shares, split-adjusted) and bring in new debt, at lower interest rates, to replace the most onerous of the acquisition debt. The equity purchase gave KKR a 47 percent interest, and cut Coniston's share to 25 percent. (Coniston's share, by the time of the 1997 bankruptcy, was just 5 percent. Some of its investment partners left the partnership and took shares of TW with them. The group may also have been able to sell some shares—though at a significant loss—during 1995 and 1996.) KKR also received warrants to purchase 15 million shares.

What possessed KKR to throw $300 million at TW is a mystery. Although the Denny's brand name was well-known, it was not an especially profitable chain of restaurants. None of the other restaurants was a market leader. The entire business had large capital spending requirements, in part because it was undisputed that Denny's and the other restaurants were getting old and needed a lot of renovation and redesign. It wasn't that there was anything terribly wrong (that KKR knew about then) with the assets; there just wasn't anything right about them either. There seemed to be no upside, especially without asset sales, which KKR did not pursue. Even with the restructuring, KKR was taking control of a company that still had more than $2 billion in debt.

During the next year, TW engaged in two cosmetic transactions that frequently foreshadow disaster: changing the corporate name and reverse splitting the stock. The company changed its name to Flagstar and called for a reverse 5-for-1 stock split.

Also in 1993, Denny's was hit with repeated charges that it racially discriminated against customers. It settled with the NAACP (which included offering more minorities franchise opportunities, which was not much of a concession, considering how badly Flagstar needed the money) and with plaintiffs in two class actions totalling $54 million.

In January 1994, Flagstar announced a $1.7 billion loss, including a $200 million restructuring charge to close or sell 270 restaurants and a $1.5 billion write-down of assets. Debt was still at $2.4 billion. Flagstar's publicly traded stock had lost one-third of its value since KKR's purchase less than two years earlier.

None of this stemmed the tide of losses. In January 1997, DLJ, which financed the original deal in exchange for 15 percent of the company, formally threw in the towel, selling its three million shares for five cents each. It must have *really* wanted to distance itself from this deal, because the stock was trading at $1.19 at the time.

Later that year, Flagstar filed a prepackaged bankruptcy, in which KKR agreed to give up its equity position. It lost its entire $300 million investment in the deal. Coniston lost substantially all of its equity investment. DLJ, which sold out for a nickel a share, got the best deal.

## What Went Wrong

KKR did not follow its usual plan. Rather than taking on a company which has bloated overhead (which it could cut), Flagstar had large capital spending requirements. The company did not, as was traditional in KKR takeovers, own valuable assets that could be sold off to pay down debt.

# Novell's acquisition of WordPerfect (1994)

Novell's decision in 1994 to diversify from computer network operating systems into applications software led to three separate failures. First, it cost one of its acquisitions, WordPerfect, its leadership in the word processing market. Second, Novell failed to make the transition into application software and lost about a billion dollars. Third, and most important, the time and money devoted to this fruitless effort caused Novell to lose its leadership in the network operating systems market.

At the beginning of 1994, Novell had the leadership in the operating system market for computer networks. Microsoft was developing a competitive product, Windows NT, but Novell controlled the market. Novell CEO Ray Noorda, soon to retire, chose this moment to diversify into applications software, mortgaging the company's future and devoting its energy to become number two behind Microsoft in that area.

In March 1994, Novell announced two deals. The first was the acquisition of WordPerfect Corporation, maker of the leading word processing program, for 59 million Novell shares. At the pre-announcement closing price of $23.75 per share, this amounted to $1.4 billion. The market viewed this acquisition so negatively, though, that Novell's stock price went into a dive. When the transaction took place later in the year, Novell's stock price had dropped to $15 per share, so the 59 million shares were then worth only $885 million. The second deal was Novell's purchase of the Quattro Pro spreadsheet program from Borland for $145 million.

The near-unanimous opinion of investors and analysts was correct. Novell overpaid, forcing itself to take on Microsoft where Microsoft was strongest. Novell's best chance of competing against Microsoft was to devote its resources to maintaining the preeminence of NetWare, its operating system, while Windows NT was in its early and inferior stages.

Microsoft was a tough competitor, and Novell had already failed to catch Microsoft on its turf. Novell bought Digital Research three years earlier for $80 million in stock for its personal computer operating system, which had actually been predominant before Microsoft's MS-DOS. By the time of the purchase, however, MS-DOS was the leading operating system for personal computers, and Digital's product was dying out. Novell did nothing to halt that trend.

Immediately after the acquisitions, Novell announced a quarterly loss, and earnings for this larger, more "integrated" enterprise lagged behind Novell's results for the year before it made these acquisitions. Windows NT's acceptance grew substantially, while the presence of Novell in the application-software market did little to stem Microsoft's successes in that area.

Novell's sales department was inexperienced at selling shrink-wrapped software to consumers and small businesses. It did not take steps to improve WordPerfect's customer support. Novell also repeated the prior owners' failure to recognize the importance of making WordPerfect integrate with Windows. While Microsoft Word, naturally, integrated seamlessly with Windows 95, most WordPerfect users were still using the DOS version of that program. As a consequence, WordPerfect lost its position as the leading word processing program.

In November 1995, only 18 months after the acquisitions, Novell announced that it was abandoning the strategy. It sold WordPerfect and Quattro

Pro to Corel Corporation in February 1996. Corel bought the programs at fire-sale prices: $10 million cash, $70 million in royalties paid over five years, and 10 million shares of Corel stock (worth about $100 million).

Novell lost at least $800 million on the transaction. The company also recognized losses of about $250 million on the purchase of a Unix company from AT&T in 1993, another white elephant purchased by Noorda at the end of his reign, and of most of its purchase price for Digital Research. Worse, the confusion at Novell allowed Microsoft's networking division to develop, improve, market, and sell successively better versions of Windows NT, dislodging Novell's NetWare from its position as the unquestioned number one in network operating systems.

## What Went Wrong

Novell achieved the worst of all possible worlds with its diversification strategy. It acquired assets it was ill-prepared to manage, and the time and money spent dealing with the business application software market allowed its upstart competitor (Microsoft) to gain a foothold in Novell's previous strength: network operating systems.

# CHAPTER 2

## RULE 2: Take advantage of your adversary's weakness

$ The Louisiana Purchase (1803)

$ J.P. Morgan's purchase of Tennessee Coal, Iron & Railroad stock (1907)

$ The Boston Red Sox's sale of Babe Ruth to the New York Yankees (1919)

$ Pierre du Pont's buyout of William Durant's General Motors stock (1920)

$ John Kluge's buyout and bust-up of Metromedia (1984)

$ Peter Diamandis' acquisition of CBS Magazines (1987)

What could be better than wanting something and finding out that whoever has that thing desperately wants to get rid of it? You have an outstanding chance of striking a good deal if you find the fabled Desperate Seller.

The first great Desperate Seller deal was the Louisiana Purchase. The U.S. government wanted better access to the Mississippi River, where its territory ended. Authorized by President Jefferson, ministers Robert Livingston and James Monroe offered France about $2 million for some property on the southern part of the river. France shocked the ministers by offering to sell the entire Louisiana Territory (which later became 13 states) for $15 million. In those kinds of circumstances, there is no shrewdness or artifice involved; your goal is to finish the deal fast without screwing it up!

The greatest baseball deal of all time was also the result of a Desperate Seller. Harry Frazee, who owned the Boston Red Sox and produced plays, was over his head in debt from his theatrical operations and was being hounded by the former Red Sox owners to make good on some notes included with his purchase of the team. When he told one of the New York Yankees owners of his predicament, a deal was quickly arranged to sell Babe Ruth to New York.

Although it may be callous to say so, great opportunities arise from the financial catastrophes of others. Pierre du Pont, brought into General Motors in 1915 by forces friendly to founder William Durant, bailed Durant out of a dangerous speculation in GM stock by buying out Durant's stock at a bargain price in 1920. Along with some other GM stock purchases in 1918, the DuPont family held that stock until the Justice Department, backed by the United States Supreme Court, ordered the DuPonts to sell it. In 1962, the investment of less than $100 million had grown to $3 billion.

Another scion of the Industrial Age, J.P. Morgan, happened on one of his great business deals by accident, an incident to his heroic efforts to rescue the U.S. financial markets from the Panic of 1907. Working with a team of bankers and other industrialists, Morgan worked around the clock for weeks to stem the tide of runs on banks, brokerage firms, and trust companies. When nearly finished, he found a brokerage firm about to go bankrupt. Concerned that liquidating the firm's securities would restart the panic, Morgan offered to buy its main asset: controlling interest in Tennessee Coal & Iron, one of the few competitors to his U.S. Steel. Like du Pont with Durant, Morgan was able to pay based on the seller's desperate needs rather than based on the value of the assets.

Buyers, as well as sellers, can be desperate. The 1980s were kind to active purchasers and sellers of media companies. The sudden desire to own such companies and build media or communications "empires" created fortunes for those who owned them. Of course, in the cases of Peter Diamandis (CBS Magazines) and John Kluge (Metromedia), they had both just bought the properties in LBOs and, in liquidating to pay the debt, found huge demand among strategic buyers. Both made fortunes flipping the proper-ties—that is, buying and then quickly selling. (In these instances, the profit is made on the skill of working out the purchase and sales on favor-able terms rather than actually owning and running the businesses.) Although Kluge got $1.55 billion from Rupert Murdoch (more than the entire purchase price, a year earlier, for assets later sold for $8 billion) for six television stations, Murdoch used the assets to start the Fox Network, so it could hardly be concluded that he got a bad deal. In contrast, Diamandis sold out to French publishing giant Hachette, which, though not ruined, struggled for years with the premium price it paid to enter the U.S. market. (It did bounce back, though, with such magazine successes as *Woman's Day*, *Elle*, and *Premiere*.)

Of course, the contrary is also true. If you are acquiring a damaged property or encounter a Desperate Seller, make sure to get the discount. Failure to heed this advice has led to business failure. The bankruptcy of Montgomery Ward, 10 years after its big-money leveraged buyout (see Chapter 9 for a profile), is a good example.

Montgomery Ward, unlike many of the 1980s retail LBOs that ended up in bankruptcy court, did not fail because of excessive debt. The company's operations simply were not strong enough to be consistently profitable. When GE Capital and management completed the buyout in 1988, the com-pany had the same problem with small, run-down stores in bad locations that it had for 40 years. A couple of years of profits, the result of some short-term measures, made everyone forget about the chain's weakness. Mobil, excoriated for the purchase, got out with a profit. Management, lauded for the riches they would no doubt soon realize, ended up with worthless paper.

Although you can't pick your adversaries in a business deal, you can pick up on their motivations. If the deal is a matter of necessity to them, they are at the mercy of an observant adversary, who is now in a position to dictate terms or walk away, a circumstance the Desperate Buyer or Seller wants to avoid at all costs.

# The Louisiana Purchase (1803)

The Louisiana Purchase was the greatest real estate deal in history.

The Louisiana Territory consisted of more than 800,000 square miles of land, bordered by the Mississippi River on the east and the Rocky Mountains on the west. By conquest, the land originally belonged to France. It ceded the territory to Spain in 1762 as payment of a war debt, but regained it in 1800 by the secret Treaty of San Ildefonso. At the beginning of the 19th century, Spain still physically monitored the territory, but it did so for France's benefit, as the two nations recognized that France now owned the land.

The western border of the United States at the time, therefore, was the Mississippi River. The river served important U.S. interests for both trade and travel. France, controlled by Napoleon, was an aggressive power with numerous Colonial interests in the Western Hemisphere. When the 1800 treaty was revealed (sometime in 1801 or 1802), there was also concern about whether the river would remain accessible. When the right of deposit at New Orleans was temporarily withdrawn in 1802 (meaning that the U.S. no longer had the right to enter the port there), acquiring a seaport along the Mississippi became a matter of great importance to the United States.

President Thomas Jefferson authorized French minister Robert Livingston and special minister James Monroe to purchase New Orleans from the French. Livingston was authorized to offer $2 million for a small tract of land on the lower Mississippi so the United States could build its own seaport. After not hearing from Livingston for a period of several weeks, and knowing the importance of access to the Mississippi River from the south, Jefferson grew impatient and sent Monroe to offer $10 million for a larger tract, including both the New Orleans area and western Florida.

Unbeknownst to Jefferson, Napoleon and France were anxious to sell. Control of the Mississippi was originally important to Napoleon because he imagined building a French colonial empire in the Western Hemisphere, with its center on Hispaniola. The Mississippi valley would serve as a food and trade center to the new empire. These hopes were dashed when the French suffered costly losses securing the island following a Haitian slave rebellion in 1802. In addition, facing a renewed war with Great Britain reduced France's likelihood of being able to hold the territory, and its sale could help finance this new war effort.

On April 11, 1803, French foreign minister Charles Maurice de Talleyrand surprised Livingston by asking what the U.S. would pay for the entire Louisiana Territory. Negotiations began the next day when Monroe arrived in Paris and continued through the month. Negotiations concluded on April 29, and the treaty is dated April 30, 1803.

Under the agreement, the United States would pay France $11.25 million and assume claims of U.S. citizens against France of $3.75 million, for a total of $15 million. In exchange, the United States would receive the entire Louisiana Territory.

The deal was so good that Thomas Jefferson, generally regarded by history as one of the nation's greatest constitutional theorists, shrugged off arguments that the purchase was unconstitutional because the Constitution did not give the federal government the power to purchase land. Jefferson said, "What is practicable must often control what is pure theory." The Senate ratified the treaty on October 20, 1803. In ceremonies on November 30 and December 20, the Spanish and then the French turned the Louisiana Territory over to the United States.

The U.S. received a total of 600 million square acres, doubling its size, and instantly became one of the largest nations in the world. The Louisiana Territory was eventually divided into 13 states. The purchase cost the United States less than three cents per acre.

## What Went Right

Although France had grand designs for the Mississippi River, the eastern border of the Louisiana Territory, a series of circumstances made it a Desperate Seller at the time the United States was interested in buying some of the Territory. Instead, the U.S. got it all—and at a bargain price.

# J.P. Morgan's purchase of Tennessee Coal, Iron & Railroad stock (1907)

It's hard to imagine the power J.P. Morgan had in financial matters in 1907. No one today—not Bill Gates or Jack Welch or Sandy Weill or even Alan Greenspan—has the level of influence Morgan had then. Morgan was 70, at the end of a long successful career. He was instrumental in building U.S. Steel, General Electric, and numerous other companies and trusts, and he had bailed the country out of at least two national economic crises. In the process of getting the U.S. out of a widespread financial panic in 1907, Morgan made a business deal worth as much as a billion dollars.

Morgan's influence was so great that as the stock market and the economy tumbled during the summer, he was advised not to cut his European trip short, lest he give the appearance of a crisis. Likewise, he attended a three-week Episcopal conference in October and would not leave early, to prevent a further panic.

The panic was touched off by an attempt to corner the stock of United Copper Company. When the takeover failed, the stock plunged. A bank, using F. Augustus Heinze's—the speculator involved—UCC shares as security, had to shut down, along with two brokerage firms that handled his accounts. The plummeting price of United Copper and the closure of the bank and brokerage firms were like tumbling dominoes: Other firms interdependent with the failed companies were in danger; stocks in general fell to four-year lows; other banks, trusts, and brokerage firms using those fallen stocks as collateral were in danger of collapse; and public depositors, seeing the spreading conflagration, demanded their money in amounts in excess of what the financial institutions had on hand.

Since Andrew Jackson closed the Bank of the United States in the 1830s, the government had no central bank, and no means (other than by depositing funds in troubled institutions to provide money for depositors) of propping up institutions to turn the tide. J.P. Morgan, along with a small group of elite bankers and industrialists, had to fill the role. For two weeks, working all day and most of the nights, Morgan, subsisting primarily on cigars, drew together the resources to restore confidence in the nation's leading financial institutions.

Knickerbocker Trust Company, which assisted Heinze's speculation, was deemed beyond repair, and failed. Trust Company of America, however, held a significant portion of Knickerbocker stock, and Morgan and his group determined that Trust had sufficient collateral for a $10 million bailout fund. On a daily basis, Morgan and his group had to make fast decisions on the fate of large financial institutions. The New York Stock Exchange had insufficient funds to finance its own and its members' operations and was in danger of closing during trading on October 24. Morgan and his group raised $25 million in 10 minutes to prevent its collapse. The following week, the group organized a syndicate to keep the city of New York from becoming insolvent, buying $30 million in city bonds. By November 4, a trust-company rescue fund of $25 million was put together to provide capital to trust companies experiencing a run of depositors.

The combination of these steps stopped the spread of the crisis, and the confidence of depositors and stock traders increased. The stock market finally began ticking upward, which relieved the pressure on all the companies using stocks as collateral. The panic, and Morgan's response, prompted changes in the laws, culminating in the creation of the Federal Reserve System in 1913.

Toward the end of the crisis, however, there was one situation that required Morgan's personal (and U.S. Steel's) financial commitment. It provoked massive criticism, as well as a huge windfall for U.S. Steel. Brokerage firm Moore & Schley, due to the drop in stock prices, had lost huge amounts in financial speculation and was in danger of becoming insolvent. Fearful that Moore & Schley's closure would spark another chain reaction, Morgan tried to develop a plan that would replace its bad assets with good ones.

It just so happened that the firm's chief asset was a controlling interest in Tennessee Coal, Iron & Railroad Co. (TCI). TCI was one of U.S. Steel's few remaining competitors, and it also controlled large mineral reserves and railroad interests. Selling TCI shares on the open market was out of the question; it was an original Dow Jones component, prices would plummet, and the market would follow it downward.

Morgan's purchase of Moore & Schley's interest in TCI would avert a further crisis, and it coincided with his U.S. Steel interests. U.S. Steel arranged to purchase the TCI stock for $30 million in its own highly rated gold bonds. Because the sale was sure to raise antitrust concerns, Morgan dispatched two of U.S. Steel's officers to get permission from President Theodore Roosevelt.

Considering the bad blood between the men—Roosevelt was known as a trust-buster and had previously all but blamed Morgan for the era's economic problems—it speaks well of Roosevelt that he recognized how Morgan had saved the country and was acting to save it again through the purchase. He agreed not to challenge the transaction on antitrust grounds. (Despite Roosevelt's assent, when the former president went on safari in 1909, Morgan said, "I hope the first lion he meets does his duty.")

Although TCI's stock had been slumping and no one else was willing to pay more, Morgan stole this one for U.S. Steel. The deal was so good that Congress held two sets of hearings, in 1909 and 1911, to condemn the deal. Despite the testimony of witness after witness, including both Roosevelt and Schley, that Morgan's action was the only way to prevent a catastrophe, the legislators could not pass up the opportunity to grandstand, some even claiming that Morgan *caused* the panic in order to enrich himself by acquiring TCI.

Nevertheless, it was a great deal for U.S. Steel. For $30 million, it purchased assets estimated in value soon thereafter at between $90 million and $2 billion. Legendary financial analyst John Moody estimated the value of TCI at $1 billion.

## What Went Right

J.P. Morgan was in the right place at the right time. In the midst of his efforts to save the financial system from collapse, he had an opportunity to buy the stock of one of U.S. Steel's last competitors. He was able to purchase it for the price necessary to stave off financial disaster, rather than the value of the company. And because of the crisis, the antitrust barriers to the purchase disappeared.

# The Boston Red Sox's sale of Babe Ruth to the New York Yankees (1919)

The history of major league baseball neatly pivots around the 1920 season. Two tragedies, both of which threatened baseball's future, occurred during that season: the death of Ray Chapman, by a pitched ball, on August 16; and the indictment of eight members of the Chicago White Sox, on September 28, for their involvement in a conspiracy to throw the 1919 World Series. Fortunately, baseball rebounded immediately from these events and ascended to unheard-of heights in popularity during the 1920s due to a third event: the sale of Babe Ruth from the Boston Red Sox to the New York Yankees on December 26, 1919.

Although Babe Ruth he had not yet reached legendary status—he was only 24—he had already established himself as a player of unique talents and a larger-than-life character. Starting in 1915, he became one of the top pitchers in the American League, leading the league in winning percentage in his first year and in earned-run average in his second year, and winning 24 games in his third. In 1918, he began playing the outfield in addition to pitching, but he still won 13 games in the regular season as well as two in the Red Sox's victorious World Series as a pitcher.

As Ruth began playing in the outfield, a limitless future appeared. In just 95 games in 1918, he led the American League in home runs with 11. In 1919, playing nearly every day (and still pitching in 24 games), he led the league in runs scored and runs batted in, and annihilated the league home run record by hitting 29. Ruth became the biggest draw in baseball, and he was just getting started.

Harry Frazee, the Boston owner, however, had more pressing problems. Frazee, a theater owner and producer, bought the Red Sox in November 1916 from Joe Lannin for $675,000. It was a debt-driven transaction, however, and three years later, Frazee still owed half the purchase price. Lannin was pressuring him to make good on the notes. In addition, Frazee's shows were doing poorly and he had another $250,000 in bank debt that was coming due.

After the 1919 season, in which the Red Sox dropped to sixth place, Frazee was complaining about his financial troubles to Tillinghast Huston, part-owner of the New York Yankees. (Based on what is known of both men, it's likely they were drinking at the time.) Huston gleaned from Frazee's ranting that Babe Ruth was available for sale. His market value was high and he was dissatisfied with his $10,000 per year contract, which had two years remaining.

Huston passed this news to his partner, Jacob Ruppert. Though Ruppert and Huston did not get along, they agreed to buy Ruth from Frazee. Ruppert's family had made a fortune in the brewery business, but he was conservative in business deals, particularly at this time because he recognized that prohibition was coming (less than a month after the trade, in fact) and figured the stadium-sharing arrangement with the New York Giants would someday end, requiring him to build a new stadium. (The Giants told the Yankees to get out after 1920, and Yankee Stadium opened in 1923.)

Frazee was so desperate for money that an agreement was quickly reached. According to the contract, dated December 26, 1919, the Yankees would pay the Red Sox $100,000 for Ruth, $25,000 in cash and three 6-percent notes for $25,000 each, due on November 1 for each of the next three years. Frazee quickly worked to sell the notes at a discount. By a letter dated the same day, Ruppert agreed to loan Frazee $300,000, secured by a mortgage on Fenway Park. In April 1920, with the details of the loan not worked out, Frazee wrote Ruppert, pleading for him to work quickly in arranging the loan.

In 1920, Babe Ruth hit 54 home runs, more than any other *team*, and the Yankees (with only two second-place finishes to show for their first two decades) finished a close third, staying in the pennant race until the last week of the season. Ruth arguably had the greatest season ever. In addition to shattering his own home run record, he led the league, by wide margins: 158 runs, 137 runs batted, an .847 slugging percentage (still a major-league record), and 148 walks (the second-place player had 97). His batting average was .376.

The Yankees drew more than 1.2 million fans in 1920, breaking the Giants' 12-year-old record by more than 300,000, and doubling the previous year's attendance. Things got even better for Ruth and the Yankees. Led by Ruth, the Yankees won seven league championships and four World Series between 1921 and 1935. Ruth provided the foundation for the franchise that dominated baseball until the mid-1960s, winning 20 world championships in 45 years.

The Red Sox, world champions in 1915, 1916, and 1918, never won another World Series. After finishing in fifth place in 1920 and 1921, they finished last in eight of the next nine seasons. In addition to Ruth, Frazee sold most of his top players to the Yankees: pitchers Carl Mays, Waite Hoyt, Joe Bush, Sam Jones, and Herb Pennock; catcher Wally Schang; and infielders Everett Scott and Joe Dugan.

Hall of Fame outfielder Harry Hooper, in *The Glory of Their Times*, takes an uncharitable view toward Frazee: "All Frazee wanted was the money. He was short of cash and he sold the whole team down the river to keep his dirty nose above water. What a way to end a wonderful ball club! I got sick to my stomach at the whole business. After the 1920 season, I held out for

$15,000 and Frazee did me a favor by selling me to the Chicago White Sox. I was glad to get away from that graveyard."

Frazee finally sold the Red Sox in 1923, for a big profit: $1.25 million. He also returned triumphant to the theater, producing the still-famous musical *No, No, Nanette*, which was a huge hit in 1925.

The contract of sale from December 26, 1919, sold at a Sotheby's auction 80 years later for $189,500.

## What Went Wrong

This deal, which altered baseball history and created the foundation for the New York Yankees becoming the greatest sports dynasty ever, depended on the faltering fortunes of Red Sox owner Harry Frazee. Because some plays he produced had bombed and the previous owner was pressuring him to make good on some financial commitments, Frazee was forced into selling Ruth, and all the other components of Boston's championship team.

# Pierre du Pont's buyout of William Durant's General Motors stock (1920)

During a 1915 management struggle involving founder William Durant's return to General Motors (GM), Pierre du Pont and his chief advisor, John Raskob, were invited to join the company's board of directors. The DuPonts were already among the wealthiest families in the United States, with a fortune in the chemicals business (initially gunpowder) going back more than a hundred years. Although du Pont and Raskob each owned only 500 shares of GM stock at the time, Raskob soon became heavily involved in GM's affairs. He was shocked that the company relied so heavily on Durant, who more or less kept everything needed to run GM's increasingly complex and far-flung operations in his head. Inventory and accounting systems were virtually nonexistent. For example, GM could not find out how many cars it was producing.

During a 1920 economic downturn, which hit the auto industry particularly hard, the price of GM stock plummeted. From its high of $558 per share in September 1915, it dropped as low as $13 in November 1920.

As the stock fell, Durant, a lifelong market speculator, began buying shares. By the time the stock reached its low, he owned 3 million shares, and had borrowed $27 million, mostly recently, to buy the stock. Margin calls were imminent. Not only would Durant face personal bankruptcy, but also there was a risk that publicity about such an event could trigger a collapse in GM. He needed $940,000 before the market opened on November 19 to make margin calls.

Durant was desperate for a solution, and Pierre du Pont offered one. He loaned Durant an immediate $1.17 million and acquired Durant's stock, in a complex series of transactions, for $9.50 per share. In total, through the transactions, Durant received $24 million for his stock and another $1.5 million in severance and in exchange for waiving various claims.

Along with other stock purchases, du Pont owned about one-third of GM stock. It turned out to be a profitable investment of staggering proportions. The company later paid dividends on that stock in excess of $20 million per year, and the connection with GM put du Pont's companies in a position to sell huge quantities of numerous automobile components. Finally, there was stock appreciation.

Pierre du Pont was named chairman of General Motors in 1921. He elevated a promising young executive named Alfred Sloan to the top executive position and watched as Sloan created the model for the modern corporation. With Sloan at the helm, GM weathered the stock market crash of October 1929, the Great Depression, and World War II.

In 1949, the Justice Department filed an antitrust suit against the DuPont family, claiming that its control of both E.I. du Pont de Nemours & Co. and General Motors violated the Clayton Act. (The Clayton Act is an antitrust statute that prohibits certain interrelations between companies.) At the time, the family owned 25 percent of DuPont and DuPont owned 23 percent of GM. The case dragged on for eight years, before the U.S. Supreme Court ruled against the family. After years of additional litigation, the DuPont family was ordered to divest itself of GM by 1965. By that time, the GM stock was worth $3 billion. (The family successfully lobbied Congress for tax relief on its $750 million share.)

## What Went Wrong

William Crapo Durant was one of the most brilliant businessmen of the twentieth century. His foresight and drive created General Motors and provided the components that Alfred Sloan molded into the model of the modern corporation. But Durant was also a financial speculator, and the failure of his speculations cost him control of General Motors on two occasions. After the first time, in 1912, Durant was able to engineer a return to a position of control. After a much larger financial reversal in 1920, however, he was forced to cede control, at a bargain price, to the DuPont family, who made billions from their GM investment.

# John Kluge's buyout and bust-up of Metromedia (1984)

John Kluge started with nothing and now, in his early eighties, is one of the wealthiest men in the world, with a net worth estimated by *Forbes* at $11 billion. In a long career of successful business deals spanning more than 50 years, the bulk of his fortune is still the result of one very smart move he made in 1984.

By acquiring substantial media and cellular assets just before those assets became coveted by numerous strategic buyers, Kluge was able to sell individual assets at prices greater than that which he paid for the entire company.

In 1959, Kluge bought 22 percent of the old Dumont Broadcasting Company for $4 million and started Metromedia. Buying and selling broadcasting properties, he enriched himself and his public shareholders for nearly 25 years. Metromedia became the largest owner of non-network broadcasting assets, owning nearly as many television and radio stations as the federal communications laws allowed. It also owned the Ice Capades, the

Harlem Globetrotters, and an outdoor advertising business. After taking some financial risks in the early 1980s—buying a Boston television station for $220 million (a record at the time) and paying $300 million for radio paging businesses in six cities—the stock price of Metromedia plummeted.

In 1984, Kluge (already a 25-percent owner) decided to buy the rest of Metromedia. He paid $1.4 billion, consisting of $100 million of his own money and $1.3 billion lent by a syndicate of banks, led by Manufacturers Hanover. Metromedia's financial advisors, Bear Stearns and Lehman Brothers, determined the price was fair and in the best interests of Metromedia's shareholders. They tried unsuccessfully to find another buyer who would have paid more.

The deal hit a snag at the outset. Metromedia missed an early interest payment—the deal was really premised on the sale of assets and their escalating value rather than cash flow—and had to refinance within six months. In fact, even as Kluge was selling a fraction of the assets for more than the entire purchase price, the financial press was referring to his company as "financially troubled Metromedia."

After completing the refinancing, Kluge began selling assets, and he was masterful at finding the top of the market for each piece of his media conglomerate. Although he paid a record $220 million to acquire WCVB in Boston in 1982, he then sold it for a record $450 million to The Hearst Corporation in May 1985. At the same time, he set another record—the highest price received for a group of television stations—in selling Rupert Murdoch Metromedia's other six television stations for $1.55 billion. Murdoch, putting together the Fox network, paid a price beyond which the stations could have fetched on a stand-alone basis.

Just one year after the deal, Kluge's $100 million investment had already reaped $2 billion, considerably more than the entire LBO price. He still owned numerous other assets, though, and all were sold at premium prices to strategic bidders who had reasons for paying stratospheric prices. Metromedia's $300 million investment in radio paging turned out to be a steal. Each of the businesses, at the time Metromedia purchased it in 1982 and 1983, had applied for a cellular license. Within a few years Metromedia had, essentially, acquired access to 36 million potential cellular customers for free. In a series of transactions between 1986 and 1993, to strategic buyers such as Comcast, Bellsouth, and Southwestern Bell, Kluge sold the paging and cellular assets for more than $4.5 billion.

By 1993, Kluge had dismantled the entire business. In 1985, Metromedia sold the billboard advertising company to Patrick Media Group for $710 million, when Patrick was attempting to become the leading outdoor advertising company. In 1986, Metromedia sold the radio stations, the Globetrotters, and the Ice Capades for nearly $350 million. In all, Kluge sold the Metromedia assets he acquired in 1984 for approximately $8 billion.

Kluge and his chief deal maker, Stuart Subotnick, did not rest on their laurels. They built a new Metromedia, finding value with varying success in Laundromats and steakhouses, and engaged in an ambitious venture providing communications services in Russia and the Far East.

As successful as Kluge had been before, during, and after the Metromedia buyout and divestiture, he made at least one wrong move. Kluge had a known dislike of minority or passive investments, and he had such an investment in WorldCom, a long-distance service. In August 1995, Kluge sold his 16 percent stake in the company for $865 million, for a gain of $600 million. As a result of WorldCom's aggressive acquisition policy, most notably the acquisition of MCI Communications, WorldCom now has a market capitalization of more than $100 billion.

## What Went Right

John Kluge took advantage of the developing market for communications properties. His company, Metromedia, had acquired undeveloped properties such as pager companies that had applied for cellular licenses. When the market for cellular properties heated up, Kluge was able to sell for a premium price, without having to spend the billions to develop the properties.

# Peter Diamandis' acquisition of CBS Magazines (1987)

When Laurence Tisch took control of CBS in 1986, he sought to reverse the company's sagging financial fortunes. He instituted waves of layoffs and cost-cutting measures, and sold divisions to refocus the company on its core broadcasting assets. Between 1986 and 1988, he raised nearly $3.5 billion by selling parts of the company devoted to music publishing ($125 million), book publishing ($500 million), and records ($2 billion), as well as a number of other assets for smaller amounts. These moves were widely criticized later, even though each sale was considered fully priced at the time. While other media companies were seeking to diversify and expand their asset base, Tisch went in the opposite direction.

The most criticism was reserved for Tisch's sale, in October 1987, of CBS Magazines to a management group led by Peter Diamandis and Prudential Insurance Co. The group paid $650 million, which was considered a rich price at the time. French communications giant Hachette had earlier made an unsolicited bid of somewhere between $500 and $600 million (depending on whether you believe Diamandis' or Tisch's version, both after the fact). Securities analysts had valued CBS Magazines at $520 to $575 million immediately before the transaction.

The management group put up about $5 million in equity. Prudential arranged financing for the rest, as well as working capital of $30 million. Management got 30 percent of the company, and Prudential got 70 percent. For this price, the group obtained 21 consumer magazines, including *Woman's Day, Modern Bride, Road & Track, Car and Driver, Field and Stream,* and *Popular Photography.* On the October 1 closing day, the company was renamed Diamandis Communications Inc. (DCI).

DCI was an independent company for only seven months, but they were very busy months. After only two weeks, DCI announced the sale of four magazines for $167.5 million. A month later, DCI sold *Modern Bride* for another $63 million. In total, DCI sold $242 million worth of magazines in late 1987 and early 1988.

The main difference between "duplicity" and "salesmanship" is whether anyone gets hurt. That said, Peter Diamandis did one excellent sales job. For example, he told *Forbes* before the buyout that, in his division, "There isn't any fat here. We have all but eliminated bureaucracy, before cost-cutting became in vogue." He later boasted that he cut expenses after the buyout by $20 million. In February 1988, he had the unpleasant task of considering making some layoffs. He emphasized that he would cut just the minimum and said, "I think that it is very fortunate for the employees of this company that the management took it over." Although staff cuts were imminent, he noted, "What everyone forgets is that the alternative is that we were going to have to take French lessons." Less than two months later—barely enough time to crack the spine on a French-English dictionary—he sold DCI to Hachette. In fairness to Diamandis, the offer was too good to turn down.

In April 1988, Hachette paid $712 million to acquire DCI, consisting of $367 million to pay the remaining LBO debt, and $345 million for the equity of Diamandis, the other top management, and Prudential. This constituted a gain of nearly $300 million in seven months on a virtually nonexistent equity investment. It was, at the time, the best Prudential ever did on an LBO. Diamandis and three top managers split $100 million.

For all his talk about the importance of independence and employee ownership, Diamandis sold out immediately for a good deal. He ended up unhappy working for a foreign conglomerate. Hachette's aborted auction of *Woman's Day* and critical attitude toward Diamandis-created *Memories* caused him and two other members of the original management group to quit in September 1990.

There was, of course, the satisfaction of having gotten the better of the deal. Diamandis profited at the expense of Laurence Tisch, considered one of the shrewdest asset traders in modern times, and Hachette, one of the world's largest publishing companies. For years, Hachette suffered over having paid such a rich price for DCI.

## What Went Right

Shrewd timing and promotional ability made Peter Diamandis wealthy and admired. Diamandis bought CBS Magazines when CBS ended its diversification strategy and sold it soon after, when other media companies decided to diversify. Diamandis was opportunistic on both sides of the transaction. A little of his success also came down to luck. Although it appeared CBS received a good price for its magazine division, its desperation to focus on its television network cost it dearly. The market for magazines heated up, and Diamandis was able to receive prices, only a few months later, far in excess of those he paid.

# CHAPTER 3

## RULE 3: Find value where others don't see it

$    The purchase of Alaska (1867)

$    Sir James Goldsmith's acquisition of Diamond International (1982)

$    Ronald Perelman's acquisition of Technicolor (1983)

$    Kohlberg Kravis Roberts & Co.'s acquisition of Safeway (1986)

$    Hanson Trust's acquisition of SCM Corp. (1986)

$    Berkshire Hathaway's purchase of Coca-Cola stock (1988)

If you discover something before anyone else, you should benefit significantly. To be a good deal maker, you must have a handle on the value of the company (or other object of the negotiations). The deals in this chapter demonstrate the rewards of creativity in finding value. The principals in these deals were smarter than their adversaries, because they saw value—and knew how to unlock it—where others failed to see it.

In the purchase of Alaska, William Seward, Secretary of State to Presidents Lincoln and Johnson, saw more than an unexplored, frozen wasteland. He believed that the future of the United States would be more secure if it expanded to the edge of its land mass in as many directions as possible. It didn't hurt that gold and oil were later discovered on the land, but Seward was right, both with the policy of Manifest Destiny in general and with Alaska in particular. With the rise of Russia as an international power, a Russian presence in Alaska would be undesirable.

The "discovery" can even be something that, in retrospect, seems obvious. Warren Buffett joked that he discovered the value of the Coca-Cola brand in 1936 when, as a boy, he would buy six-packs for 25 cents and sell the bottles for a nickel apiece. And, Buffett has said, it took him only 51 years to buy the stock. Buffett, starting as a Benjamin Graham–taught value investor, looked for stocks selling below their intrinsic value. That usually brought Buffett in contact with out-of-favor businesses trading at less than book value or at a tiny multiple of earnings. He expanded his definition over time to include, in his evaluation of "intrinsic value," non-balance-sheet assets such as brand name and management ability. Even though Coca-Cola, in 1988, traded at a premium to its book value and earnings, Buffett correctly recognized that the company had an irreplaceable brand name, probably the best in the world. Its management, he felt, was expert at how to maximize that value.

The remaining deals in this chapter are about 1980s-era takeovers where the financial professionals involved knew early on how to make big money from leveraged acquisitions and divestitures. It was their model that numerous others later followed, but they got there first, working with the problems of structuring these complex, large-scale transactions before the time when every investment banker was rushing to help (and take a cut). This was also the time before the multitude of buyers pushed up prices for high-profile takeovers. Sir James Goldsmith, in his acquisition of Diamond International, and Ronald Perelman, in his acquisition of Technicolor, were among the first to quickly buy and sell big companies in the 1980s, and they took great advantage of their head start by purchasing at bargain prices.

The other two deals—KKR's buyout of Safeway and Hanson Trust's acquisition of SCM—took place in 1986, when the Deal Decade was already in full swing. Each, however, seized opportunities that competitors overlooked, and reaped huge rewards. KKR made a great series of asset sales to bring down debt, then demonstrated patience—a commodity in short supply in the deal-making frenzy of the 1980s—and waited until its excellent management team rebuilt Safeway into a company far more valuable than the one it took over.

Hanson Trust was impressive in the size of its undertaking: It made its $1.3 billion off SCM as a result of eight divestitures, running the gamut from sales to third parties, to IPOs, to spin-offs. Hanson accomplished this, literally, with one hand tied behind its back; SCM's biggest asset, Smith Corona, went bankrupt with Hanson Trust owning 50 percent, costing it what was once a paper profit of $400 million.

# The purchase of Alaska (1867)

By the late eighteenth century, Alaska was internationally recognized as the property of Russia as a result of conquest by Danish explorer Vitus Bering, who, exploring the North Pacific for Peter the Great in 1741, spotted the land mass. Although Bering and many of his men died of scurvy on the disastrous voyage, those who returned told of animals such as sea otters, whose skins would be highly desired.

By the late 1700s, Russia inhabited parts of the land and the fur trade thrived. The land was also inhabited by several indigenous peoples: Eskimos, Aleuts, Tlingits, and Athabascans. These groups did not fare well under Russian occupation. Many died of diseases with which they were unfamiliar, such as smallpox. Some groups, like the Tlingits Indians, warred with Russians.

Russia's interest in Alaska waned by the 1850s. The fur trade fell off and the Crimean War lessened Russia's interest in controlling remote territories. During the administration of President Buchanan, Russia offered to sell Alaska, but negotiations bogged down and the American Civil War diverted the attention of the United States government.

For William H. Seward, Abraham Lincoln's Secretary of State, the purchase of Alaska was an important part of an overall strategy. Because Lincoln had little interest in international affairs, Seward played a dominant role in Lincoln's administration. Although he had his hands full with the delicacies of international relations while the U.S. fought the Civil War—he almost committed a monumental goof by suggesting that he could reunite the North and the South by declaring war on Europe—Seward pursued the doctrine of Manifest Destiny. Seward thought that the United States should control as much contiguous land as possible and that its security was best obtained through outward expansion.

Seward was seriously wounded in the assassination plot against Lincoln, but he recovered to serve as Andrew Johnson's Secretary of State.

When Russia renewed its offer to sell Alaska in 1867, Seward jumped at the chance and negotiated the terms in a matter of hours. The price: $7.2 million, or just two cents an acre. The Alaska land mass is one-fifth the size of the continental United States.

The Senate was less enthusiastic about the purchase, and ratified it by a margin of a single vote. With so little known about Alaska, the purchase was popularly derided as "Seward's folly." The U.S. was slow to encourage settlement or even exploration of the Alaska territory. The discovery of gold at the end of the nineteenth century changed that, and the discovery of huge oil reserves during the 1960s established Alaska as the most resource-rich part of the country. In addition, with the emergence of the United States as an international power, the doctrine of Manifest Destiny has served the country well; it would be hard to imagine a Russian presence in contemporary North America in the place where the state of Alaska now stands.

## What Went Right

Secretary of State William Seward recognized the importance of the United States' outward expansion. Alaska was such a remote territory that it was decades after the purchase before there was even an official map of Alaska. Its rich resources and strategic importance validated Seward's foresight.

# Sir James Goldsmith's acquisition of Diamond International (1982)

The press never tired of reporting that Sir James Goldsmith was larger than life: the separate homes he maintained for the families he created with both a wife and a mistress; the duality of his religious background and nationality (a British-Jewish father, a French-Catholic mother); his gambler's mentality (he once resolved a million pound difference in an acquisition price over a game of backgammon); and his mysterious sense of timing (he largely sold out of equities immediately before the 1987 crash).

Lost in all this were Goldsmith's brilliant and daring financial maneuvers. In a career that included so many successes, and a fortune estimated at $2 billion by the time of his death in 1997, the biggest and most dramatic is still the largely forgotten takeover and dismantling of Diamond International in 1982.

Goldsmith began in his takeover in 1979, at the height of the U.S. recession. He acquired 6 percent of Diamond International, an integrated forest-products concern. In addition to owning 1.7 million acres of timberland, Diamond had subsidiaries that made and sold cans, paper, lumber, and even wooden matches.

In June 1980, in the face of a threat from Goldsmith to acquire the entire company, and the presence of another potential acquirer, the management of Diamond made peace with Goldsmith. Diamond allowed Goldsmith to acquire up to 40 percent, provided he did not go further. He was also allowed to pick one-third of the board.

After Goldsmith and two associates joined the board and he bought 40 percent, the price of Diamond stock slumped. The expected takeover premium for Diamond shares was not forthcoming, and pulp prices were low. Numerous other dissident shareholders emerged. With Goldsmith having lost a quarter of his investment and other raiders distracting management, Goldsmith made an offer for the rest of the company at the end of 1981: $44.50 per share, while the stock was trading at $29. Goldsmith paid approximately $600 million for the company. A majority was borrowed from a banking syndicate, a minority borrowed from a web of companies controlled by Goldsmith from Lichtenstein to Panama.

Goldsmith financed the transaction largely with short-term debt at very high interest rates, guaranteeing that he would pay for the acquisition by selling assets. He arranged to sell the Heekin Can division to Wesray for $98 million, including assumption of debt, before the acquisition of the remainder of the Diamond stock was even completed.

Although the deal was not completed until almost the end of 1982, Diamond was practically liquidated by the end of 1983. In addition to the sale of Heekin Can, Goldsmith sold the paper mills and inventory for $149 million, the retail lumber chain for $120 million, the paper packaging operations for $84 million, and the match business for $13 million. A series of smaller divestitures raised enough money for Goldsmith to pay off all the bank debt and leave only the debt to his holding companies.

After all this, Goldsmith still owned the timber assets, which were the reason he bought the company. For almost nothing, Goldsmith bought 1.7 million acres of timberland. He spent the next decade liquidating the trove, fetching prices between $150 and $400 per acre.

Tracking the prices Goldsmith obtained is difficult, due to the frequent splitting of the parcels and multiple partners and corporate entities. The corporation managing the timberlands, Diamond Occidental, sold the Maine assets in the mid- and late-1980s for $150 million. James River acquired Diamond Occidental when it had only its last 550,000 acres of timberland for $225 million. Numerous sources estimated Goldsmith's haul at $700 million. Goldsmith was able to use the same formula with similar results in the takeover of another forest-products company, Crown Zellerbach, just a few years later.

## What Went Right

James Goldsmith was so certain of the value of Diamond's timber assets that he was willing to engage in the long and complex process of acquiring Diamond during a recession to get control of those assets. By selling off Diamond's operating assets, he was able to obtain Diamond's timberland almost for free, and he was able to sell the timber assets at premium prices after economic conditions improved.

# Ronald Perelman's acquisition of Technicolor, Inc. (1982)

Ronald Perelman and his acquisition company, MacAndrews & Forbes, have been involved in many notable deals in the last 20 years; his outfoxing the government in negotiations for the purchase of five S&Ls in 1988 is profiled in Chapter 10. For a return on assets, however, his biggest victory was the acquisition in 1982, and sale in 1988, of Technicolor.

Technicolor is in the film-processing business. Though it is best known for processing film for movie studios, it had numerous other commercial and consumer operations, including a string of One-Hour Photo shops.

In 1982, Perelman, who had made several successful smaller acquisitions, purchased Technicolor for $120 million. He used $2 million of MacAndrews & Forbes' money and borrowed the rest. (At the time of the deal MacAndrews & Forbes was a public company; Perelman took it private—that is, he bought the publicly held stock so that it no longer traded on a public stock exchange or had shareholders other than Perelman or partners he brought in—four months after the deal's completion.)

Perelman courted Technicolor's CEO, his advisor, and several board members in a matter that was aggressive and challenged in courts for years as illegal. According to deposition testimony, Perelman had implied separately to both the CEO and his rival on the board that each would run the company post-acquisition. The CEO's advisor was also promised a place in Perelman's budding empire. Several other board members were informed of the deal, presented as a *fait accompli*, only hours before they were asked to approve it, which they did. Perelman paid $120 million for 81 percent of the shares ($23 per share) in November 1982, and the same price for the remainder in a second-step merger in January 1983.

Although these facts were disputed and came to light in the years of legal wrangling after the deal, to most observers, Perelman did not have to go to the trouble. In the year before Perelman bought Technicolor, it earned just $3.4 million on sales of $229 million. One-Hour Photo was an expensive money loser.

Perelman knew better. The one-hour photo labs were closed. Some businesses and excess real estate were sold for more than $50 million. Perelman focused on the commercial film-development business, and Technicolor thrived, even making some acquisitions during the mid-1980s.

In September 1988, Carlton Communications, a British firm in the business of supplying television services, agreed to pay $780 million for Technicolor. MacAndrews & Forbes (now wholly owned by Perelman) owned 100 percent of Technicolor. Having purchased Technicolor six years earlier with only $2 million in equity, Perelman made nearly $780 million.

As Perelman was well aware, gains this big do not come without legal challenges. One of Technicolor's minority shareholders, 4.5 percent owner

Cinerama, Inc., challenged the deal and the price in two separate Delaware actions in 1982 and 1986. Despite numerous rulings and reversals, the deal finally passed the court's muster in 1995, nearly 13 years after it was concluded and seven years after Perelman sold the company. Cinerama's appraisal action, seeking a fair price for its shares, was still pending at the end of 1999. It took a good part of the late 1990s to determine whether the fair value of the shares should be determined as of November 1982, when Perelman took control, or January 1983, when he completed the second step of the merger. The action has the dubious distinction as the longest corporate action ever pending in the Delaware courts.

## What Went Right

In Technicolor, Ronald Perelman discovered a company loaded with unprofitable assets that could be sold, leaving the core of a profitable company that Perelman acquired at almost no cost. When the main assets of Technicolor appreciated in value, Perelman cashed out for a huge gain. Although Perelman did not invent the buy-to-sell acquisition, it was rare in 1982 for someone to buy a company with little equity and act so aggressively to maximize the value through a series of asset sales.

# Kohlberg Kravis Roberts & Co.'s acquisition of Safeway (1986)

In the mid-1980s, grocery chains became favorite targets of corporate raiders. The chains tended to be among the last businesses to recover from the corporate malaise of the 1970s. Their size made them vulnerable to being bought then sold piecemeal. And their high employee and capital spending costs made would-be acquirers visualize large cost savings.

Safeway owned more than 2,300 stores in 29 states and in Europe, Central America, and the Middle East. Although it had performed well in the stock market during the early 1980s, the stock was still widely seen as undervalued. Buying $145 million worth of Safeway stock during mid-1986, Dart Group, controlled by the Haft family, threatened a takeover.

Safeway did *not* want to be taken over by the Hafts, who had a reputation as quick-buck artists and were not especially good managers. Later, they would run part of the family business into bankruptcy and fight each other in court for four years, during which time their business would fall apart.

Enter Kohlberg Kravis Roberts & Co. (KKR). KKR managed investments for pension funds, specializing in high-risk, high-yield transactions. For the previous several years, KKR had been buying public companies, usually with management's involvement. The plan was to find undervalued assets, stay for the long haul, get good management, improve the company, and then go public again. To maximize the return, KKR borrowed heavily to finance its transactions, so its deals—again, generally with the blessing of management—often involved a good deal of bloodletting. Aggressive asset sales and layoffs were usually part of the operating plan.

At the time, KKR wasn't as famous as it would become. Its buyout of RJR Nabisco, for years the largest U.S. takeover, still the largest leveraged buyout, put its principals' pictures on the front pages of newspapers and magazines and made them the subjects of books and movies. But KKR had already completed several large deals; it had just bought Storer Communications for $2.5 billion and Beatrice for $6.2 billion.

Dart Group had offered $64 per share for Safeway's 61.1 million shares and was rebuffed. KKR reached an agreement in late July 1986 to buy the company for $69 per share (cash for 73 percent, securities for the rest). The deal was valued at $4.1 billion.

This was, by far, the best the Hafts ever did on a deal. They made $80 million by selling their Safeway stock. They also made KKR give them an option to buy a portion of the new company, which they sold back several months later for $60 million.

The money the Hafts made was dwarfed by KKR's return on investment. KKR's principals put up about $1.5 million of their own money. The rest—$175 million—was put up by their limited partners. The company was thinly capitalized, even by the debt-to-equity ratios of the day. Although they had a very small shareholding stake in the new enterprise, their deal with the limited partners entitled them to 20 percent of the profits. So, for less than $2 million—and, of course, their financial acumen, which made the deal happen—they owned more than 20 percent of the new, highly leveraged company.

Up front, KKR charged its investors $60 million for making the deal happen. After that, it developed a sound, patient strategy for making a profitable exit. It sold assets, including all non-Safeway stores' assets and the European operations, for $2.4 billion, 40 percent more than expected. Many of these operations were not even profitable, so the remaining company had a strong base of operations to pay off the much-reduced debt.

The remainder of KKR's profit depended on its sale of Safeway stock, as profits from the ongoing enterprise were committed to reducing debt. Safeway went public again in 1990, though KKR did not sell any of its shares.

The 1990s were good to Safeway. By August 2000, Safeway's market capitalization was more than $24 billion. KKR and affiliates, between 1996 and 1999, sold nearly $5 billion in stock in five secondary offerings and still held 50 million shares, worth nearly $2 billion more.

This bounty did not come without a significant cost. Immediately after the deal was struck, both houses of Congress introduced resolutions to investigate the deal and its effect on workers. Susan Faludi wrote a now-famous article in *The Wall Street Journal* in 1990, for which she won a Pulitzer Prize, cataloging the suicides, heart attacks, mental anguish, families torn apart, and communities left in shambles, as KKR and management fought Safeway's unwieldy structure to shed assets, cut costs, and boost productivity. Numerous commentators have suggested that KKR's principals were stung by the criticism, and lowered their profile—this occurring after the RJR Nabisco deal, which also put KKR in the glare of the public spotlight, usually in an unflattering way.

KKR may even have done fewer deals, and been slower to exit its investments, so as not to attract a lot of attention and ire. Of course, if this was true in the case of Safeway, it just served to make the company more money.

## What Went Right

Few investors are better than KKR in discovering value and exploiting it. The acquisition of Safeway was one of its best. KKR bought Safeway for what appeared to be a fair price, but was able to sell fringe assets for substantial money and improve the remaining operations. Its patience has been extravagantly rewarded.

# Hanson Trust's acquisition of SCM Corp. (1986)

Hanson Trust is a British conglomerate, founded and operated until recent years by Lord Gordon White and Lord James Hanson. It owned several U.S. companies, but made its biggest (and best) deal in 1986 when it acquired SCM Corp. for $930 million. Hanson Trust, led in this deal by Lord White, executed a nearly flawless exit strategy. Even though one of the main assets of SCM later went bankrupt, Hanson Trust made more than $1 billion on the deal, mostly within three years.

SCM was an old-fashioned industrial conglomerate. Started a century earlier as Smith Corona and still a famous brand name in typewriters, it also owned interests in paper, office supplies and equipment, paints, chemicals, food, and flavors and fragrances.

In defense against a $60-per-share offer by Hanson in August 1985, SCM agreed to be acquired in a Merrill Lynch–led management buyout for $70 per share. In the midst of a bidding war between Merrill and Hanson, SCM agreed to a $74-per-share offer from Merrill that included an auction-ending lockup option for Merrill to buy two of SCM's best divisions, Durkee Foods and Glidden Paints, at bargain prices if SCM accepted a higher offer.

Hanson made a higher offer, premised on invalidating the lockup. The U.S. District Court ruled in favor of the Merrill Lynch offer, but the Second Circuit reversed the decision. One day after the appellate decision in January 1986, Hanson completed this $75-per-share ($930 million) tender offer.

Hanson began immediate, aggressive asset sales. Within a year, the entire acquisition price had been recouped. Glidden Paint sold for $624 million. The two Durkee foods divisions sold for $185 million and $140 million. Allied Paper sold for $160 million. Along with other asset sales, Hanson earned $1.25 billion, giving it a profit of $300 million. It still owned the office equipment division (Smith Corona), a metal division (SCM Metals), two chemical companies (SCM Chemicals and Glidco), and a flavors-and-fragrances company (Baltimore Spice).

Each asset was disposed of in a favorable manner. Baltimore Spice sold in 1990 for $24 million. SCM Metals became part of a spin-off of certain U.S. assets of Hanson in 1995 to Hanson shareholders, into a company called U.S. Industries. U.S. Industries sold SCM Metals in 1996 for $122 million. The two chemical companies were packaged with Quantum Chemicals into another part of the 1995 spin-off, given to shareholders as publicly traded Millennium Chemicals. Of its initial $1.4 billion market capitalization, approximately 30 percent of the operating income came from the former SCM divisions.

Hanson even made money from Smith Corona, and it was practically the only one to do so. It was the maturing of Smith Corona's market that originally led it to conglomerize, but Hanson was able to package the computer, office equipment, and typewriter assets into a separate company, Smith Corona Corporation, in which it sold a 52-percent interest to the public in 1989. The IPO (initial public offering) led to Hanson receiving a special dividend of $428 million.

It still held nearly half of Smith Corona, valued at the IPO price at approximately $400 million. That value was never realized, however, as Smith Corona began reporting disappointing operating results as soon as the offering was completed. The stock soon dropped from its IPO price of $21 per share to $5 per share. From there, it began a long, slow slide into bankruptcy in 1995. Although Hanson had to give back about $20 million to shareholders to settle a class action in 1992, it was a wonder they were able to get as much as they did from a dying asset.

Even with the worthless 48-percent ownership in Smith Corona, this deal ranks as one of the savviest bust-ups of the era. Hanson Trust made back its purchase price in less than a year, and cash profit of $750 million in less than three years. In addition, Hanson's shareholders later received stock that derived at least a half-billion dollars of its value from later asset sales or assets contributed from the SCM acquisition.

## What Went Right

SCM was a jumble of different businesses: paint, foods, paper, office equipment, chemicals, and several others. The principals of Hanson Trust had to make numerous smart deals to get a good price for each asset. They succeeded to such an extent that even when one of the "trophy" assets, the office equipment division, went bankrupt, Hanson Trust still made $750 million from SCM.

# Berkshire Hathaway's purchase of Coca-Cola stock (1988)

Warren Buffett is the most successful investor in history. Even with the price of his investment company, Berkshire Hathaway, slumping for two years, a $10,000 investment in Berkshire when Buffett took it over in 1965 would be worth $50 million in 2000.

Buffett owes his success to value investing, a doctrine most eloquently espoused by Benjamin Graham, a professor of Buffett's at Columbia in the 1930s, and author (with David Dodd) of *Security Analysis*. According to Graham, stocks have an intrinsic value based on their asset values, separate from the stock market's valuation. The key is to find and exploit the disparity between the two valuations. The analysis is rigid and technical, requiring investment only in stocks selling at discounts to book value.

Buffett admits that Graham would not have bought Berkshire Hathaway in recent years, nor would he have bought any of the stocks Buffett has bought. Buffett has gone beyond Graham's definition of value investing. He has learned about additional definitions of "value," and, with all the investments Buffett has had to make, especially in the predominantly rising market of the last 20 years, he has had to expand his definitions a bit.

It was in this process that Buffett made his greatest investment: purchases on the open market of $1 billion in Coca-Cola stock in 1988 and 1989. Coca-Cola could not possibly meet Graham's concept of a value investment, selling at a large premium to book value. (For example, the company carries its trademarks at no or nominal value, and those trademarks are generally regarded as the company's most valuable assets.)

During 1988, Buffett began buying Coca-Cola stock. Trying to keep news of his purchases from driving up the price, he began buying after Berkshire's annual meeting and continued through the summer. (Because Buffett was renowned as an investor, people often assume that if he's buying, they should be buying, too.) By the time Berkshire was required to disclose the purchases, it had bought more than 176 million shares (adjusted for four subsequent stock splits), or 6.3 percent of the company, for just more than $1 billion. Buffett spent another $200 million to raise the stake to 200 million shares during 1994.

For obvious strategic reasons, Buffett generally discloses his investments and philosophy only as the law requires or when it suits his purposes. He likes the image of simpleton and is happy if people accept his initial explanation that he made the purchases because of his fondness for Cherry Coke. On other occasions, however, he has given some of his reasons, and they are consistent with many of his stock purchases of the last two decades.

Buffett had a high regard for Coca-Cola's management and its deployment of assets. Coke's COO, Don Keough, was an old acquaintance of Buffett's from Omaha, and Buffett had great respect for his abilities. Buffett also admired CEO Roberto Guizueta, who reversed the company's conglomerization (including the moves Guizueta himself instituted), focusing solely on building and exploiting Coca-Cola's brand awareness around the world.

Most important, Coca-Cola's brand name was an asset, according to Buffett, of phenomenal value. The most recognized brand name in the world, it simultaneously (if managed properly) assured premium prices and fought off competitors. Even though 80 percent of Coca-Cola's business is outside the U.S., there are huge portions of the world still to conquer. With its brand awareness, its management, and its experience in winning over foreign markets, there was enormous value in those untapped markets.

In a lifetime of successful investing, this was Buffett's most profitable investment. In less than three years, the price of Coca-Cola stock doubled. The next year, in Berkshire's 1991 annual report, Buffett noted that "[w]hen we loaded up on Coke three years ago, Berkshire's net worth was $3.4 billion; now our Coke stock alone is worth more than that."

After a couple slow years, the stock price started accelerating again. The investment gained $1 billion in 1994, another $2.5 billion in 1995, and yet another $2.5 billion in 1996. Even though Coca-Cola has slumped in the stock market for the past two years, in August 2000, Berkshire's $1.3 billion investment was worth more than $12 billion.

## What Went Right

Even though Warren Buffett has been known for his conservative investment philosophy, he has been willing to change (some) with the times, expanding his definition of value to include intangible, yet real, assets such as brand awareness and management acumen. In targeting Coca-Cola, he picked a stock that was overvalued by his traditional standards, but which profited Berkshire Hathaway by more than $10 billion.

# CHAPTER 4

$   Robert Campeau's acquisition of Federated Department Stores (1988)

$   William Farley's acquisition of West Point Pepperell (1989)

$   Gibbons Green van Amerongen's LBO of Ohio Mattress (1989)

$   Quaker Oats' acquisition of Snapple Beverage Co. (1994)

$   Seagram's sale of DuPont stock to acquire MCA (1995)

If you convince yourself that you *must* have something, the chances that you will overpay for it rise dramatically. The most powerful weapon the deal maker has is the word *no*; without it—especially if the seller recognizes this—the buyer is easy prey.

Many of the flameouts of the late 1980s came from buyers and advisors who could not say no. William Farley was practically forced by Drexel Burnham Lambert to make a deal. They raised him a big pool of cash, and he had to pay a high rate of interest on it. He literally could not afford to stay on the sidelines. Naturally, his advisors (also Drexel) would not dissuade him from trying another big deal, even as the price of the deal rose and the junk-bond market fell apart. Drexel wanted to show the world it was still business as usual, and wanted to do a big junk-bond financing to prove it. When the principal and the advisor are both under the gun, what chance is there to back away if the deal is not right? There was plenty of evidence that West Point Pepperell was not a good target, but no one in that deal would say so.

The advisors of these late-1980s failed deals deserve a large share of the blame. While Drexel was sliding toward extinction, its competitors lost their common sense in an effort to catch up to its successes of a few years earlier. First Boston was particularly guilty of this in its role of advising upon and financing both Robert Campeau's takeover of Federated and Gibbons Green van Amerongen's LBO of Ohio Mattress. First Boston became a force in mergers and acquisitions, so it was very aggressive about convincing the principals that deals should go forward, despite warning signs. When some of its stars (who pushed the firm in this direction) left to start a rival firm, the remaining investment bankers pushed even harder, to hold First Boston's position. This attitude nearly put First Boston out of business.

Even in the upper reaches of big business, ego can get the better of the participants. Merv Griffin, a successful producer and syndicator of game shows, made a bid for Resorts International on the request of a minority shareholder. (See Chapter 10 for a profile of this deal.) He and Donald Trump fought like cats and dogs over the company for most of 1988. Several times, Griffin threatened to pull out of the deal, leading to speculation that he recognized that the deal was not viable. But still, he completed the takeover at too high a price, traded the unfinished Taj Mahal casino to Trump (but kept the huge debt of the Taj Mahal), and went bankrupt in less than a year.

Even where ego is not primarily responsible, deal makers and companies can put themselves in positions where, strategically, they think they *have to* complete a deal. Quaker Oats, for example, thought the acquisition of Snapple Beverage would make sense. The acquisition of Gatorade several years earlier did wonders for the bottom line. In addition, there were rumblings on Wall Street that Quaker was stagnant, a threat to be taken over. Snapple, however, was a lot different from Stokely-Van Camp (Gatorade's parent). Thomas Lee, Snapple's primary owner, insisted on top dollar. Quaker was hooked; even an unexpected 75-percent drop in earnings did not dissuade it from agreeing to the deal. Quaker lost nearly $1.5 billion in three years and its CEO quit as a result of the debacle.

There was not much chance of Edgar Bronfman, Jr. quitting Seagram while his family controlled the company. Still, his interest in making his own mark and in doing it in the entertainment business cost the company dearly. In acquiring MCA, he got some good music assets and good theme parks, but also a lot of dead weight in movies and television. Worse, he had to sell the company's 24-percent stake in DuPont to finance the purchase, costing Seagram about $10 billion in stock appreciation in three years.

# Robert Campeau's acquisition of Federated Department Stores (1988)

Robert Campeau grew up poor in Ontario. Becoming successful in home building, he continued leveraging his success into larger deals. Not satisfied with becoming a Canadian real estate developer, he moved into retailing and to the United States, acquiring Allied Stores in a public, hostile takeover fight in 1986. At one point, his personal fortune—primarily his holdings in Canadian-traded public-company Campeau Corp.—was estimated at $500 million.

But it was a house of cards. Although Campeau had some successes, his skills were primarily as a promoter, not as an evaluator or manager of assets. His last several years in the spotlight were spent overpaying for assets, then moving on to the next, larger, transaction.

The last transaction, in 1988, was the takeover of Federated Department Stores. *Fortune* called this "the biggest looniest deal ever." Campeau was in no position even to consider this deal. He had just completed the highly leveraged acquisition of Allied Stores and, though he had sold off divisions and paid off the most onerous debt, left himself with a company that was clearly not able to service the remaining debt.

Campeau's original offer ($4.2 billion plus the assumption of more than $2 billion in preexisting debt) was probably feasible. But Federated's board of directors rejected his $47 per share hostile takeover bid and courted other suitors. (Tellingly, May Department Stores, a conservatively run retailing chain, came within a hair's breadth of agreeing to buy Federated.) Macy's, itself highly leveraged as a result of its own management buyout less than two years earlier, came in as a white knight, bidding up the price. The involvement of Macy's, led by experienced retailer Edward Finkelstein, was used as evidence that the price was reasonable, because Finkelstein was willing to have Macy's pay nearly as much; Macy's slid into bankruptcy two years after Campeau-led Federated. This maneuver raised the price by approximately $2.5 billion. The deal closed on April Fool's Day in 1988.

Federated, like Allied Stores, was simply not big enough to generate enough money to make interest payments, especially with the most desirable divisions sold to pay the short-term debt. In addition, Campeau stumbled over the financing, and his erratic style—once putting his psychiatrist on the board of directors, refusing to pay his financial advisors, and frequently firing or causing managers to quit, to cite just a few examples—scared off competent managers.

The deal was advertised as having more equity than most. Campeau was supposedly contributing 20 percent equity; other deals were accomplished with 90 percent or more of the funds coming from loans. This was fictitious, however, and demonstrated how Campeau was overextended from the start. Although it appeared $1.4 billion of the $6.5 billion purchase price would be equity, Campeau had to borrow, at very high rates, the money he used for "equity." Campeau Corp. borrowed $260 million from the Reichmann family of Toronto, owners of Olympia & York. (These brilliant investors lost money on their extensive association with Campeau, but they lost much more in their attempt to redefine the London skyline on a project called Canary Wharf. See Chapter 6 for a profile of that deal.) Edward DeBartolo lent a Campeau Corp. subsidiary $480 million. Another $500 million was in the form of loans, due in one year.

The Campeau-Federated takeover is the financial community's version of *The Emperor's New Clothes.* Campeau led some of the shrewdest minds in high finance down the drain with him. Apart from the Reichmanns and DeBartolo, the fingerprints of M&A whiz Bruce Wasserstein are on this failure, along with those of First Boston, PaineWebber, Citibank, and a host of others.

Apart from the fat fees the advisors and bankers stood to earn from the deal (and the later divestitures), many of these otherwise-savvy players had additional motives for getting a deal done regardless of prudence. Bruce Wasserstein had made a significant reputation for himself and his company, First Boston. But one week into the deal, he and partner Joseph Perella left to open their own shop. How better to announce your presence than by snagging the biggest deal of the year? Because Campeau continued to retain First Boston, that firm had to go along for the ride to demonstrate that, even without some of its stars, it was still a force in mergers and acquisitions.

At one point, Campeau needed an emergency bridge loan of $2 billion to complete the deal. One of the banks he turned to was PaineWebber, who had to sue him to get its fee in the Allied Stores deal. But PaineWebber jumped at the opportunity to climb aboard this leaky ship; bridge loans to complete takeovers were becoming big business, and PaineWebber wanted to demonstrate that it was a player. PaineWebber ended up holding $96 million in unsecured debt.

Campeau, obviously, was the biggest loser. His net worth dropped from $500 million to barely anything. Of course, it is questionable how much he was ever worth, because all these transactions were highly leveraged and, when his company's stock was valued at a high number, it was based on the (incorrect) assumption that he could service the debt on all his acquisitions.

Less than two years after the closing, on January 15, 1990, Campeau-run Federated filed for protection from its creditors under U.S. bankruptcy laws. Robert Campeau lost the bulk of his fortune, but still lives comfortably, even by tycoon standards: He lives in a $10 million Austrian chateau he built in 1991 and has been attempting a reentry into the Berlin home-building market.

## What Went Wrong

Robert Campeau and his advisors—perhaps even the advisors more than Campeau himself—were so motivated to acquire Federated that all common sense went out the window. They convinced themselves of the soundness of ridiculous projections for cash flow and asset sales, because everyone in the deal had some powerful reason for doing the deal, at any price. After completion of the deal, reality interceded. There was no conceivable way Campeau could, through asset sales and operations, service the debt, and Federated quickly went bankrupt.

# William Farley's acquisition of West Point Pepperell (1989)

William Farley's 1989 acquisition of textiles maker West Point Pepperell was emblematic of the Takeover Decade: aggressiveness, ego, and risk, fueled by Michael Milken's debt financing. His failure, which occurred, not coincidentally, at the same time as the bankruptcy of Drexel Burnham Lambert, symbolized the excesses of the decade: wildly optimistic estimates of cash flows and divestitures, ignorance of economic cycles, out-of-control bidding, and deal making without regard to risk.

Farley, until the West Point debacle, was a poster child for Milken's methods. Starting with only about $25,000 of his own money at the beginning of the decade, he completed several small leveraged deals and one large one, a $2 billion acquisition of Northwest Industries in 1985. After selling most of Northwest's assets, Farley ran its jewel, Fruit of the Loom, even appearing in its commercials. He briefly considered running for president in 1988.

Like many bad business deals at the end of the 1980s, the takeover of West Point Pepperell originated in bad motives. Drexel had raised a blind pool of $500 million for Farley in early 1988, and, after refinancing some of his other junk-bond debt, he was left with $300 million. Paying between 14.5 and 15.5 percent on the money, Farley was strongly motivated to put the money to work by attempting a takeover. The candidate, West Point, had just finished a leveraged, hostile takeover of J.P. Stevens and itself had $1 billion in debt. Although it had some assets that could be sold off, it was regarded as an efficient operation, so there were no easy improvements that could be used to boost the bottom line, a common feature in the successful deals earlier in the decade.

Farley's financer and advisor, Drexel Burnham Lambert, was also pushing for a deal. Wounded by the loss of Michael Milken and the specter of criminal charges, the firm wanted to complete big deals to maintain its presence. Individual investment bankers, fearful of the possible demise of the firm, wanted to secure their fortunes by completing as many deals, and snagging as much in bonuses, as possible.

Less than six months after raising the blind-pool money, Farley bid $48 per share for West Point Pepperell. In a hostile five-month fight, Farley eventually raised his offer to $58 per share and obtained the company's agreement to be taken over in March 1989.

The financing was a hard sell for Drexel. Many prospective buyers considered the optimistic cash-flow projections accompanying the $700 million junk-bond offering to be unbelievable. To complete the bond offering, Drexel had to buy all the bonds it was unable to sell. In this case, it ended up holding 20 to 30 percent of the issue.

The total cost of the deal was $2.8 billion, consisting of $1.8 billion to buy out West Point's shareholders and $1 billion to assume its existing debt. Farley was so tightly stretched that he acquired 95 percent of West Point stock rather than a full 100 percent. Even so, $1 billion of the money raised was in the form of a short-term, high-interest bridge loan.

That outstanding 5 percent cost Farley the entire deal. Under the terms of the deal, Farley could not use the cash flow of West Point Pepperell to pay the acquisition debt until he acquired 100-percent ownership. In a deal of nearly $3 billion, his inability to raise $80 million sent him spiraling toward bankruptcy.

It took a year for Farley to sell any assets. When he finally sold Cluett Peabody (Arrow shirts, Gold Toe socks), it was for $400 million, some $200–400 million less than projected.

Farley never made interest payments on the acquisition debt. He defaulted in April 1990, lasting only that long because of a negotiated extension in the term of the bridge loan. Simultaneously, creditors pushed Farley, Inc., parent company of Fruit of the Loom, into bankruptcy, closing the door on any chance that Farley could fashion some rescue from that entity. (As the price of West Point's junk bonds plummeted, the portion of the bonds in Drexel's inventory continually worsened its balance sheet, playing a role in its collapse in early 1990.)

In August 1991, Farley reached an accommodation with lenders that led to a prepackaged bankruptcy of West Point Products. Farley would give up 95 percent of his ownership to lenders, who would convert $1 billion of the debt into equity. Farley lost virtually all of his equity, somewhere between $150 and $300 million. Following the reorganization in September 1992, Farley sold his 5-percent stake back to the company and resigned.

The reorganized company finally cashed out the last 5 percent of its shareholders in 1993 and operated profitably without the massive debt imposed by Farley before the bankruptcy. Farley devoted his energies to a largely unsuccessful attempt to operate Fruit of the Loom profitably. Since mid-1999, Fruit of the Loom has fired and sued Farley and filed for bankruptcy.

## What Went Wrong

When Drexel raised the blind pool money for Farley, it almost guaranteed something bad would happen. Farley and, later, Drexel were forced to complete a transaction, and all common sense went out the window. They planned poorly and overpaid, and the company immediately went bankrupt.

# Gibbons Green van Amerongen's LBO of Ohio Mattress (1989)

The rush to get in on the deal frenzy of the 1980s struck few companies harder than First Boston. The investment bank, led by the ambitious Bruce Wasserstein, clawed its way to a leading position. The defection of Wasserstein, Joe Perella, and some other M&A professionals, plus the ever larger and more famous fees paid to Drexel Burnham Lambert, pushed First Boston into an aggressive role financing deals.

Its aggressiveness was more evident than its judgment. Two of the worst deals were Robert Campeau's acquisition of Federated Department Stores (profiled earlier in this chapter) and LBO firm Gibbons Green van Amerongen's (GGvA) LBO of Ohio Mattress, owner of the Sealy brand.

CEO Ernest Wuliger encouraged the preliminary expressions of interest the company received in November 1988, and publicly put Ohio Mattress up for sale. Six different buyers made bids, three of which were increased. On March 6, 1989, Ohio Mattress announced GGvA was acquiring it for $960 million plus assumption of debt.

The initial capitalization was as follows:

▸ $495 million of secured debt, managed by a syndicate of three banks;

▸ a $457 million bridge loan by First Boston, to be replaced by permanent financing; and

▸ a $170 million equity contribution by GGvA.

The deal later developed a vile reputation on Wall Street, and was nicknamed "The Burning Bed." It had problems from the beginning for several reasons. First, although there was competition among buyers, the price was nearly double Ohio Mattress's market capitalization shortly before the company put itself up for sale.

Second, although Sealy was a strong brand name, Ohio Mattress had been built on Wuliger's hands-on salesmanship. Despite Wuliger's interest in remaining, GGvA immediately hired a new CEO and wanted Wuliger to report to him. GGvA also fired or failed to retain the other top managers. The equity group did not include experienced managers in the company.

Third, the transaction was not planned with the idea of selling assets. Ohio Mattress's main assets were the Sealy name and its nationwide network of factories and sales organizations. Ohio Mattress did own a few mattress brands in addition to Sealy, but the company dragged its feet and lost out on a chance to sell the Stearns & Foster division for $87 million to Wuliger after he left. In addition, the company's reliance on marketing made it difficult to cut costs after the deal.

Fourth, only weeks after the acquisition of Ohio Mattress was complete, GGvA broke up, with Mark Green leaving to start his own company. The partners publicly fought over who was at fault when the Ohio Mattress deal went bad.

In this environment, with the junk bond market collapsing, First Boston was trying to sell $475 million of unsecured debt. Unlike Drexel Burnham, which had Michael Milken and his stable of captive buyers, First Boston could not raise the money before the deal closed. It had to front GGvA a bridge loan of $457 million. The loan left Ohio Mattress thinly capitalized and also required that the owners pay very high interest. Furthermore, the longer it remained outstanding, the more First Boston's abilities came into question.

On August 11, 1989, only five months after Ohio Mattress announced the deal with GGvA, First Boston had to withdraw its $475 public offering of subordinated debt. Eight months later, First Boston converted the bridge loan to permanent debt, but the interest rate on the debt was 14 to 15.5 percent and GGvA had to give First Boston 40 percent of the company's equity.

First Boston became the main owner of the company in September 1991, when it exchanged the subordinated debt for equity. It then owned 94 percent of the company. GGvA did not get completely shut out; it received warrants which, when exercised, could be worth a 21-percent equity stake.

First Boston and GGvA finally ridded themselves of Sealy (the new name for the company) for good in early 1993. A partnership run by Sam Zell (known in business circles as "the Gravedancer" for his ability to pick up and profit from troubled companies) bought Sealy for $250 million, plus the assumption of the long-term debt.

First Boston lost about half of the $450 million it put up for the original bridge loan. First Boston itself would have gone belly-up had Credit Suisse not bailed it out by transferring some of the bad loan on its books. Coming along with the company's problems with the Campeau-Federated deal, this deal killed First Boston's ambitions to be a leader in mergers and acquisitions. Zell scored a huge gain on the transaction, selling Sealy to Bain Capital in 1997 for $800 million.

GGvA got sucked into an auction process, perhaps assuaged by the logic that they couldn't be overpaying if other buyers were willing to pay nearly as much. They made an equity investment of $170 million, nearly all of which they had to give away by the time of the second debt-for-equity swap.

## What Went Wrong

There were several solid reasons why Ohio Mattress was not a good candidate for a leveraged transaction: It had few assets that could be sold to pay down debt, and its success was due to incurring heavy marketing costs (which could not be cut). Still, GGvA and First Boston were seduced by the presence of other bidders and all the surrounding mergers-and-acquisitions activity. The acquisition debt, however, could not be sold, and GGvA and First Boston suffered huge losses.

# Quaker Oats' acquisition of Snapple Beverage Co. (1994)

In 1992, a leveraged buyout firm, Thomas H. Lee Co., headed by the eponymous Mr. Lee, purchased Unadulterated Food Corp. for $130.2 million.

Unadulterated Food Corp. was an attractive purchase primarily because its main asset was the Snapple line of soft drinks. After selling 13 percent to the public only six months later for $60 million—roughly eight and a half times what the Lee group paid for it—most investors would have been content to sit back after making such a shrewd purchase and sale.

But Tom Lee and his company did not make hundreds of millions of dollars for themselves and their investors by patting themselves on the back and sitting on the sidelines. In November 1994, only two and a half years after the initial purchase, Lee's group sold its remaining shares in the now-public Snapple Beverage Corp. to Quaker Oats in a transaction that cost Quaker $1.7 billion, counting the price of buying out the other public shareholders and assuming Snapple's debt.

The big winners, of course, were Lee and his investors. Excluding borrowed money, which was paid back at relatively nominal interest, they invested $27.9 million in 1992 to obtain Snapple, and received $900 million when they sold their shares in several transactions between 1992 and 1994, most of that money coming in the Quaker acquisition.

Had the deal strengthened Quaker's beverage division, as its purchase several years earlier of Stokely-Van Camp, which allowed it to obtain the Gatorade brand, had, it probably could have handled Lee making the huge profit. But Quaker lost big, and did not look especially smart in doing so.

There were clear signs during negotiations that all was not well with Snapple's operations. The same day the negotiations concluded, Snapple announced an unexpected 74-percent decline in earnings, due to increased competition and excess inventory. This would have given most buyers reason to pause, reassess, even run for the hills. Analysts immediately criticized the high price and blamed Quaker's fear of being taken over itself, forcing the company to make a deal.

The effect of those competitive and inventory problems on Snapple accelerated over the next two years. At the time of the acquisition, Snapple was selling approximately 70 million cases of product per year. In two years, that figure fell to 45 million cases and was declining at an annual rate of 20 percent.

And the problems that Quaker did not inherit, it created. Key to Snapple's success was its image, in large part due to its heavy spending on advertising: a quirky campaign featuring Wendy, a Snapple employee, reading letters from Snapple customers. Quaker cancelled the campaign, imposed a four-month media blackout while it studied repositioning the brand, and developed a new campaign based on the slogan, "We want to be number three."

Finally, in early 1997, Quaker unloaded Snapple at the fire-sale price of $300 million. (The purchasers were Nelson Peltz and Peter May, whose exploits with Triangle Industries are profiled in Chapter 1.) When Quaker announced its first quarter results that April, those results included a $1.4 billion loss and the resignation of Quaker's longtime CEO and Chairman.

Making Quaker look even worse, the new owners returned the brand to profitability. They returned Wendy to the advertising campaign, amidst great fanfare (and free publicity). They also restored sufficient credibility to the brand to introduce several brand extensions, including a line of sports drinks and a smoothie-type drink.

## What Went Wrong

Quaker was concerned about being taken over itself, so it bought Snapple. Because of its success in acquiring Gatorade years earlier, it jumped to create parallels between the two transactions, ignoring some of Snapple's obvious and immediate problems, including a 74-percent decline in earnings, right in the middle of negotiations. Completing the deal anyway, it became a huge failure.

# Seagram's sale of DuPont stock to acquire MCA (1995)

If you have a goose that lays golden eggs, is it better to sell the eggs or sell the goose? The answer, naturally, depends on the prices you can get. Clearly, however, it is *riskier* to sell the goose, particularly if you are already used to getting a good price for the eggs.

This was the situation facing Egdar Bronfman, Jr. and Seagram in 1995. Bronfman, whose family owned 36 percent of Seagram, had been in the spirits business since before the days of Prohibition. It was a reliably profitable, mature business. It had thrown off sufficient cash for Egdar, Sr.

in 1981 to take a large position in Conoco in an abortive takeover attempt. When DuPont took over Conoco, Seagram converted its ownership into a 24-percent stake in DuPont.

By 1995, Bronfman had a successful, easy-to-manage, but unexciting business. DuPont paid a cash dividend and its stock appreciated, and the spirits business allowed Seagram to make some spirits (Martell and Absolut) and soft drink (Tropicana) acquisitions, as well as a passive stock purchase (15 percent of Time Warner). Bronfman, however, upset this stability by radically recasting Seagram as an entertainment company.

There has been much speculation behind the series of large-scale moves undertaken by Edgar, Jr. during the latter half of the 1990s. The most common was that Edgar became star-struck and preferred the exciting entertainment business to the mature liquor business and passive ownership of DuPont stock. This, however, ignored Egdar's life story: He was previously a movie producer and a songwriter, his family was worth billions, he was friends with big stars, and he controlled internationally known brand names such as Martell and Chivas Regal. Less discussed was the possibility that he felt a need to establish himself as the leader of the family company and put his own stamp on the family fortune.

In April 1995, Seagram bought 80 percent of MCA for $5.7 billion. MCA owned Universal Studios, the Universal theme parks, a TV production company, extensive film and TV libraries, half of the USA Network, and record companies (MCA, Geffen, and half of Interscope). The price was not outlandish. The seller, Japanese electronics giant Matsushita, had bought MCA five years earlier for more, and had lost its stomach for the costs and tribulations of doing business in Hollywood.

The assets, however, required management acumen not possessed by then-current MCA management or at Seagram. The studio was not making much money. Its cash cow (Steven Spielberg) had just left to start his own studio (Dreamworks SKG); its television and film libraries were languishing; and it was in complex co-ownership agreements with Time Warner and Paramount (later acquired by Viacom) for some of its music and television assets.

Bronfman did not choose the right people for the job. Some, including Ron Meyer, Sandy Climan, and Howard Weitzman, were inexperienced. It took Bronfman a year to get a management team in place, including Frank Biondi as CEO (he formerly had a similar position under Sumner Redstone at Viacom). He then sold the television assets that Biondi was experienced at managing. In less than five years, all but Meyer were gone.

Although the music business has done well, aided by another huge acquisition (PolyGram), and the theme parks have continued their expansion, Seagram has a lot of dead and underperforming assets. The film and TV libraries remain underutilized, and the opportunity to use USA Network as an outlet to maximize their value (as Disney and Ted Turner have done, combining entertainment libraries with cable outlets) was forgone. When Seagram acquired control of the USA Network, it sold a majority at a bargain price to Barry Diller. (Seagram has the opportunity to reacquire USA if Diller leaves, but this merely makes the transaction an extremely expensive management contract to secure Diller's services.) Universal Studios has been a millstone and an embarrassment. Bronfman has all but said that it exists primarily to provide theme rides for the parks. Of course, without Spielberg, those kinds of hit movies are not being made.

This deal's failure, however, was mostly the result of what Seagram gave up, not what it got. To finance the acquisition, Seagram sold its stake in DuPont back to the company for $8.8 billion. This was nearly $3 billion less than its market value, but the transaction was structured to have fewer tax consequences for Seagram. DuPont had tripled in value since its acquisition in 1981, and it provided Seagram with $300 million per year in cash dividends.

Prior to the announcement of the $10 billion acquisition of PolyGram in May 1998, the market value of Seagram, including all the MCA assets, was about $19 billion.

It is not necessary to perform a complex valuation analysis to see that Bronfman cost Seagram many billions of dollars. In May 1998, Seagram's 312 million (split-adjusted) shares of DuPont alone would have been worth $23 billion. In three years, the market value of Seagram (with MCA) rose about $5 billion, while the value of the DuPont shares it gave up rose by more than $10 billion.

Despite Bronfman's gaffes, he may get the last laugh. On June 20, 2000, Seagram announced that it was merging with a French company, Vivendi. Vivendi would pay, in stock, $77 per share for the outstanding Seagram's stock, or $34 billion. The deal, still subject to numerous regulatory approvals and the fluctuations of Vivendi stock, seems the embodiment of the Greater Fool theory. Apart from the music assets, everything Seagram owns is either losing money, is expected to be sold, or does not fit Vivendi's "vision" of itself as a global media powerhouse. There is no reason to believe such a venture will create value for Seagram's shareholders, unless they can unload their shares on an upswing in the stock price prior to the merger.

## What Went Wrong

Seagram had a stable, mature business, along with a passive ownership in DuPont, another stable, profitable company that paid a rich dividend. Although we can only speculate as to Edgar Bronfman, Jr.'s motives, it appeared that he was willing to throw away safety, stability, and profitability to show that he could make his mark on the company. Although he may have escaped with a profit, the sale of DuPont stock to buy MCA made no economic sense.

# CHAPTER 5

# RULE 5: Innovate

$     The purchase of Manhattan from the Canarsee Indians (1626)
$     Ray Kroc's agreement to franchise McDonald's (1955)
$     The merger of the Pennsylvania Railroad and New York Central (1968)
$     Wesray's LBO of Gibson Greetings (1981)
$     Wesray's LBO of Avis (1986)

If you can develop a method of doing deals—an innovation in financing or selling—you can profit in ways that others cannot. Although there is no substitute for clear thinking and a smart plan, developing something extra in your plan can provide an extra edge.

Innovation in deal making can reveal value, or make it accessible, where it would not have otherwise been apparent. When Ray Kroc obtained an agreement with the McDonald brothers to franchise McDonald's, he actually made a very poor agreement. So anxious to get their assent to duplicate their method of operation, he had to agree, as franchiser, to take little in fees, as well as to have his activities unduly restricted. Kroc was a visionary, not a deal maker. His financial officer, Harry Sonneborn, developed the idea of having McDonald's rent, then buy, the real estate and lease it to franchisees at a profit. The idea was so innovative and so successful that when Kroc needed to buy out the McDonald brothers but lacked the money to do so, Sonneborn was able to get a loan from several endowments, impressing them with the real estate angle on McDonald's.

One of the greatest real estate deals ever, the purchase of Manhattan from the Canarsee Indians, was innovative in its way of dealing with a complicated and recurring problem. Rather than trying to take the land from the Indians by bloodshed, the Dutch offered a fairly nominal sum. The settlement of Manhattan was thus accomplished with less fighting than most expansions of Indian-inhabited territories.

Among all the LBO firms, Wesray Capital was probably the most innovative. Although Kohlberg Kravis Roberts & Co. completed more large deals and made more money, Wesray, led by former Treasury Secretary William Simon and Raymond Chambers, introduced numerous financing innovations in its deals. Wesray's acquisition of Gibson Greetings is credited with starting the leveraged buyout craze of the 1980s. When Wesray was able to finance the $80 million deal with less than $1 million in equity and make it work so convincingly, banks and other funding sources (who could charge more in fees for leveraged acquisitions) warmed up to the idea of transactions with little equity. Wesray also popularized pre-sales of assets and using leasebacks to get more up-front money out of the company.

Wesray's acquisition of Avis was so profitable, in part, because it revolutionized the use of an employee stock ownership plan (ESOP) as an exit strategy. Because of the tax advantages of an ESOP, Wesray was able to get a richer price from the ESOP than a private purchaser or public stockholders would pay. Of course, the mechanism is also an invitation to abuse, as described in Wesray's sale of Simmons Mattress to an ESOP. (See Chapter 6 for a profile of that deal.)

Similarly, a lack of innovation can destroy a business deal. This happened to the federal government in its regulation of the railroad industry. The Interstate Commerce Commission (ICC) always had a reputation of being heavy-handed in its regulation of railroads; that became fatal in the merger of the Pennsylvania Railroad and New York Central into Penn Central. The ICC, still regulating railroads as in the days when it had monopoly power over transportation, held up the merger for years and required that the two railroads take on a third, bankrupt railroad in the combination. It took only two years for Penn Central to go bankrupt, and the government spent billions maintaining Amtrak and Conrail, the publicly subsidized successors.

# The purchase of Manhattan from the Canarsee Indians (1626)

The 1626 purchase of Manhattan is interesting to study not just because of its historical and financial importance, but because it illustrates the difficulty of evaluating business deals. For that matter, it illustrates the difficulty of reconstructing historical events. In both instances, it sometimes just depends on whom you ask.

The Dutch began claiming parts of what would become America's east coast (which they called New Netherland) in 1609. In 1626, Dutch representative Peter Minuit purchased the island of Manhattan (which the Dutch called New Amsterdam) from a group of local Indians. The Netherlands' economic and political problems during the period that immediately followed the purchase led it to cede the property to the English in 1674. At this time it became known as "New York." As a result of the Revolutionary War, the land became the property of the United States.

Everything else about the deal is in dispute, including the identity of the seller and the price. According to most accounts, the seller was the Canarsee Indians, though some claim it was the Shinnecock Indians or the Algonquin Indians. The price has been described in many ways, among them: 60 gilders; 60 florans; $24 worth of beads; the value of 10 beaver pelts; 30 beaver skins (the equivalent of one musket and a bale of tobacco); a load of cloth, beads, hatchets, and other odds and ends; and the equivalent of one and a half pounds of silver (worth $72 today).

Minuit did not get a good deal because he paid the equivalent of 60 gilders, versus 600 gilders or 6,000 gilders. He got a good deal because he bought peace and security at a price he could afford and then developed the area so it could become the foundation for modern-day Manhattan.

The deal, from a pure economic perspective, is not as good as the previous paragraph's one-sentence summary conveys. The local Indians did not do badly for themselves. Many accounts explain that the Canarsees had not settled the area and were just passing through. Therefore, they sold something they did not even own, and took advantage of Minuit's fear of Indians, desire for peace, and unfamiliarity with the area.

A second perspective is that the local Indians did not recognize "ownership" of property. They took the offer as a gratuitous gesture. They did not vacate the area following the deal, nor were they charged for occupying the property.

A third perspective is that the transaction was not a purchase but a ransom. According to this view, Minuit was buying peace rather than land. Historical accounts explain, for example, how the Raritan Indians in the Staten Island area "sold" Staten Island six times.

The fourth perspective is that, by getting anything, the Indians made a great deal. The purchase of Manhattan was one of the few instances where Europeans, as part of their conquests, recognized property rights of the indigenous people. In most other instances, those rights were ignored—and, in fact, the Indians did not consider themselves "owners" of the land—which led to later conflicts, destroying most of the Indian tribes and much of their culture. Perhaps history would have been significantly changed for the better if settlers had viewed the territories as properties rather than conquests, and reached early economic accommodations with the indigenous population. This is not to say that there was never any bloodshed in connection with the development of New York by the Dutch, but the process was accomplished in a less violent way than in most expansions through the American territories inhabited by Indians.

## What Went Right

The Dutch, for a relatively nominal sum, reached an accommodation with the Canarsee Indians for Manhattan and avoided much of the strife and bloodshed associated with European conquest of Indian-occupied territories in the Western Hemisphere. Unfortunately for The Netherlands, its economic and political problems cost it its colonies, and it ceded control of New Amsterdam to England, who renamed it New York in 1674. Just more than a hundred years later, the new sovereign, the United States of America, obtained the land through the Revolutionary War.

# Ray Kroc's agreement
# to franchise McDonald's (1955)

In 1954, in a story that is now part of business legend, 52-year-old salesman Ray Kroc went to San Bernardino, California, to pay a sales call. Kroc, a lifelong salesman and entrepreneur who had achieved, at most, modest success, was selling Prince Castle Multimixer machines at the time, which had the capacity to make five milk shakes at once. When a restaurant in San Bernardino ordered eight, Kroc traveled from Illinois to find out what kind of business would need to mix 40 milk shakes at once.

There, he met the McDonald brothers and saw their hamburger stand in action. At their small, spotlessly clean shop, with a limited menu, low prices, and lines around the block, Kroc saw his future. The brothers were reluctant to expand. They had sold franchises and received little in return.

Kroc, desperate, made them an offer too good to refuse: The McDonalds would have to put up no money for the expansion; all expenses would come from Kroc's end. Kroc would sell franchises for only $950 per store, and would receive less than 2 percent of total sales. Of this amount, the McDonald brothers would receive 30 percent. They reluctantly agreed, and a very wary arrangement ensued.

According to the legend, that's practically the end of the story. Popular accounts focus on Kroc's single-minded drive, his control of all aspects of the operation, and his near-religious fanaticism, all of which contributed to McDonald's becoming one of the world's most well-known brand names, with 25,000 locations worldwide, $30 billion in annual sales, and a market value of more than $40 billion. How Kroc built the business, from the initial agreement with the McDonald brothers, to its level of success when he stepped down as CEO in 1968, when he died in 1984, to the present day, is the story of superb deal making and managerial skill.

Kroc started by developing a branded product. By enforcing rigid product specifications and quality control, he assured that every McDonald's eating experience would be the same, regardless of the location. The formula worked, and by 1960, 200 McDonald's restaurants had $75 million in total sales.

All Kroc had really succeeded in doing, by that time, was to create the foundation for a high-profile business failure. Because of the franchise agreement with the McDonald brothers, the company earned only $159,000 in 1960. Further, the master franchise agreement he struck with the brothers in 1955 was a legal nightmare, which Kroc could remedy only by repeatedly violating it, jeopardizing future financing and his position with the company. (As much as Kroc sought to create uniform operations, he had developed modifications from the San Bernardino store, which he was prohibited from doing under the agreement. He was also prohibited from becoming a franchisee, which he needed to do to build a prototype store in Des Plaines, Illinois, in 1955.)

Two brilliant moves put his company on firm footing. First, at the suggestion of Kroc's first financial officer, Harry Sonneborn, McDonald's entered the real estate business, first leasing and later buying the properties on which the franchisees would operate. This was consistent with Kroc's goals of control (allowing franchisees a sweet deal in the franchise agreement but imposing operating conditions in the rental agreement) and entrepreneurship (the types of people Kroc sought as franchisees did not have the wherewithal to purchase the land themselves). It produced huge profits because McDonald's set the base rent by marking up its carrying costs on the properties by up to 40 percent, and included a computation of rent based on a percentage of sales, when sales reached a certain level. McDonald's also required that franchisees post a security deposit, which the company used as capital to buy real estate. Later, Sonneborn would tell stock analysts that "McDonald's is a real estate company, not a fast-food company." Shortly before Kroc's death, he credited Sonneborn with saving the company, saying, "Harry alone put in the policy that salvaged this company and made it a big-leaguer. His idea is what really made McDonald's rich."

Second, Kroc stretched his resources and bought out the McDonald brothers. He never got along with them, eventually concluding that they were not meeting the standards he was imposing on other franchisees, and learning that they were selling franchises in Kroc's home territory. Most important, he had to get out from under the legal cloud of the master franchise agreement with the brothers.

The McDonald brothers insisted on $2.7 million, in cash, nonnegotiable. For a company that earned less than $200,000, that was a lot of money. Kroc realized, however, that the business was expanding and he was getting a bargain by saving the future royalties.

In 1961, Sonneborn arranged a loan of $2.7 million from several college endowments and pension funds. The money manager, John Bristol, had not heard of McDonald's but was impressed by McDonald's plans to profit from its real estate investments. Although Sonneborn was able to prevent Bristol from getting equity in McDonald's as part of the deal—McDonald's was far too risky an investment to get a straight loan—Sonneborn and Bristol engineered a repayment term and bonus payments based on McDonald's profitability.

These moves provided the foundation for McDonald's rapid and profitable expansion during the 1960s. Kroc also developed a unique relationship with franchisees, insisting on uniformity in service and basic menu, but at the same time, encouraging innovation. Ronald McDonald, the Big Mac, and the Egg McMuffin are all ideas originally developed by individual franchisees. (The original Ronald McDonald was then-25-year-old Willard Scott.)

When Ray Kroc died in 1984, he was one of the wealthiest men in the United States, and the international expansion of McDonald's was well underway. He also unleashed his pent-up frustrations on the McDonald brothers. Immediately after closing the deal to buy them out in 1961, he built a McDonald's one block from their San Bernardino store, which they renamed Big M. Big M's business faltered, their store was finally sold in 1968, and the next owner went out of business in 1970.

## What Went Right

The real financial genius behind McDonald's displayed itself after McDonald's got its franchise system off the ground. By figuring out how to make real estate profits from the franchises, Ray Kroc and Harry Sonneborn put the company on firm financial footing, after which it was about to become an American institution.

# The merger of the Pennsylvania Railroad and New York Central (1968)

The federal government was the culprit of, and a big loser in, the 1968 merger of the Pennsylvania Railroad and New York Central Railroad into Penn Central. Still penalizing the industry for the sins of the railroad barons from the turn of the century, railroads were harshly regulated during the 1950s and 1960s, while they were forced to compete, largely unsuccessfully, with air and highway travel for passenger and freight business.

Although the creation of Penn Central was presented as a merger of equals, it was really a takeover by Pennsylvania of New York Central. Pennsylvania was the healthier, more diversified company (not that it helped the combination after the merger), its CEO ran the merged company, and Penn Central maintained its headquarters in Pennsylvania's old offices.

The two railroads had been competitors for traffic along the East Coast and between the East and the Midwest since before the Civil War, so there was a lot of bad blood. Purely as a means of survival, the two companies considered a merger starting in 1957. Discussions were cut short, however, when New York Central's CEO, Robert Young, committed suicide shortly after cutting the railroad's dividend in 1958. Although the two early-1960s CEOs, Stuart Saunders of Pennsylvania and Alfred Perlman of New York Central, did not like each other, a merger proposal was presented for approval to the Interstate Commerce Commission (ICC) in 1962.

The ICC was established in the 1870s to stop abuses by the then-all-powerful railroads, as well as by a few of their powerful customers (such as John Rockefeller), who were able to cut deals not available to competitors. It became the federal regulatory agency most involved in the affairs of its regulated businesses. By the early 1960s, the landscape had changed; the ICC did not respond to that change. Air and highway travel took away profitable passenger and freight business (sometimes with subsidies from the government) while the railroads were stymied in attempts to increase prices, merge, or close unprofitable lines.

The ICC took three years to approve the Pennsylvania-New York Central merger, and it took two trips to the U.S. Supreme Court before the merger could finally take place in 1968. In the meantime, Saunders began diversifying Pennsylvania away from railroads and into minerals processing, real estate development, air charters, and even amusement parks.

The two companies formed Penn Central, the nation's largest railroad, on February 1, 1968. The merger was a mistake from the start, especially for Pennsylvania, which had the resources to weather the poor conditions for railroads at the time. Apart from Saunders (Chairman and CEO of the combined entity) and Perlman (President and COO) barely speaking, there was little attempt made to combine the managements. In addition to wasting money on two corporate staffs—$80 million in merger-related savings never materialized—the companies had different management structures. At Pennsylvania, teams were organized geographically; at New York Central, they were organized by function.

There was also the matter of a third party to the merger. Before it would approve the merger, the ICC required Penn Central to take in New York, New Haven & Hartford Railroad, a bankrupt old railroad that was losing $20 million a year.

That the enterprise didn't flounder from the outset was only accomplished by creative accounting. By milking the subsidiaries for dividends (even beyond their earnings), Penn Central claimed a small profit at first, despite railroad operating losses of $140 million.

The mismatch between the merger partners, and the failure to even attempt to coordinate operations, made the combination worse than either of the two railroads could have been on their own. Trains went to the wrong cities and major industrial customers complained frequently that shipments were not arriving on time. Penn Central became a legendary symbol for bad service. The trucking industry feasted on Penn Central's inefficiency.

In 1969, Penn Central again milked its subsidiaries to make up for deficiencies in operating income. For example, a trucking subsidiary with a $2.8 million profit remitted a $4.7 million dividend. Another with $4.2 million in profits remitted $14.5 million.

It was just a matter of time before somebody, or something, called a stop to this inefficient enterprise. The bond market took care of the job. In early 1970, with $100 million in debt due to mature, Penn Central attempted a bond offering. Although the bonds offered a premium interest rate of 10.5 percent, a recently announced loss killed the offering.

Penn Central stock began falling rapidly. In June 1970, the company appealed to the Nixon administration and to Congress. It appeared that an emergency cash infusion, along with loan guarantees, would be approved. Senator Vance Hartke said at the time that, if Penn Central failed, "there would be a shortage of sufficient coal to keep the utilities going, so you'd have blackouts, you'd have no heat, you'd have actual shortages of food and the rest of the United States would come toppling down and you'd have a depression bigger than the depression of the 1930s." (Ironically, this attitude, which far overstated the power of the railroads, justified the myriad of regulations that ultimately doomed the railroads.)

On Friday, June 19, 1970, after the stock market closed, the Nixon administration announced that it reversed its position and was *not* supporting government-backed loans for the railroad industry. On June 22, Penn Central filed for bankruptcy, claiming liabilities of $3.3 billion.

According to some reports, the railroad was losing $2 million per day. It was the largest bankruptcy ever, up to that time.

Out of this wreckage, and a wave of railroad bankruptcies in the early 1970s, the government started two subsidized companies, Amtrak (to handle passenger traffic) and Conrail (to handle freight). Both cost the government billions over the next several years. The ICC finally got the message (with the help of Congress gradually legislating it out of existence), and the federal government lessened the level of regulation over the railroads.

## What Went Wrong

The federal government failed to innovate and realize that the ICC's heavy-handed enforcement tactics were inappropriate to a now-struggling railroad industry. The Pennsylvania-New York Central merger would have trouble succeeding under the best of circumstances, but the government's delay and requirement that a third, bankrupt railroad be included in the merged company doomed the deal. That failure led to the largest-ever bankruptcy (until that time) and a federal bailout costing taxpayers billions.

# Wesray's LBO Of Gibson Greetings (1982)

Wesray Capital, owned by former Treasury Secretary William Simon and his partner, Raymond Chambers, an investment banker, was formed in 1981. Its first significant transaction was the leveraged buyout of Gibson Greetings, a greeting-card company that was then a division of RCA. This deal, more than any other deal or single event or circumstance, made the 1980s the Deal Decade.

RCA, after years of acquiring assets, started shedding those assets as the high inflation of the 1970s caused its stock price to stagnate and increased debt-servicing costs. High inflation during the 1970s hurt business earnings, but it hurt the price of publicly traded stocks even more. The uncertainty of the effects of inflation and the attractive, guaranteed returns from government bonds drove money from the stock market. Even quality companies with good earnings were trading at huge historical discounts. This was worse for conglomerates, which had built up assets (many of them stellar performers) only to see their stock prices stagnate and their interest expenses grow. In the early 1980s, these assets were selling at prevailing prices, which were cheap compared with earnings, and ridiculously cheap when compared with earnings in an era of low inflation, which was just starting.

In January 1982, Wesray bought Gibson Greetings for $80 million. Simon and Chambers each put up only $330,000 in cash and, even with other equity contributions, provided only $1 million of the purchase price in the form of equity. This was not the first leveraged buyout ever. In fact, Kohlberg Kravis Roberts & Co. had been doing leveraged deals since at least as far back as 1978. The high profile of this deal and its dramatic success ushered in the dawn of an era.

The financing of the deal was groundbreaking, and was later adopted in numerous leveraged transactions. They mortgaged Gibson's machinery in exchange for a $13 million loan from an affiliate of Barclays. They received the balance from General Electric Credit Corp., in its initial foray into LBO financing. GE Credit was willing to take the risk because of the other innovative financing planned by Wesray, and an equity stake in Gibson. Both methods were used to lure lenders in future LBOs.

The innovative financing consisted of selling Gibson's real estate and a factory for $31 million, then arranging to lease back the use of those assets, pursuant to a simultaneously executed 20-year arrangement. The money was used to pay down the GE Credit loan. Wesray was actually able to negotiate the sale, mortgage, and leaseback of assets before it owned them, with all transactions taking place nearly simultaneously.

The deal quickly proved to be a steal. Gibson Greetings had been strongly profitable before the transaction, and its profits increased. Wesray took the company public only 13 months later. Although Wesray did not sell any stock, the IPO valued the company at nearly $300 million, with Simon's and Chambers' ownership worth more than $130 million. In subsequent offerings between 1983 and 1986 and other sales, Simon and Chambers each made about $75 million on the investment, for a more-than-200-fold return, in less than four years.

The deal ushered in the era of leveraged buyouts. The speed with which Wesray obtained its windfall made the financial world take notice.

Simon's credibility made the complex, leveraged structure work, and the success signaled to the players in future deals—equity investors, management, secured lenders, unsecured lenders, advisors—that such deals could make the participants a lot of money. The public's enthusiastic response to the IPO showed that investors would not shun these leveraged entities when the financial purchasers wanted to exit. Investment banks such as Drexel Burnham Lambert sprang to prominence because of their willingness to sell unsecured debt. Financial services companies, such as GE, Citibank, and First Chicago, became heavily involved in both debt and equity investments in leveraged transactions. And numerous investors started leveraged buyout funds to cash in.

Simon and Chambers split in 1986, though Wesray continued to manage its ongoing deals. Each of the principals was worth more than $250 million. Simon attempted to start a similar firm, but feuded with that partner. He later started a company with his sons to manage his business interests. Chambers devoted himself to helping rebuild urban New Jersey. He also owns the New Jersey Nets.

## What Went Right

Wesray Capital's acquisition of Gibson Greetings was one of the earliest LBOs. Even so, it pushed the envelope, with very little equity and a host of sales and leasebacks, all executed quickly. William Simon's high profile provided the credibility to attempt these moves, and their success (a 200-fold return in four years) spawned a wave of similar deals.

# Wesray's LBO of Avis (1986)

In 1986, when Wesray bought Avis, only $10 million of the purchase price was equity. In 14 months, Wesray engaged in a number of financial maneuvers to improve Avis' balance sheet. Then it sold the remainder of the company to an ESOP. Its profit—an amazing $740 million—is one of the greatest short-term investment profits in history. The crowning achievement was the innovative use of the ESOP, which allowed Wesray to realize a return far greater than from any other exit strategy.

Avis is an ongoing experiment in corporate ownership. Since its founding in 1946, it has had 14 owners. It has been part of five different conglomerates, spent time with both KKR and Wesray as owners, and gone public twice. In 1986, KKR acquired Beatrice, Avis's then-owner. In the first of a long series of divestitures, it sold Avis to Wesray in April 1986.

Although Wall Street expected Avis to fetch $400 million, KKR sold it to Wesray for an amount estimated at $250 million. Wesray was willing to move fast on the deal, and assume more than $1.3 billion in debt in connection with the deal. Wesray allowed some top management to participate in the deal and put up only $10 million in equity; it financed the rest. Impatient to make a bunch of asset sales in a hurry, KKR let Wesray get the better of the deal. It turned out that even at $400 million, the company would have been a steal for Wesray.

Wesray quickly sold off some subsidiaries. In July 1986, it sold Avis Leasing's domestic fleet management operations for $280 million, half of which was assumption of debt. It announced a public offering of Avis Europe the next month and raised approximately $300 million.

CEO J. Patrick Barrett, who invested in the deal, was quoted at the outset as saying he thought Avis would be a "permanent investment" for Wesray: "I got the feeling that Wesray has an interest in this business and feels it's a good investment." In September 1987, just 14 months after closing on the LBO, Wesray announced it was selling Avis. (Barrett later disclosed that he made $50 million on the transaction.)

Wesray was selling to an ESOP for $1.75 billion. Because the deal included the assumption of Avis's $1 billion in debt (preexisting and relating to the Wesray acquisition), Wesray would receive approximately $750 million on its original investment of $10 million. Wesray took about $500 million in cash and the rest in securities of the new company.

For workers, the deal was rocky but ultimately turned out well, in part because no one can own Avis for too long. Operating results improved dramatically after the sale to the ESOP, and employee morale and ownership became the subject of news stories and advertising. During the economic slowdown from 1990 to 1992, however, momentum was lost. Avis stopped increasing in profitability. Long seeing its main competition as Hertz, it was suddenly confronted by aggressive discounters, such as Budget and Alamo. A share of ESOP stock worth $5 in 1987 was worth $9 in 1994. A buoyant economy lifted the company soon after, though, and the lure of new ownership worked its usual wonders. HFS, owners of Century 21 Realty and Days Inns, bought the company from the ESOP in 1996 for $800 million, or $25 per ESOP share. (In 1997, HFS conducted an IPO for Avis.)

## What Went Right

To start, Wesray was much more shrewd than KKR, Avis' seller. Wesray then made some aggressive financial moves to reduce significantly the acquisition debt. With nearly any exit strategy, Wesray would have achieved a phenomenal return on its $10-million investment. Because of the tax advantages to lenders to an ESOP, it could borrow more money, and pay a higher price, than any other kind of buyer. Wesray used the ESOP in an unprecedented way to maximize its return.

# CHAPTER 6

## RULE 6: Take care of the little people

$ Gordon Cain's acquisition of Cain Chemical (1987)
$ The Reichmanns' attempt to build Canary Wharf (1987)
$ Kohlberg Kravis Roberts & Co.'s acquisition of Duracell (1988)
$ Wesray's sale of Simmons Mattress Co. to an ESOP (1989)

Deal making, with its numerous complexities, can be seen as an art, but it is important to remember that the object of the deal is generally something tangible. Making a good deal improves the likelihood of a venture's success once the buyer or seller gets the spoils, but the venture must, to some degree, succeed or fail on its merits. It is too easy, especially in the business conditions of the past 20 years, in which assets have been able to move freely among various owners, to consider the deal as an end in itself. If you buy a company, even if you got a great price, you still have to run the thing.

In many good and bad deals, this comes down to how you treat employees. In numerous deals, employees are regarded as a big expense, and the possibility of mass layoffs can be regarded by acquirers as a positive thing; think of the savings. That certainly helped KKR make its money on Safeway, but it came at a price. The negative publicity may have altered KKR's subsequent operations. (See Chapter 3 for a profile of that deal.)

Many fine deals, rather than treating employees as an expense to cut, have succeeded because the buyer used employee ownership to improve the operation. Again, a KKR deal demonstrates this. KKR's acquisition of Duracell included significant equity for employees. KKR's deals typically include employee equity, but in Duracell, the structure seemed tilted toward increasing ownership in the rank-and-file, rather than just making equity partners of the top managers. (The top managers also had significant equity in this deal.) Properly motivated, these employees increased cash flow by 20 to 50 percent and made KKR one of its biggest-ever profits on a deal.

Gordon Cain, in taking over seven commodity chemical businesses under the name Cain Chemical, may have gone even further, spreading equity to nearly every employee. They helped Cain cut costs significantly. Along with cyclical improvements in commodity chemical prices, everyone made a huge profit. More than 90 percent of the rank-and-file employees participated in the ESOP, and they each made at least $100,000 in one year.

The ESOP mechanism can work well for employees and the deal makers both, as the experience with Cain Chemical and Avis (see Chapter 5) indicates. ESOPs can be subject to abuse, however, and Wesray abused the ESOP it created as an exit strategy to its Simmons Mattress acquisition. Although Wesray still profited significantly, it had to give back portions of its profits on four separate occasions.

Deals can fail based on the treatment of people other than employees. The Reichmann family, building a real estate empire on massive debt, should have had very cordial relationships with the bankers who made it possible for them to borrow $20 billion. The Reichmanns' successes isolated them and made them careless. Bankers rushed to loan them money, so they treated bankers accordingly. When, in building the giant Canary Wharf project near London, the economy turned against them, Paul Reichmann continued the same treatment, and the bankers responded by kicking the Reichmanns off the project and throwing their company, Olympia & York, into bankruptcy.

Drexel Burnham Lambert's bankruptcy, to some degree, was the result of a similar payback. Although Drexel is not the subject of any one deal in this book, it played a role in financing at least five of the deals profiled. In addition, as a pioneer in the field of leveraged financing, Drexel cast a large shadow, causing other firms to jump into the deal business, leading to several other deals profiled in this book.

The beginning of the end for Drexel, obviously, occurred when Michael Milken was indicted. Drexel struggled to survive, but decided to pay big fines to settle charges lodged against it. When it was in financial distress, no banks or governmental entities came to its defense. Unlike the situation when J.P. Morgan worked to shore up temporarily weakened financial institutions to end the Panic of 1907, no one was interested in saving Drexel. Other firms felt that Drexel shunned them by not sharing deals and expertise when it was on top. When the tables turned, no one on Wall Street stepped up to help—and many were secretly glad Drexel came to that end.

# Gordon Cain's acquisition of Cain Chemical (1987)

Gordon Cain was regarded as the father of petrochemical LBOs. A career executive at DuPont, he returned from retirement twice to lead employee buyouts of chemical operations. Cain's formula was not complicated. It was based on the truths he learned during nearly a half century in the business.

First, take advantage of industry trends. If the chemical business favored specialty chemicals, buy the commodity chemical businesses on the cheap. Second, take advantage of cyclical pricing. Buy when chemical prices are low, and benefit when they go up. Third, cut overhead ruthlessly. Cain was able to reduce overhead by 75 to 80 percent in his most successful buyouts. Fourth, spread employee ownership. (This also helps smooth things over with employees after you have cut overhead to the bone.)

In early 1987, Cain, then 75 years old, organized his most ambitious effort. Focusing on ethylene plants, Cain bought seven commodity chemical plants from four different companies. The companies all wanted to unload ethylene assets because of the chemical's low price and devote their resources to higher-margin specialty chemicals. The purchase price was approximately $1.1 billion. There was virtually no equity component to the purchase price. Gordon Cain put up $2.3 million himself, out of approximately $25 million in equity put up by employees, other executives, and

Morgan Stanley. Cain's credibility, plus the equity kicker (the portion of he ownership of the company granted to the lender, along with interest on the loan, in exchange for being able to borrow the money), motivated bankers to finance 98 percent of the transaction.

Nearly everything went right in the deal. Cain had purchased the assets for a fraction of the price of building ethylene production capacity. He paid, on average, between 25 and 50 percent of the replacement cost of the plants to acquire them. Therefore, anyone trying to enter the business to compete—and it would take approximately three years to build such plants—would have to spend much more than Cain to enter the field.

In addition, Cain had correctly recognized that ethylene prices were bottoming out. Within six months, increased prices raised cash flow by nearly 25 percent more than acquisition projections. Cain succeeded in reducing expenses and keeping morale high. The top executives owned significant portions of the company, all managers had equity, and the rank-and-file employees owned 12 percent through an ESOP.

It took only about a year for Cain's efforts to bear fruit. In April 1988, he sold his company to Occidental Petroleum for $1.25 billion. Occidental also assumed the remaining $830 million in debt from the LBO. The $25 million put up by the investor group grew 40-fold in one year.

Gordon Cain made $100 million on the transaction. Three executives, who put up $900,000 each, received a total of $120 million. Morgan Stanley and Chase Manhattan, which put up some of the $25 million and were responsible for the financing, each made $120 million. The biggest winners, though, were Cain Chemical's 1,300 employees.

The employees, concerned at the time of the buyout and again upon learning of the sale to Occidental that they would be out of jobs, made at least $100,000 apiece. Seventy managers received an average of $2 million apiece. All but 90 of the 1,300 workers shared $155 million through the ESOP. Workers who joined too late to qualify for the ESOP received an extra year's salary. Even workers who declined to participate in the ESOP received $10,000 each.

# The Reichmanns' attempt to build Canary Wharf (1987)

The Reichmann brothers—Paul, Albert, and Ralph—and their company, Olympia & York Developments, deserve inclusion in this book for their financial acumen in becoming Manhattan's biggest landlord. At the height of New York's financial crisis in 1977, they leveraged their Toronto holdings and bought eight Manhattan office towers for $320 million. In the mid-1980s, they refinanced those buildings for $1.5 billion and built the World Financial Center, completed in 1988, increasing the family fortune still again.

In the scope of the financial catastrophe that followed, however, based in part of what they did with that fortune, their earlier success and its fruits were swept up in a much larger business failure. In 1987, Paul Reichmann (the leader of the brothers' real estate ventures) purchased 71 acres on the Thames riverfront in London named the Isle of Dogs. Christened Canary Wharf, Reichmann predicted that Prime Minister Margaret Thatcher would lift London back to its place as the financial center of Europe and the world's largest financial institutions would eventually bristle at the size and cost of accommodations in London's financial district a couple miles away. Thus, he sunk somewhere between $2 and $3.6 billion of the family's fortune into developing a massive office complex. In total, the project would include construction of 21 buildings and would cost more than $10 billion. To finance even the first part of this monolith, the other properties of Olympia & York Developments had to be leveraged.

That Robert Campeau and Donald Trump were laid low by excessive debt surprised very few people. Although their high public profiles and lavish lifestyles had little to do with their financial problems, it was easy to imagine how bad judgment and adverse circumstances caught up with them. Such a thing was considered unthinkable with Paul Reichmann, his brothers, and their company.

The Reichmanns, at least in appearance, were the embodiment of conservative lifestyles and financial responsibility. They were devoutly religious, shunned the press, and lived an insular, conservative lifestyle. But lifestyle and business sense do not always coincide. Although the Reichmanns made some very smart business deals, making billions in the process, they committed the same errors as their flashier compatriots. They took reckless risks and alienated people and institutions upon which their future depended. Their ambitions for Canary Wharf met the same end as their flamboyant counterparts.

The first phase of Canary Wharf was completed in September 1991. The Reichmanns had extended themselves to complete it, but it was clear that they would need even greater reserves. At opening, the first-phase buildings were only 57 percent leased. The timing was awful: London was going through its worst real estate recession since World War II. Vacancies in London's financial district were rising, and rents were coming down. It was a buyer's, and lessee's, market. For the Reichmanns, who built their fortune in Toronto and New York on purchasing properties during similar downturns, it did not bode well that they not only couldn't take advantage of this London downturn, but they were frozen in place as victims of it.

Slumps in the North American real estate market also hurt Olympia & York's cash flow. Its attempt to diversify beyond real estate cost it money better spent shoring up its properties. Its other investments—Gulf Canada Resources, Abitibi-Price (the world's largest producer of newsprint), and others—fared poorly as well. The family got a black eye, and took a loss of several hundred million dollars from its $700 million investment in Robert Campeau's disastrous takeovers. By the end of 1991, the Reichmann empire, built on $20 billion in debt, was threatening to collapse.

With the prime assets owned throughout the world by the Reichmanns, and Paul Reichmann's unquestioned integrity, the family could have saved most of its fortune through one of two steps: sale of some properties (at, unfortunately, depressed prices) or negotiation with lenders for forbearance of debt in exchange for some equity. Real estate workouts are complex—and this would have been the most complex one ever—but they happen all the time, and the Reichmanns had the savvy, the quality assets, and the integrity to emerge relatively prosperous.

Here Paul Reichmann committed his next, and most costly, gaffe. He refused to give in to his creditors. He would not give them equity, a voice in day-to-day operations, or even up-to-date financial information. So certain was he of his correctness that he practically dared banks to throw Olympia & York into bankruptcy in the United States, Canada, Great Britain, and Japan. He did not think the bankers could handle the massive write-offs of a bankruptcy, or would take the blame for risking a chain reaction of negative impacts on the world's real estate, banking, and financial markets.

With the Reichmanns, the traditional banking relationship was turned on its head. Paul Reichmann, rather than being a supplicant eager to please banks in exchange for loans, had so much influence that he could raise tens, or even hundreds, of millions of dollars without providing financial information or making any effort to be accountable. When the Reichmann family's financial situation worsened in March 1992 and it had to restructure or default on the original terms of its loans, Reichmann did not change his attitude toward his lenders. The restructuring plan he presented in nearly 100 banks provided little in the way of equity or financial information. All it really did was ask for forbearances—and more money, which was desperately needed to continue development of Canary Wharf.

In May 1992, creditors called his bluff and began foreclosing on collateral. Reichmann overestimated the strength of his hand. Because, in part, Olympia & York owed to so many banks, and was indebted to all the world's largest financial institutions, those institutions were able to shoulder the blow, and no one bank had gone too far in lending to the Reichmanns. Olympia & York filed bankruptcy petitions around the world. When the dust settled, the family, according to one magazine, went from "super rich" to "very rich." The family's net worth, estimated by *Forbes* in 1991 at $7 billion, was less than a tenth of that by 1993. The Reichmanns lost their entire interest in Canary Wharf.

The story does not end there, though. In a stunning reversal of fortune, today Paul Reichmann is back in charge of Canary Wharf. Immediately after being deposed from his position in 1992, he tried to form a group of investors to buy the development back from the banks who owned it in bankruptcy. Naturally, they turned him down.

In 1995, however, bringing in the Tisch family, Michael Price, Edmund Safra, Saudi Prince Alwaleed bin Talal, and other investors, Reichmann reacquired Canary Wharf. This time, however, he owns only a small minority stake. That stake, however, originally valued at about $30 to $60 million, has increased significantly in value. London's long-promised transportation improvements from downtown to the area—the Limehouse Link tunnel and the Docklands light-rail—have finally been completed. An upturn in the real estate market has jacked up rents and occupancy rates. A public offering reduced the debt on the project. Reichmann's stake, based on the market capitalization of the company in 1999, was worth between $200 and $400 million.

## What Went Wrong

So great was the Reichmann family's reputation that bankers begged to loan the Reichmanns money. Paul Reichmann's arrogance in dealing with bankers came back to haunt him when the family overextended itself in 1992. The Canary Wharf project required massive amounts of debt and enormous cooperation from lenders. They provided it, but the Reichmanns did not reciprocate. When the project fell behind schedule and local economic conditions worsened, the lenders remembered this attitude, crushing the family's hopes for the project.

# Kohlberg Kravis Roberts & Co.'s acquisition of Duracell (1988)

In May 1988, Kohlberg Kravis Roberts & Co. (KKR) engineered the buyout of Duracell from Kraft for $1.8 billion. This deal succeeded grandly for KKR and its investors, not because KKR did a superior job of buying and selling assets, but because it did a superior job of *managing* them. It got management working much more effectively than it worked for its previous corporate parent, and KKR, its fund investors, and Duracell management were handsomely rewarded.

The terms of the deal were not dictated solely by economic interests. Kraft was pursuing a two-year strategy of divesting itself of its non-food businesses. At $1.8 billion, KKR outbid its competitors by at least $500 million and shocked analysts with the price, who thought Duracell was worth no more than $1.2 billion. Part of the disparity can be attributed to the market's recognition around this period of the premium value of recognizable brand names. (Warren Buffett, in his greatest financial maneuver, bought $1 billion in Coca-Cola stock at the same time KKR was buying Duracell. See Chapter 3 for a profile of that deal.) KKR could also afford the full price because it had management's eager participation.

The deal called for $350 million in equity financing. In addition, KKR convinced 35 Duracell managers to take 9.85 percent of Duracell's stock, either paying cash for it or taking it in the form of stock options as compensation. (By the time KKR sold the company eight years later, the value of this stock jumped 11-fold.)

Management soon bailed KKR out of any charges that it overpaid. Freed from Kraft's giant corporate bureaucracy, which was experienced primarily in food companies, management was able to convince its new owners, despite the heavy debt levels, of the importance of improving research and development. Management's financial participation assured that the money was spent wisely.

All aspects of performance improved with management ownership. They boosted cash flow by more than 50 percent in the first year after the buyout and by nearly 20 percent per year after that.

In May 1991, KKR took Duracell public, issuing 34.5 million shares at $15 per share. In October 1991, KKR sold enough stock to recoup its $350 million in equity. It made additional secondary offerings in November 1993 and March 1995. Although it sold no stock initially, its participation in the secondary offerings and payment of cash dividends allowed it to realize $1.3 billion on its investment by 1996. The secondary offerings also trimmed $600 million from the acquisition debt by the end of 1991.

In September 1996, KKR sold Duracell to Gillette. Gillette had been looking for a new venture for five years, requiring, among other things, a strong consumer brand and a commitment to research and development.

Each Duracell shareholder would receive 1.8 shares of Gillette for each share of Duracell, for an initial value of $7.2 billion. (All stock figures account for a 2-for-1 stock split declared by Gillette in 1998.) By the time of this transaction, KKR still owned 34 percent of Duracell. The deal closed at the end of December 1996.

Just before the deal closed, Kravis (who would be joining the Gillette board of directors) got into a fight with Warren Buffet, who was on the board. KKR wanted Gillette to pay it a $20 million fee for negotiating the sale. Buffett thought the fee should be $8 million because that was the fee Gillette paid each of its two investment banks. Kravis threatened to pull the deal unless he got the $20 million, and he got it.

Some of the limited partners wanted to see KKR immediately turn the Gillette stock into cash, but the strategy of patience paid off. The stock was trading at $39 at the time of the merger, and was trading at $48 six months later.

In February 1998, KKR sold 20 million shares for $1 billion. A weakness in Gillette stock in 1999 interfered with KKR's plan to sell at least half of its remaining stake. As of September 2000, it still owned 51 million Gillette shares, worth $1.5 billion.

KKR and its investors have received $2.3 billion in cash and still hold stock (which is arguably undervalued) worth $1.5 billion. The total profit to date has been $3.8 billion, and KKR's cut (comprised of fees collected on the purchase and sale, management fees, and 20 percent of profits) has been about $800 million.

## What Went Right

KKR arguably overpaid for Duracell by a significant amount. Although the brand name was more valuable than analysts thought, KKR's secret weapon was management participation. With a properly motivated management, cash flow increased dramatically, and both management and KKR made huge amounts of money.

# Wesray's sale of Simmons Mattress Co. to an ESOP (1989)

In 1989, Wesray sold Simmons Mattress Co. to an ESOP for $249 million. This was not one of the biggest deals of the 1980s, but it was one of the most abusive. The deal was so bad for the ESOP that the principals of the deal had to give back some of the proceeds on four separate occasions over the next four years. Wesray still made more than $100 million on the deal and, though it appears the ESOP neither ruined the company nor cost employees their retirement plans, it came close to doing both.

Wesray bought Simmons from Wickes Cos. in 1986 for $120 million. The deal was similar to many instituted by Wesray. It contributed only $5 million in equity, gave a piece of equity to top management, and sold the deal to lenders based on aggressive asset sales. In two years, Simmons retired 75 percent of the debt, selling three large plants and its international operations. All that remained was for Wesray to implement the next step in its well-rehearsed business plan: the exit strategy.

In this instance, Wesray determined not to go public or sell Simmons to a third party. It had Simmons create an ESOP and had the ESOP buy the company. This was a legal practice and it was not uncommon at the time. In fact, Wesray did the same thing with Avis, another of its LBOs. (See Chapter 5 for a profile of that deal.)

ESOPs are a favored financing tool because of the tax benefits involved. The company receives tax deductions on the stock dividends that it pays to the ESOP and on the interest that it incurred to create the ESOP. Banks lending money to set up the ESOP can exclude 50 percent of the interest earned from their taxable income.

Despite the benefits, the structure also invites abuse. The seller automatically dominates a sale to an ESOP. The ESOP has no prior existence, so it has no individual personality or personnel capable of hard bargaining or simply walking away if the deal seems unfavorable. Under federal law, a trustee must be appointed, but the trustee is not a principal and, even in doing its fiduciary best, is not a perfect substitute for a party with its own money on the line.

Although Citizens & Southern Bank, an experienced ESOP trustee, was chosen as the trustee, Wesray and the selling shareholders seemed to roll over it with whatever terms it could get the bank to finance. Chemical

Bank, the lender to the ESOP, played a much more active role in the deal, but caved in to Wesray at every opportunity. Chemical, like many other financial institutions in the late 1980s, wanted to get into the lucrative business of LBOs, and the prospect of lucrative fees and working with Wesray (though it was technically the adverse party, because it was the seller and Chemical supposedly represented the buyer) was irresistible.

In January 1989, Wesray and senior management sold Simmons to the ESOP for $241 million, including the assumption of $40 million in debt. The original LBO group, therefore, received $200 million on its original $5 million investment. It did not receive the entire amount in cash, however; $20 million came in the form of junior subordinated debt, and Wesray also gave one of the lenders, Rockefeller Group, an option to "put" its $30 million of paid-in-kind equity back to Wesray. (As the terms "junior" and "subordinated" imply, this debt placed Wesray at the back of the line for any claims on assets.)

In this instance, the deal went bad before it even started. Simmons was $7 million behind in its payables at the time of the closing. Within four months, management was meeting with Chemical (which postponed the planned syndication of most of the debt as these details became known) to explain that it had a cash shortfall of $17 million, including past due payables of between $11 and $13 million, $3 million in Canadian taxes, and $2 million in letters of credit.

Notwithstanding Simmons's poor cash position from the outset, how could this business sell for $120 million in 1986, sell off all its best assets, and still be worth nearly $250 million less than three years later? The answer was contained in some fanciful projections floated to Chemical and Citizens & Southern at the time of the deal.

For the company to have any chance of surviving under this capital structure, it needed to make miraculous improvements. Simmons projected a $6 million profit for a division that lost $4 million the previous year. Three real estate properties, not especially valuable because Wesray could not or did not sell them, would have to be sold immediately.

Within months, Rockefeller Group exercised its option and returned the paid-in-kind securities to Wesray, making this the first of four give-backs the group would have to make on the deal. By the end of 1989, Simmons defaulted on Chemical's $15 million bridge loan. During 1989 and 1990, Simmons went through two debt restructurings.

Raymond Chambers, one of the investors with Wesray, broke a dead-lock in negotiations to bring in Merrill Lynch Capital Markets (MLCM) as an equity investor in a restructured Simmons with the second give-back. He forwarded $5 million in cash and $5 million in Simmons securities from a trust he controlled.

In March 1991, MLCM invested $32 million and received preferred stock, giving it 60 percent of the equity in Simmons. Wesray made its third give-back by forgiving the $70 million in Simmons debt it held.

The ESOP's ownership fell from 100 to 31 percent. The value of the ESOP stock had dropped from $48 million to only $6 million. Because part of the formation of the ESOP included eliminating the company's contributions to its 401(k) plan, the ESOP constituted the main retirement plan for most of its employees.

In November 1991, employees filed a class action against Wesray, the trustee, and a dozen managers who sold the company to the ESOP. In 1993, in connection with a settlement of the class action and after intervention by the Department of Labor, Wesray and management agreed to a fourth give-back, of $16.5 million.

It appeared that both Simmons and the ESOP were on firm financial footing with the infusions of capital. Wesray made well in excess of $100 million on the transaction. But the immediate failure of Simmons to handle the financial terms, and the four subsequent give-backs, suggest Wesray took advantage of the structure of the deal and significantly overreached.

## What Went Wrong

The structure of an ESOP opens it to abuse in a takeover situation. Although Wesray had used the mechanism both to its benefit and the benefit of the employees in other deals, it overreached, loading Simmons with debt it could not service. Wesray still profited, but it looked greedy and had to give back money on four occasions.

# CHAPTER 7

## RULE 7: Be a pest

$ The ABA's financial settlement with the Spirits of St. Louis (1976)

$ T. Boone Pickens' "unsuccessful" takeover attempt of Gulf Oil (1984)

$ Conseco's acquisition of Green Tree Financial (1998)

Gordon Gekko tells Bud Fox in *Wall Street*, "If you want a friend, get a dog." Although the principals in big deals often appear to be cordial—shaking hands in front of the cameras, conducting joint news conferences, agreeing to generous severance packages for the old guard, and such—you can probably get further ahead in deals by being mean. There may be times that being friendly will best meet your objectives; those times are in the minority. More often, if something is worth negotiating for, it is worth getting all you can.

There are certainly instances where participants in the deal did much better for themselves simply by becoming pests. Nobody likes that kind of adversary, but often it is possible to wear down a negotiating adversary and get the better of the deal.

One of the greatest examples of that kind of behavior is the little-known deal struck by the owners of the Spirits of St. Louis in the defunct American Basketball Association (ABA). The St. Louis franchise would not be joining the NBA, and the other ABA franchises—the Denver Nuggets, Indiana Pacers, New York (now New Jersey) Nets, and San Antonio Spurs—had to negotiate a financial settlement. The Spirits' lawyer, Donald Schupak, took advantage of the fact that the negotiation with him was the end of a long, arduous process. The other owners finally caved in to his demand that each of the four franchises give him and his clients a perpetual right to one-seventh of each of their network television revenues. It wasn't worth much at the time, but Schupak and the other Spirits' owners have received more than $50 million since 1976. In contrast, another ABA owner not joining the NBA negotiated a cash settlement of $3 million, and that was considered a lot.

Corporate raiders perfected the art of saber rattling during the 1980s. By purchasing some stock in a company and threatening a takeover, the raiders usually "put the company in play," either leading the company to buy back the raider's stock at a premium or attracting someone else to take over the company. In this way, without the financing and operating risks of actually taking over a company, the raider could make a big profit in a hurry. The most profitable instance of this was T. Boone Pickens' attempted takeover of Gulf Oil. Pickens made as much noise as he could, finally driving Gulf into the arms of Standard Oil of California (which is now Chevron). Pickens and his company, Mesa Petroleum, made $500 million on the deal.

Despite the possibility that this kind of behavior can be anticipated and ignored, it continues to work, even against skilled negotiators. Conseco, the insurance and financial services company, had made more than 40 acquisitions when it encountered Lawrence Coss and Green Tree Financial. Still, Coss, even though his company was in trouble, convinced Conseco's deal-savvy CEO, Stephen Hilbert, that other acquirers were beating down the doors. Conseco paid a huge premium to acquire Green Tree, and investors have shunned Conseco stock since the deal, knocking more than 80 percent off its market capitalization. Green Tree shareholders got roughly double the price their stock had been trading at before the merger announcement. The premium was even greater considering that, upon announcing the deal, Conseco disclosed that it would have to take $500 million in charges, mostly to fix Green Tree accounting errors. If Green Tree had made such an announcement without a deal, its stock price would have plummeted further.

# The ABA's financial settlement with the Spirits of St. Louis (1976)

The most extravagant failure in the nine-year history of the American Basketball Association was the Spirits of St. Louis. The team's star, Marvin Barnes, was aptly nicknamed "Bad News." Barnes was so much trouble that the Spirits once had to use a time-out so Barnes could pay his charter pilot, courtside, after he missed a team flight. Despite a roster of heralded busts and players who later became NBA stars (such as Maurice Lucas and Moses Malone), not to mention a recent Syracuse graduate named Bob Costas as their announcer, the team's record was 67-101 in two years. They were on the brink of expiring peacefully when the NBA finally agreed to a merger with the ABA.

The NBA would take the four strong ABA franchises—the Denver Nuggets, Indiana Pacers, New York Nets, and San Antonio Spurs. All four teams were loaded with quality players and played to packed arenas. Only a few NBA teams could make similar claims. Each team paid the NBA an entry fee and bore a pro-rata responsibility for paying off the ABA teams that would not be joining the NBA.

The Nuggets, Pacers, and Spurs continued their winning ways immediately after the merger. The Nets were forced to move to New Jersey, a concession to accommodate the New York Knicks, and to sell their franchise player, Julius Erving, to pay the cost of entry. Some say they got the worst deal, and that the franchise struggles to this day as a result of those decisions.

The four new entrants had to make arrangements with the other three ABA teams from the 1975–76 season: the Kentucky Colonels, Spirits of St. Louis, and Virginia Squires. The Virginia situation was dealt with easily; that franchise shut its doors in the weeks before the completion of merger negotiations and its ownership received nothing. (Some would argue the Virginia franchise got the shortest end of the stick, but having already gone out of business, its negotiating position, obviously, was not particularly strong.) The Kentucky franchise received $3 million and was considered fortunate to get that.

That left St. Louis.

The St. Louis franchise was owned by brothers Dan and Ozzie Silna and their attorney, Donald Schupak. The negotiation with Schupak was the end of a long, complicated series of deals by the other owners. In addition to negotiating with the NBA, they had to participate in negotiations with the players' union, which had filed a class action antitrust suit to block the merger, and deal with the Kentucky franchise.

Schupak simply wore down the four owners and their representatives with his demands. The three St. Louis owners received $2.2 million in cash, as well as one-seventh of each of the four new NBA teams' network television revenue *in perpetuity*.

A portion of an NBA franchise's network television revenue was not considered particularly valuable during the 1970s. The league had a serious image problem, and NBA playoff games were frequently televised on tape delay, with virtually no complaints.

But, as Indiana Pacers president Donnie Walsh said, "Perpetuity is a long time." Long enough for Julius Erving to make a positive impact on TV ratings when he joined the NBA. Long enough for Larry Bird and Magic Johnson to join the league's two most storied franchises—Boston and Los Angeles—at the same time, bring their college rivalry to the NBA, and increase TV ratings. And more than long enough for Michael Jordan and the Chicago Bulls to dominate the public consciousness as no other sports team, or individual figure, ever has.

The owners of the former St. Louis franchise have received approximately $50 million so far and, with the current television deal, are earning $13 million per year. The four franchises have spent years trying to negotiate a buyout of the provision but, not surprisingly, the Silna brothers and Schupak want a very high price.

## What Went Right

Donald Schupak and the Silna brothers refused to give in to the other ABA owners. Their assent to the merger was necessary and, by holding out, they were able to wring out some NBA television rights, which generate more than 10 million dollars annually. For a sports franchise that was a nightmare to operate, they definitely got the last laugh.

# T. Boone Pickens' "unsuccessful" takeover attempt of Gulf Oil (1984)

T. Boone Pickens and the company he controlled, Mesa Petroleum, played a high-stakes game of chicken in the early 1980s. The game was so sophisticated that Pickens could make $40 million from flipping the stock of a company like Cities Service Co. and be regarded by *Business Week* as "defeated" because he was not allowed to spend $5 billion to buy the whole company. Pickens made similar sums on so-called unsuccessful raids on Superior Oil and General American Oil.

After playing this game several times, he set his sights on Gulf Oil, the nation's sixth-largest oil company. With the entire investing public focused on Pickens and Gulf, and the national media reporting every move, the parties went through a highly publicized sparring match at the end of 1983 and into 1984. With each parry and thrust, Gulf's stock price rose. These are the highlights:

- *October 8, 1983.* Rumors swirl that Pickens is behind the surging volume in Gulf stock.
- *October 12.* Gulf proposes reincorporating in Delaware, according to its spokesman, to prevent a "Wall Street wolf" from "shooting his way onto the board."
- *October 18.* Pickens discloses that he (mostly with money from Mesa and affiliates) has spent $630 million to buy 14.5 million shares, or 8.75 percent, of Gulf. By the end of December, he will have acquired nearly 20 million shares, or 13 percent, at an average price of around $45 per share. Pickens states his intention to take steps to produce "a significant appreciation" of the price of those shares.
- *October 19.* Four banks financing Pickens' activities withdraw, supposedly due to pressure from Gulf. One of them is Mellon Bank of Pittsburgh, which, like Gulf, was founded by the Mellon family.
- *November 1.* Pickens announces a proxy fight to prevent the reincorporation.
- *December 31.* Gulf wins the proxy contest by a narrow margin.
- *January 1984.* Gulf regards Pickens as defeated. Pickens tries, mostly in vain, to raise money to make a bid to buy the entire company.

- ▸ *February 13.* Gulf raises a $6 billion line of credit, and says it will use it to repurchase (in cash) the company's remaining shares if Pickens acquires 51 percent of Gulf's stock.
- ▸ *February 23.* Pickens offers $65 per share for an additional 8 percent of Gulf, to raise his stake to 21 percent. This move causes Gulf's stock price to rise from 52 5/8 to 58 1/4. Pickens announces the presence of additional investors, though he supposedly had been trying, unsuccessfully, for weeks to find enough investors to finance a purchase of the entire company.
- ▸ *February 24.* Pickens discloses that Gulf had, earlier in the month, tried to buy back his stock for $70 per share. He also discloses that Atlantic Richfield offered Gulf $70 per share for the company on February 1.

Each of these maneuvers caused the price of Gulf's stock to jump. By the beginning of March, it had risen to more than $70 per share, up from about $30 per share before Pickens began acquiring stock. Gulf hurriedly solicited bids from everyone but Pickens, and on March 6, 1984, it announced a deal. Standard Oil Company of California would buy Gulf for $13.2 billion, or $80 per share, in the largest corporate merger ever.

Pickens' group was the biggest winner. It owned 21.7 million shares, with an average purchase price of $45 per share. At the $80 per share merger price, the group's profit was $761 million. Mesa owned two-thirds of the shares, so it made $506 million.

Pickens' move was probably the most profitable of the takeover-dominated 1980s. He put Gulf "in play" without ever actually making an offer. Much of the money used to purchase his group's stake was borrowed. He tried for months to find partners and financing, with only limited success. (One of his advisors, Drexel Burnham Lambert, after frustrating itself attempting to find financing, shortly thereafter took the bold move of issuing a letter saying it was "highly confident" that it could raise necessary financing. The nonbinding commitment, which Drexel later on occasion proved was not a bluff, was treated like currency in numerous later deals.)

Pickens' company, Mesa, later ran into trouble, and Pickens was ousted in 1996. But for a time, he had his pick of targets among the world's largest oil companies, and they quaked when he expressed interest. The half-billion dollar profit in seven months on Gulf was his crowning achievement.

> ## What Went Right
>
> Although the classic rules of strategy dictate that someone who wishes to take hostile action move with stealth, Pickens telegraphed all his moves, sometimes even appearing clumsy. Each move, however, was calculated. Pickens admitted years later that he wasn't even sure he wanted to own Gulf. His structural plans for Gulf were thoroughly discredited as creating huge negative tax consequences for shareholders and depriving the company of the money needed to explore for additional reserves. Nevertheless, the pressure he put on Gulf forced it into a merger with Standard Oil of California, and Pickens and his group made a half billion dollars.

# Conseco's acquisition of Green Tree Financial (1998)

Since its inception less than 20 years ago, Conseco has grown to become one of the country's largest specialty insurers (largely as a result of wise acquisitions). Under the leadership of Stephen Hilbert, Conseco provided a greater return to shareholders, from 1987 to 1997, than any other Fortune 500 company. From 1992 to 1996, Hilbert was the top-paid CEO, receiving $277 million. Despite this stellar record, Lawrence Coss (who himself earned more than $200 million during the 1992–96 period) and Green Tree Financial took advantage of Hilbert and Conseco, costing Conseco more than 80 percent of its market value.

Conseco had consolidated 44 insurance companies in 17 years, but in 1997, Hilbert was looking for something bigger. He set his sights on Green Tree Financial, a sub-prime lender specializing in mobile-home financing. Green Tree had a 10-year record of strong earnings growth, and served a market similar to Conseco's. Hilbert had visions of expanding Conseco from insurance to a variety of financial services, and cross-selling the products of the two companies.

After very preliminary talks in 1997, Green Tree suddenly became available in early 1998. Unfortunately, it became available because the company developed serious problems that threatened its ability to continue operating. Green Tree had been able to grow without significant permanent debt or equity capital because it packaged and sold its mortgages. Using a controversial gain-on-sale accounting technique, Green Tree would book the profits for the entire life of a loan at the time the debt was sold. This required the company to assume rates of early redemption as well as nonpayment; those rates were assumed to be pretty low.

The conventional wisdom—that low-income borrowers would not shop for rates or refinance when interest rates dropped—proved false as continued low interest rates caused a wave of refinancing among Green Tree's borrowers. The income stream being terminated early, Green Tree had to reduce already-recognized earnings. In late 1997, Coss announced a $150 million earnings restatement, which he assured the stock-holding public would be a one-time event. In early 1998, however, he had to announce a further $40 million restatement, along with an additional $200 million restatement for 1996.

The earnings restatements started a chain of events that threatened Green Tree's existence. It made extensive use of commercial paper to finance its lending activities, and ratings reductions limited its ability to borrow. Banks providing backup financing raised rates and reduced the amounts they would lend. As a last resort, Green Tree had to borrow $500 million from Lehman Brothers, but at high rates and with warrants for Lehman to purchase 2.7 million Green Tree shares at the then-current price of $22.50 per share. (Lehman was able to make $43 million on these warrants in two months.)

When Hilbert approached Coss in late March 1998, Conseco should have had the stronger negotiating position. Green Tree was in desperate shape financially, and it was considering unpleasant alternatives to stay in business, such as finding an equity investor, selling debt or equity to the public, and being taken over. In its current condition, there was not a great deal of interest, except at bargain-basement prices.

Somehow, however, Coss seized on Hilbert's interest and took advantage. Knowing that Hilbert wanted to diversify beyond insurance into other financial services, Coss began making demands. The price would have to be more than $50 per share (nearly double Green Tree's stock price), and Conseco could have one week to put a deal together, because of all the other potential deals Green Tree was considering.

Hilbert and Conseco fell for it. Ignoring Green Tree's dire financial condition, Hilbert assumed that he needed to outbid other suitors bearing premium offers, and he needed to do it fast. In fact, there were no other offers, and potential investors would have either insisted on high interest rates for debt financing or would have paid only the market price (mid-$20s) for Green Tree stock.

On April 7, 1998, Conseco agreed to acquire Green Tree for $53 per Green Tree share in Conseco stock, or $7.6 billion. On the previous day, Green Tree stock had closed at $29 per share. The reaction to the deal by Conseco investors was immediate and negative: The next day, Conseco stock dropped 15 percent. Eventually, the value of the deal dropped to $6 billion because of the weakness of Conseco stock.

Conseco, in a very responsible move but one inconsistent with its insistence on paying a premium price for Green Tree, immediately announced that it was preparing further restatements of Green Tree's earnings. In July, when the deal closed, it announced another $350 million reduction in Green Tree's prior earnings, along with $150 million in restructuring charges. In addition, Conseco had to contribute more than a billion dollars to Green Tree immediately so it could continue operating.

Although Hilbert predicted when the deal closed that investors would change their minds and Conseco stock would hit $70 by the end of 1998, it went in the other direction. The additional charges, skepticism about cross-selling, and fears that Conseco's aggressive increases in Green Tree's lending activities would lead to future write-downs caused the stock price to continue tumbling throughout 1998 and 1999. By February 2000, it was trading at $16 per share. The loss in market value to Conseco's pre-merger investors was about $8 billion.

Stephen Hilbert insisted that Conseco is performing as expected, and investors just don't get it. Analysts have attributed the rising earnings, yet falling stock price, to a belief that Conseco's aggressive increase in lending is coming at a sacrifice of quality, and those earnings will someday need to be restated. Lawrence Coss remains a board member, but he retired from management in 1998. He received a $30 million "golden parachute," but never sold his Green Tree stock following the merger. He has more than $100 million in Conseco stock, which was worth four times that amount when the deal was announced. How he would have done had the deal never taken place, however, is difficult to say; Green Tree's future was very much in doubt.

For Hilbert and Conseco, things only got worse. The company was forced to take additional write-downs on the Green Tree investment and, in April 2000, Hilbert was finally forced out of the company he founded. Conseco announced that it was selling the Green Tree assets, recognizing that it would receive only a fraction of the price it paid only two years earlier. During the summer of 2000, Conseco stock dropped as low as $5 per share.

## What Went Wrong

Stephen Hilbert and Conseco, after 20 years of hard bargaining to acquire scores of companies, got bamboozled. They decided they wanted Green Tree so badly that they fell for every tactic Lawrence Coss and Green Tree could imagine to raise the price and minimize Conseco's due diligence and financial discipline. The Green Tree acquisition reversed decades of shrewd financial moves by Conseco, and it cost Stephen Hilbert his company.

# CHAPTER 8

## RULE 8: Do your homework

$ Sony's acquisition of Columbia Pictures (1989)

$ Minoru Isutani's purchase of Pebble Beach (1990)

$ The merger of HFS and CUC International into Cendant (1997)

The advice to do your homework might seem unnecessary, particularly in the big deals profiled in this book. This rule is occasionally ignored, however, especially because the larger the deal, the more planning and information are necessary to carry it off. These big deals are so complex that the principals could do plenty of planning and due diligence, but still ignore something that turns out to be important.

Even the most adept deal makers are not immune from lapses of judgment. Henry Silverman's building of franchise-giant HFS was accomplished by careful planning and obtaining a lot of information. Still, when he arranged a merger with CUC International, he allowed CUC to withhold its internal financial information. Even though Silverman would be the CEO of the combined enterprise, he agreed to let CUC maintain its own internal reporting systems. It was inevitable that he would find out that CUC was cooking its books, but proper due diligence—even refusing to do the deal if the information was withheld—would have saved Silverman's shareholders billions of dollars.

Apart from developing a strategic vision, Sony failed to develop an operating plan. Even though it had a longtime U.S. presence and owned a successful record company, its ownership of Columbia Pictures was, from the start, a disaster, traced to poor planning. Sony followed some bad advice about who to obtain as co-CEOs and, worse, signed up Jon Peters and Peter Guber while they had an exclusive production deal with Warner Brothers. It cost Sony about a half-billion dollars to fix that mess.

Japanese investor Minoru Isutani's purchase of Pebble Beach also failed due to fundamentally bad planning. Isutani paid an outlandish price, which he could only recover by selling golf course memberships. He neglected, however, local regulations requiring that Pebble Beach maintain public access. Floundering in debt, he finally unloaded the property at a loss of about $300 million.

# Sony's acquisition of Columbia Pictures (1989)

When Sony acquired Columbia Pictures Entertainment, Inc. in 1989, the price—$3.4 billion, or nearly $5 billion including assumed debt—was unquestionably high. Sony was looking for more than another source of earnings, however. It was looking for that elusive concept of synergy, which it never found. Further, as an outsider trying to play an insiders' game, it got scalped.

Sony never quite got over having its Betamax video recording technology surpassed because Philips, the inventor of VHS, signed up more movies to be made available on VHS. (By most accounts Betamax is superior to VHS.) It bought CBS Records in 1987 and Columbia Pictures in 1989, in large part to assure itself a certain amount of captive "software" for its developing technologies.

The purchase of CBS Records turned out well, because the label had a large roster of talent. It did little, however, to advance Sony's attempt to develop Digital Audio Tape (DAT) as the new audio industry standard. In fact, theoretically, owning a competing music company could be a disadvantage when trying to negotiate with other music companies to release their product on DAT.

The purchase of Columbia Pictures, on the other hand, was disastrous. Although Sony bought, as part of the deal, Columbia's 2,700-title film library, it was never able to make 8mm recorded tapes an industry standard to replace VHS. More important, it significantly overpaid and installed incompetent management to run the studio.

Coca-Cola had owned Columbia through the 1980s, and never quite developed the knack for filmmaking. Though the studio was not a significant money maker, Coke took advantage of what Sony perceived as its desperate need and made a $1.2 billion profit on the investment. This was enough to end Coca-Cola's diversification kick.

Walter Yetnikoff, President of CBS Records, recommended Peter Guber and Jon Peters as co-CEOs of Columbia Pictures (which consisted primarily of two studios, Columbia and Tri-Star, and a profitable television division). Neither had experience running a studio, but they were hot at the time, having co-produced *Rainman* and *Batman*.

The deal Yetnikoff offered was sweet in the extreme: $2.75 million each in salary, 2.5 percent of all profits in excess of $200 million, a bonus pool of $50 million in five years, and a percentage of the appreciation in value of the studios. In addition, Sony would buy Guber-Peters Productions, their publicly traded production company, for $200 million. This amount was far in excess of any possible value of the assets. In fact, after Sony bought it, it wrote off much of the purchase price as a loss.

The biggest mistake, however, was neglecting Guber's and Peters' contractual obligations to Warner Brothers, a competing studio. Only a few months before, the duo had signed a five-year production deal with Warner. Yetnikoff knew about the conflict. Guber and Peters knew about the conflict. For some reason, however, no one told Warner until after the agreement was reached.

Warner Brothers sued Sony, Guber, and Peters for breach of contract and sought an injunction to prevent Guber and Peters from working for anyone else. Prior to the lawsuit going anywhere, the parties settled, and the settlement was a bonanza for Warner:

- ▸ Sony agreed to sell Warner a 50-percent interest in Columbia House, the largest direct-mail club for audio and video entertainment in the United States;
- ▸ Warner received exclusive cable-TV distribution rights for all Columbia feature films;
- ▸ Warner and Columbia would swap properties, with Warner becoming the sole owner of the valuable Burbank Studios (which Warner and Columbia jointly owned) and Columbia getting the smaller, less valuable, Lorimar Studio; and

▸     Warner would keep the 50 film projects Guber and Peters had in development, including the rights to the *Batman* sequels.

Analysts estimated that Warner received between $400 and $600 million in assets for letting Guber and Peters out of their contract.

Guber and Peters might have outlived this legacy had they run the studio profitably. They merely confirmed Sony's mistake in hiring them, however, costing the company more money at every opportunity. They outspent every studio, yet gradually lost market share and had few hits. They looked bad doing it, too, as stories spread of their profligate ways. They spent as much as $200 million to refurbish the Culver City studio lot and increased overhead by 50 percent. In just the first two years after the acquisition, Sony invested another billion dollars in the company. Ironically, Sony's chairman, Akio Morita, co-authored a book not long before the purchase titled *The Japan That Can Say 'No.'* Jon Peters left after two years, supposedly having worn out his welcome with Sony long before.

In late 1994, the rest of the management team unraveled. In October, Peter Guber resigned. His severance package was worth somewhere between $20 and $40 million, and Sony agreed to invest $200 million in his new production company. (It got off cheap with Peters, paying him only between $10 and $25 million in severance.) Sony bit the bullet, announcing a $2.7 billion write-off of Columbia assets and reporting a quarterly loss of $3.2 billion. Walter Yetnikoff having long fled the scene, Mickey Schulhof, the head of Sony Corp. of America, who engineered the purchase of Columbia and the deal with Guber and Peters, was forced to resign within a year.

## What Went Wrong

A smart deal requires more than a strategic vision. When Sony bought Columbia, it was buying a business that required specific business acumen. Sony went about obtaining its management in a haphazard way, saddling itself with an untenable legal situation, which Warner exploited to the tune of several million dollars, and chose inexperienced managers who squandered money and opportunities.

# Minoru Isutani's purchase
# of Pebble Beach (1990)

Pebble Beach is one of the most exclusive resorts in the United States, and its most famous golf course, Pebble Beach Golf Links, hosts a stop on the PGA Tour annually and has hosted numerous U.S. Open championships and a PGA Championship. Tom Watson's final-round chip-in on the 17th hole to defeat Jack Nicklaus in 1982 is one of the most famous moments in golf's long history. Tiger Woods' historic victory in the 2000 U.S. Open further cements Pebble Beach's reputation as America's home course.

Financially, the resort is no less storied. Since 1980, it has had five owners and has made (or cost) various owners hundreds of millions of dollars. In 1981, Marvin Davis, an oil and real estate investor, bought Pebble Beach, along with the rest of the assets of Twentieth Century Fox Co., from public shareholders. In addition to Pebble Beach, Fox owned Aspen resort property, a Coca-Cola bottler, real estate in Century City, the movie studio, and the film library. The purchase price for the whole package was $700 million, of which only $50 million was equity.

The deal was a bonanza for Davis. He sold the studio and film library in 1985 to Rupert Murdoch for $575 million. After paying off debts and partners, Davis' gain was estimated at $300 million *plus* the Aspen and Pebble Beach resorts. Davis improved Pebble Beach by building The Inn at Spanish Bay and an accompanying golf course. After talks to sell the entire resort fell through, however, upkeep costs were kept at a minimum.

In September 1990, Japanese golf course and resort owner Minoru Isutani, and his U.S. corporate entity, Cosmo World, purchased Pebble Beach Co. for $841 million from Davis and his partners. For that grand sum—more than Davis paid in 1981 for the entire Twentieth Century Fox Corporation, including Pebble Beach, the studio, and all the other assets—Isutani got four golf courses (Pebble Beach, Spyglass Hill, Spanish Bay, and Del Monte) and two resort properties (Del Monte Lodge and The Inn at Spanish Bay). The 5,300-acre complex also included a significant amount of undeveloped forest land.

This was a heady time for Japanese investors in the United States. The booming Japanese stock and real estate markets had made numerous men wealthy overnight, and they were reveling in the opportunity to purchase "trophy" properties in the U.S. A particularly buoyant segment of the Japanese economy was golf-course development and speculation. The Japanese love of golf is legendary, and developers were pre-selling memberships to clubs for hundreds of thousands of dollars. The memberships traded like securities. (It later turned out that some of these developers just absconded with the money. Others sold far more memberships than they represented. Still others built courses only to find that, the boom times over, the members had busted out and could not make good on their financial commitments.)

It is not automatic that a huge profit for one side means a bad deal for the other, but Isutani completely ignored this, along with several other facts. The courses were steady earners, but, when factoring in the significant maintenance costs, they weren't cash cows. There was plenty of undeveloped land, but many zoning and environmental rules preventing its complete development.

To pay short-term debt of approximately $550 million, Isutani bought the resort with a plan familiar in Japan but unknown in the United States: selling preferred-time golf memberships. Under the plan, Isutani would sell 750 memberships for $750,000 apiece. The membership would entitle the holder to guaranteed tee times for life during a two-hour block each day, and up to 60 rooms set aside for members at the two resorts.

Although Isutani never got far enough to test the water, the shift in the Japanese economy imperiled the plan. The expected price per membership dropped from $750,000 to $350,000 (though the proposed number of memberships doubled to 1,500). As challenges delayed the plan's implementation, the estimated membership price dropped to $150,000.

The price ended up being academic. The California Coastal Commission nixed Isutani's plan to privatize the resort in any way. The Coastal Act of 1976 protected existing public access to 1,100 miles of California coastline and required that any new coastal development retain that accessibility. Furthermore, Pebble Beach had previously promised the Coastal Commission that it would keep the course open to the public.

As soon as the public—and, more specifically, the locals—got wind of the plan, massive negative publicity ensued and the Commission rejected the plan in October 1991, after Isutani had already received a one-year extension on $574 million in loans. The kiss of death was when Isutani's company missed the filing deadline for challenging the Commission's decision in court by 15 minutes. Shortly thereafter, Monterey County said that

Pebble Beach Co. was $3 million in arrears for property taxes, and still owed $365,000 in real estate transaction fees from more than a year earlier.

In January 1992, just five months before the U.S. Open was coming to Pebble Beach, Isutani sold the resort to another group of Japanese investors, Sumitomo Credit and Taiheyo Club. They paid between $500 and $574 million, just enough for Isutani to cover his loans but lose his entire equity stake of $267 million (and perhaps as much as $350 million). Working with PR firm Hill & Knowlton, the new owners kept the purchase secret for a month and carefully planned media relations.

Sumitomo and Taiheyo Club succeeded where Isutani failed. They made a nice profit, selling Pebble Beach to a celebrity investor group in July 1999 for $820 million.

## What Went Wrong

Minoru Isutani bought Pebble Beach with the idea that he could sell golf memberships similar to the way in which extravagant Japanese golf projects are financed. He did not gauge the demand for such memberships, nor did he account for the complex restrictions governing ownership and use of land in the Monterey Peninsula. He made numerous careless moves and was forced to sell at a large loss.

# The merger of HFS and CUC International into Cendant (1997)

Henry Silverman made a successful and lucrative career from making aggressive business deals. An admitted control freak, Silverman insisted on detailed financial information for every part of acquired businesses, and, as his company, HFS, Inc., grew, he wrestled with massive amounts of information to keep on top of operations. *Fortune* called him a genius, a term frequently used to describe Silverman's assent in the business world.

He let down his guard in one deal, however, and it cost shareholders as much as $30 billion.

Silverman, who spent the 1980s working successfully for several LBO-fund operators, started on his own in 1990, acquiring Days Inns. His strategy was to divest himself of the actual assets and operations and to make his money solely on franchise fees. HFS went public in 1992 and, for five years, used its stock as currency to expand aggressively, acquiring more hotel chains, rental cars, mortgage companies, and real estate and travel agencies. Always, the formula was the same: Acquire only the franchising rights (or sell everything but the franchising rights) and expand the brand name, bringing in new franchisees. Although Silverman was not well-known to the public at large, between 1992 and 1995, HFS stock rose 2,000 percent, from $4 to $79 per share.

In May 1997, HFS announced that it was merging with CUC International. CUC International could be considered the first e-commerce company. In 1973, Walter Forbes promoted a concept of people buying consumer goods electronically instead of in stores, keeping overhead at a minimum and passing on the savings to consumers. There being no Internet then—there weren't even personal computers in 1973—Forbes' idea went nowhere, but he developed the concept of shopping clubs, where the power of a large number of buyers could be used to obtain goods at lower prices. CUC made its money primarily on yearly membership fees, and did not own any of the products it was selling (or, perhaps more accurately, arranging for consumers to buy), so it was able to pass all the price breaks it could obtain to consumers.

The existence of synergy between HFS and CUC was questionable, and it was undeniable that the two companies had radically different cultures. Where Silverman ran a tight ship, personally conducting meetings involving every division and becoming intimately familiar with monthly financial information on every business segment, Forbes regarded himself as a strategist and marketer. Although CUC maintained and met aggressive profitability goals, Forbes professed ignorance about the details of operations and did little to promote financial controls at his expanding company.

This was not the type of operation Silverman had become successful acquiring. Prior to the merger, HFS' requests for nonpublic information were denied on the grounds that, if the deal fell through, HFS might acquire a competing business. Similarly, HFS' auditors were unsuccessful in getting nonpublic information. HFS had to rely on CUC's auditors, Ernst & Young, for the opinion that CUC's books were clean.

Further, the two companies agreed to keep their separate headquarters after the merger, and Silverman and Forbes agreed to a bizarre revolving

CEO set-up. From inception until January 1, 2000, Silverman would be CEO and Forbes would be chairman. Then, they would switch jobs. Significantly, Forbes insisted on and received a promise that the companies would keep their internal financial reporting systems.

The deal was completed in December 1997, creating a company with an initial market capitalization of more than $25 billion. (During the next few months, as the news of the merger highlighted these two relatively unknown high fliers, the market capitalization would climb to nearly $40 billion in April 1998.) The problems, however, started almost immediately.

CUC's separate financial reporting system was supposed to prepare consolidated monthly reports for Silverman. As of late February 1998, however, the January 1998 report had not been completed. Cendant, as the combined entity had been named, was also in danger of missing the deadline for filing its annual report with the Securities and Exchange Commission. Silverman repeatedly asked Forbes and his staff for more access to financial information, both for the annual report and for corporate planning and strategy.

In early March, Cendant's chief accounting officer met with CUC executives and was shocked to see a list of "adjustments" designed to boost revenue by $165 million for the first quarter of 1998. He then learned that CUC had done something similar in 1997, boosting revenue by $100 million.

In April, three of CUC's top financial and reporting officers were forced to resign. (Forbes claimed ignorance and resigned several months later.) On April 15, Cendant announced that it uncovered accounting irregularities requiring that it lower 1997 earnings by as much as $115 million. Trading the week before at $41 per share, Cendant dropped to $19 per share, on the heaviest one-day single-stock volume in NYSE history.

Throughout July and August 1998, as Cendant officers—HFS' former officers, as CUC's former officers were leaving or were being fired from the company—and new auditors and lawyers pieced together the fraud, the company had to announce that the overstatement had grown. The restatement figure grew to $300 million in operating profits for 1997. In total, Cendant had to restate three years of earnings, reducing the total earnings by more than $500 million.

Cendant stock eventually dropped to as low as $9 per share. From the early April high of $41, shareholders had lost $29 *billion* in market value. The company spent 1999 trying to repair the damage, paying $400 million to call off one acquisition, selling off some old CUC divisions, buying back stock, and agreeing to the largest-ever securities class action settlement ($2.8 billion). CUC's auditors, Ernst & Young, separately settled for $335 million, the largest securities-fraud settlement reached with an auditor.

Silverman has had some success in rehabilitating Cendant. The stock price doubled from its late 1998 lows by early 2000. His reputation, however, is forever tarnished. Forbes, with his $44 million severance package, continues to maintain he was duped by his underlings.

## What Went Wrong

For people familiar with Henry Silverman and his methods, it is inconceivable that he would fail to do due diligence. That was exactly where he failed in the CUC acquisition, however. He let Walter Forbes and CUC withhold operating information until after the deal was concluded, and even then revealed, only when it was impossible to withhold it any longer, that its financial reports were a sham.

# CHAPTER 9

## RULE 9: Predict the future and seize it

$ Microsoft's purchase and license of DOS to IBM (1980)
$ GE Capital's acquisition of Montgomery Ward (1988)
$ Michael Robertson's purchase of the domain name MP3.com (1997)
$ Sabheer Bhatia's and Jack Smith's sale of Hotmail to Microsoft (1997)

There is a premium on seeing assets and imagining them not just as they are but as they will become. The deal maker who can master this skill has an advantage in assessing the value of a transaction over adversaries who take only a short-term view.

Naturally, this skill is essential to deal makers in high technology businesses. It is no accident that Microsoft, historically, has been the company with the best handle on the future trends in computing. Its best deal, the purchase and licensing of DOS to IBM, succeeded on such a grand scale because Microsoft recognized that IBM's entry into the personal computer market would transform the computer business. IBM's entry would signal both to potential buyers and competitors that the computer was a development worth big money, and was here to stay. Consequently, Microsoft took a relatively small up-front license fee to keep the license nonexclusive. They then licensed 100 million copies of DOS, mostly to IBM's competitors.

Of course, Microsoft is occasionally criticized for not anticipating the development of the Internet. Because it did not establish itself as a leader in Internet products at the outset, the founders of Hotmail were able to strike a good deal with Microsoft. Providing free e-mail, accessible through the Web from any computer, Microsoft found it easier to buy it than build it. Hotmail's founders, in contrast, made this fortune off little more than an idea—but it was an idea that 50 million people seized upon after Hotmail became available.

Michael Robertson, founder of MP3.com, also made a fortune off a vision. With very little understanding of the technology, Robertson foresaw that MP3 compression technology would be popular on the Internet, so he paid $1,000 to buy the MP3.com domain name. Many regard his business plan as an afterthought, but the market has valued Robertson's ownership in the hundreds of millions of dollars.

When a business has had short-term success, the potential acquirer must determine if that success has masked long-term problems. When GE Capital bought Montgomery Ward in a management-assisted LBO, the purchasers were swayed by a few good years, primarily in Ward's fringe businesses, such as their credit-card operation and the introduction of stand-alone Electric Avenue stores. They ignored Ward's long-term problems and, when those problems overwhelmed the quick fixes, Montgomery Ward had to file for bankruptcy.

# Microsoft's purchase and license of DOS to IBM (1980)

In 1980, the main players in the computer business were small, upstart companies. Their products were generally designed with very little software, for use by people who developed their own simple programs. This had recently changed when Apple Computer entered the market, with computers for the ordinary consumer. Microsoft was a tiny company with 40 employees and a niche business selling programming languages, such as BASIC, to be packaged with computers.

Apple's proprietary Apple-DOS was the dominant operating system, because Apple had the biggest share of the market. The most successful operating system for non-Apple computers was CP/M, developed by Gary Kildall of Digital Research. Microsoft did not sell an operating system.

In secret, IBM decided that it had to enter the "microcomputer" market, and fast. IBM segregated a small team and told the team to bring a product to market in one year. Bill Lowe was placed in charge of the team.

The rush to market was very unlike IBM, and it forced Lowe's group to take another uncharacteristic step: outsourcing. IBM traditionally built as much of its own technology as possible, but the one-year deadline made that impossible. Virtually all the hardware and software came from third parties.

Not disclosing its revolutionary plans and wielding a very restrictive nondisclosure agreement, Lowe talked with Bill Gates about packaging Microsoft's programming languages with some as-yet-undisclosed IBM product. Lowe's team was under the impression Gates also controlled the rights to CP/M, but he corrected them, and they made an appointment to see Gary Kildall.

Three things about Kildall irked IBM. First, he did not show up for the start of the meeting. Second, his wife (who was also his business manager), unlike Microsoft, refused to sign the nondisclosure agreement. Third, the IBM PC would be a 16-bit machine (the then-current version of CP/M supported only 8-bit machines). The failure to reach a nondisclosure agreement meant that IBM did not tell Digital of its grand plans (which would have included CP/M with every computer) and Digital did not tell IBM of the 16-bit operating system it had on the drawing board.

With Microsoft a party to the nondisclosure agreement, and the strong likelihood that Microsoft would provide programming languages, IBM and Microsoft representatives began a series of presentations on the new machine as well as negotiations. Gates was hungry for the business, so he offered to try to provide a 16-bit operating system.

Paul Allen, Gates' partner, knew of a local company, Seattle Computer, run by Tim Paterson, which was developing a 16-bit program similar to CP/M. There is a dispute about exactly *how* similar, and Kildall maintained that a lot of the code was just lifted from CP/M. Paterson's program was called QDOS ("quick and dirty operating system").

Gates and Steve Ballmer (then a new Microsoft employee) negotiated the operating system agreement while, almost simultaneously, Allen negotiated to buy QDOS from Paterson. There was a short period of time when Gates and Ballmer had obligated Microsoft to provide the operating system before Allen had actually concluded negotiations to purchase it.

Either deal could probably stand alone as one of the best business deals of the Computer Age. Allen got Paterson to agree to sell QDOS outright for $50,000. Paterson did not know Microsoft was turning around and licensing it to IBM, but he tried unsuccessfully to angle for a licensing deal. Allen played hardball, and Paterson sold out.

Gates immediately recognized the importance of retaining ownership of the program. Because of IBM's size and antitrust history—not to mention the virtual nonexistence of competing 16-bit operating systems around—IBM could not negotiate so easily for total ownership.

More important, it was not an exclusive license. Because IBM was required by a 1956 consent decree to publish extensive information about all its hardware and software, Gates and company believed that IBM's entry would transform the market and make it expand rapidly, and clone makers would develop to challenge IBM. Microsoft was in a position where it could sell DOS to each of IBM's competitors.

Kildall remained a pioneer, though the preferred position of MS-DOS in IBM's computers doomed CP/M with IBM and the coming clones. Kildall eventually sold Digital to Novell in 1991 for stock then valued at $80 million. He died following an altercation at a bar in Monterey, California in 1994 but remains a part of Silicon Valley folklore.

Microsoft later hired Tim Paterson as a programmer. Paterson worked sporadically for Microsoft for the next 20 years. His biggest mistake may not have been selling QDOS—he did not have the size of Microsoft even then to develop the relationship Gates started with IBM—but rather leaving Microsoft in 1982 and letting his stock options expire before Microsoft went public. Those options had an estimated worth in 1997 of $30 million.

The IBM Personal Computer (PC, for short) spawned the next generation of the computer revolution. IBM made billions from PCs, but by setting the industry standard with open architecture and a nonproprietary operating system, it may have cost itself hundreds of billions in sales lost to competitors.

Microsoft, of course, emerged victorious. Accurately foreseeing the future, IBM's entry coincided with an unprecedented boom in computer development and sales by other companies, which tended to use an operating system compatible with IBM's. Microsoft was able to strike much better deals with these other companies, and it eventually sold more than 100 million copies of MS-DOS. This income stream and market presence allowed it ample time to develop application software and dominate that market, as well as go through several unsuccessful versions of the most successful product in the history of computing: Microsoft Windows.

## What Went Right

Microsoft expanded beyond its niche market of programming languages into operating systems only because it obtained the confidence of IBM when IBM was embarking on the then-secret project of entering the personal computer market. Seizing the opportunity when IBM could not reach an agreement with an operating-system company, Microsoft foresaw the gigantic impact of IBM's entry into the personal computer market. It snatched up an operating system and licensed it to IBM on terms that would allow it to capitalize on the explosion in the personal computer market after IBM's product hit the market.

# GE Capital's acquisition of Montgomery Ward (1988)

The collapse of Montgomery Ward & Co., ending in July 1997 with a bankruptcy filing, was really 50 years in the making. Bad management decisions after World War II doomed the company; it just took a lot of savvy minds a half-century to figure it out.

Sewell Avery was considered a legendary CEO of Montgomery Ward during his time in the 1930s and into the 1940s. He skillfully led Ward through the Depression-era, even building new stores and closing the lead in retail sales held by Sears. He also positioned Ward properly for the dislocations caused by World War II. He was, oddly, unprepared for peacetime prosperity, stockpiling cash for another depression just around the corner instead of modernizing old stores and expanding to take advantage of the increased consumerism of the middle class and the suburbanization of America.

As Sears and JCPenney moved further ahead, and a crop of new retailers developed, Ward lagged. "Dowdy" was the term used countless times to describe its stores. Periodic attempts were made to expand and update stores, but Ward was always behind the times, or too cash-poor to follow through. Montgomery Ward merged with Container Corporation of America in 1968, and Marcor, the name for the combined entity, was purchased by Mobil in 1974.

Mobil, in a series of transactions, paid $1.9 billion and was excoriated for the purchase. Attempting to diversify because of the recent uncertainties regarding the future of oil production, Mobil was criticized politically for running away from the problem. As Montgomery Ward continued to struggle in the late 1970s and early 1980s, Mobil was criticized for making the purchase and for not doing more to improve the company.

Mobil got the last laugh. It sold Container Corp.'s assets for $1.15 billion in 1986 ($700 million in cash, $450 million in assumed debt). Although Mobil eventually provided cash infusions of $600 million in 1980 through 1982 (during which Montgomery Ward lost more than $400 million), a series of effective short-term management moves restored Ward to profitability in the mid-1980s.

In 1988, GE Capital, with the involvement of management, bought Montgomery Ward for $3.8 billion ($1.5 billion cash and $2.3 billion in assumed debt). For more than a decade, the purchase by Mobil was described as the poster child for bad business deals, but Mobil escaped without injury. It acquired the combined company for $1.9 billion, spent $600 million to resuscitate Ward, received $2.2 billion in cash in the two sales, and, in the end, was able to take nearly $2.8 billion in debt off its books. As a bonus, it received a $50 million dividend from Montgomery Ward the year before the buyout.

Conversely, GE Capital looked like it was structuring a sound business deal, but it later ended up in shambles. Immediately after the group (40 members of management, led by CEO Bernard Brennan, put up $5 million for a 50-percent stake) bought Ward, it sold the credit card division to GE Capital for $2.7 billion ($500 million cash and $2.2 billion in assumed debt). Although the credit card division was very profitable—GE Capital earned as much as $200 million from it in peak years—management was actually taking over a company with less debt than before the buyout. Post-buyout, Ward was capitalized with $100 million in equity and $1 billion in debt.

Brennan, like all the CEOs before him who experienced short-term success with Montgomery Ward, promised expansion and renovation. Although the buyout had not saddled the company with an unmanageable debt structure, it was hardly positioned to make the huge (and, in many cases, decades overdue) investments necessary to put Montgomery Ward on a par with WalMart, Target, Sears, JCPenney, or with specialty retailers, such as Best Buy and Circuit City.

In the early 1990s, focusing on a specialty-store concept while ignoring the larger problem of the scores of old, dingy stores in bad locations, Montgomery Ward earned about $100 million per year. In 1995, *Forbes* estimated that Brennan's stake was worth $450 million. In just three years, it was worth one-thirtieth of that amount.

Ward's Electric Avenue and other specialty stores were an initial success, but competitors who were better capitalized eventually surpassed them. The new stores based on this concept were not profitable for long, and any small profits generated by those stores were dwarfed by the losses from the large number of bad stores. Brennan's hard-charging, micromanaging style, though praised in 1990, was blamed for management defections and bad decisions a few years later. He resigned at the end of 1996, with a five-year $7.5 million consulting contract and a $12.5 million interest-free loan secured by his 30-percent ownership interest.

Less than a year later, the contract was cancelled and the loan was worth far more than the stock. In July 1997, Montgomery Ward filed for bankruptcy. In the previous 18 months, the company had lost nearly $500 million, surviving only on cash infusions by GE Capital.

GE Capital was both the largest shareholder and largest lender of the company. In 1999, when it emerged from bankruptcy court protection, it emerged as the 100-percent owner of the retail chain, its direct-mail business (named Signature, it was always profitable and had an estimated value of $1 billion), and the credit card operation (with estimated losses in 1998 of $110 million). It gave up claims to about $1 billion in debt and paid $650 million to be divided among the unsecured creditors (who got about 28 cents on the dollar).

The scorecard from GE's perspective does not look good. It paid $2.3 billion for the credit card business in 1988, and more than $1.6 billion for the direct-mail and retail businesses in 1999. It has made money from the credit card business and may again, and the direct-mail business has always been profitable. Still, both of those businesses depend in large degree on the retail operation, which, even with 100 store closures during the bankruptcy, is still poorly positioned in the competitive retail field. There is, however, talk of some new store designs.

## What Went Wrong

Since the end of World War II, Montgomery Ward has fundamentally been out of step with the direction of American retailing. A group of savvy purchasers mistook a fluctuation for a trend, however, imagining a rosier future for Ward that its outdated look and poor store locations made possible.

# Michael Robertson's purchase of the domain name MP3.com (1997)

In 1997, Michael Robertson was an enterprising, but unsuccessful, businessman. He had tried to start three companies, two of which failed and a third that was failing. He was 31 years old and looking to hook up with something big.

Robertson was looking at Internet traffic sources and noticed the term "MP3" was being searched a lot. He knew nothing of the technology, but learned that MP3 was a free technology developed in 1991 for digitally compressing music. Robertson decided to buy the domain name "MP3.com."

The owner was a fellow named Martin Paul, who wanted a domain name with his initials. Paul sold Robertson the rights to the address for $1,000. This, obviously, gave Robertson no rights in connection with the technology. It just gave him the right to call his as-yet nonexistent Web site by that name.

Robertson's approach to product was simple: Anyone could upload music on the site, provided they owned it and would offer one song for free. Robertson would make money on homemade CDs ordered by visitors on the site (offering a more favorable royalty split than the big labels) and from on-site advertising.

The first day the site was open, it got 10,000 visitors. By October 1999, MP3.com was getting 350,000 hits per day, and had 35,000 contributors on the site.

Very little cash was necessary to get the site up and running. The relationships with 35,000 individuals and bands have virtually nothing in common with the usual artist-recording company relationship. Robertson's company did not scout or audition these acts, pay them to join the site, cover any of their expenses, advance them any money, or even pay the costs of recording their music. The artists just log onto the site and upload their music.

Still, running a busy Web site requires some money, and Robertson wanted to market MP3.com aggressively, so he raised $11 million from Sequoia Capital, which had a role in the founding of such companies as Apple, Oracle, and Cisco Systems. He struck a favorable deal, keeping two and a half times as much stock as Sequoia, despite not bringing anything to the relationship other than the idea that owning the MP3.com domain name would be valuable.

Arguably, the odds of success for this company are long. It owned no technology, had no rights to its artists' work, and gave away its product. Even with 35,000 artists, MP3.com was selling only 320 CDs per day during the fall of 1999. The company did not engage in the promotional activities of the major labels. It had no clout in radio which, even with the growth of the Internet, should be a major force in defining or reflecting musical tastes for some time. There are competing technologies and competing Web sites.

Robertson's foresight, timing, and marketing aggressiveness, however, made his investment an initial success with investors. The initial public offering price tripled during the pre-offering process, and was finally set on July 21 at $28 per share, valuing the company as a whole at $1.86 billion. Initial investors treated the company even better. The stock briefly traded at more than $100 per share on the first day of trading, closing at $63 per share.

In one day as a public company, Robertson's stake—more than 24 million shares—was valued at more than $1.5 billion. MP3.com's stock has plummeted since then, dropping to $8 per share in August 2000. The lack of a profitable operating plan has hurt MP3.com, along with many other Internet companies, in 2000. In addition, MP3.com has had legal problems in connection with some music available on the site. Finally, it is far from clear that MP3 will become an industry-standard format, and Napster has become the flavor of the month (with its own legal problems) in the area of online music transfer. Still, Robertson's stake is worth $200 million.

## What Went Right

Although the vagaries of the aftermarket for Internet stocks have not been kind to Michael Robertson, his vision put him in the right place at the right time. Without any technological expertise or music-industry background, foresight alone put him at the center of a storm of controversy with a fortune valued in 2000 at $200 million.

# Sabheer Bhatia's and Jack Smith's sale of Hotmail to Microsoft (1997)

In 1988, Sabheer Bhatia came to the United States from India. He was a 19-year-old student, going to study at Cal Tech. In 1996 he and a colleague at Apple Computer, Jack Smith, developed an idea: free e-mail, accessible through the Internet. E-mail services were exclusively the domain of Internet Service Providers (ISPs), so the mail was accessible only when obtaining access through the ISP. In addition, the ISP had access to the e-mail.

Bhatia and Smith imagined a Web site where people could access their e-mail over the Web from any computer, and it would not be subject to the whims (or prying eyes) of the system proprietor, such as an employer. The idea came primarily from the two young entrepreneurs' attempts to communicate about their business dreams and goals without using the office e-mail.

In early 1996, Bhatia was pitching another idea to venture capitalists (Smith handled engineering, Bhatia handled money-raising): JavaSoft, a

Web-based database program. It evolved into a Trojan Horse for the free e-mail system. To keep unscrupulous venture capitalists from turning him down and stealing the idea, Bhatia would pitch JavaSoft and, if he felt he had the confidence of his audience, would describe the free e-mail feature.

On his 20th try, Bhatia convinced a venture capitalist to come up with initial financing of $300,000. Draper Fisher Jurvetson agreed to provide the financing in exchange for 30-percent ownership. Bhatia, though desperate for money and with nothing more than an idea, insisted that the Draper firm get only 15-percent ownership for its $300,000. Although they were at first shocked at Bhatia's hard bargaining, they eventually agreed.

It is typical for a Web venture to go through several levels of financing, raising enough money to do the things necessary to advance the idea, which allows it to raise more money. Bhatia and Smith wanted to keep as much equity for themselves as possible, so they wanted Hotmail—the name is derived from "mail" and HTML, the dominant Web programming language—to be running and gathering subscribers before they needed more money. This would keep them from the bind of most budding entrepreneurs: being subservient to the money source because the project is unfinished and untried.

They managed to make the $300,000 last until July 4, 1996, when Hotmail began operating and signing up subscribers. This made it possible to raise additional money without giving up much equity. The immediate success of Hotmail also allowed them to revise the financing plan; word-of-mouth was so strong that it wasn't necessary to spend much on marketing.

By mid-1997, Hotmail had six million users. Not only did they dispense with marketing costs—a major expense for most Internet start-ups targeting consumers—but they were able to provide content on the site without paying for it. Better still, Hotmail charged content providers for the privilege of carrying the content, on the theory that the content was a form of advertisement for the provider's site.

Many people disparaged the original success of Hotmail, claiming that anyone could have come up with the idea. Those same doubters then said that as soon as a big company (such as Microsoft) became a competitor, Hotmail would crumble.

Microsoft indeed became interested in the business, but by this time Hotmail had twice as many subscribers as Microsoft Network, so it wanted to acquire Hotmail rather than compete with it. Just a year after starting, Microsoft offered $160 million for the company.

Bhatia turned it down. Negotiating alone against as many as a dozen Microsoft employees—occasionally including Bill Gates—Bhatia held his ground. Microsoft, despite howling at Bhatia's unreasonableness, began raising its offer. It offered $200 million, then $250 million, then $300 million, then $350 million, all of which Bhatia turned down. By this time, Bhatia's employees were begging him to accept and one of Bhatia's venture capitalists, Doug Carlisle, offered to build a life-sized bronze sculpture of him in Menlo Ventures' office. The delays also increased Hotmail's value; it now had 10 million subscribers.

Bhatia finally relented, and Hotmail agreed to be acquired by Microsoft on December 31, 1997, for 2.7 million Microsoft shares, which were at the time worth $400 million. Owning Microsoft stock is in some ways better than cash, as it has more than doubled in value between the time of the deal and August 2000.

On the other hand, some analysts think Bhatia and Smith sold Hotmail too cheap. The service added 20 million subscribers in 1998 and another 20 million in 1999 (though some of this is attributable to Microsoft's marketing muscle). Bhatia was quoted in mid-1999 as saying, "When we sold, it was considered an outrageous amount. In hindsight, yes, we sold too low. But I don't regret it because at that time it was considered a great deal."

Still, Bhatia and Smith, if they are still holding it, have more than a half-billion dollars in Microsoft stock. The venture capitalist who put up $300,000 has more than $200 million, and would have had twice as much if Bhatia had not initially struck such a hard bargain. Neither works for Microsoft anymore. Both are younger than 35. Bhatia has started an e-commerce company called Arzoo! and plans to participate in the wiring of his native India. Smith has started N3.net, which works with the hardware and software needed to speed up Web sites, and bought a winery in his community.

The sculpture of Bhatia was never completed. He attended a sitting but his mother made him stop.

## What Went Right

Bhatia and Smith foresaw the value in freeing e-mail from ISPs. They also recognized that they could offer it for free and still generate multiple streams of revenue. With fast execution and hard bargaining, they built a company from scratch to a sale to Microsoft for $400 million in 18 months.

# CHAPTER 10

## RULE 10: Don't negotiate with your betters

$ Ronald Reagan's negotiation of residuals for the Screen Actors Guild (1960)

$ Merv Griffin's acquisition of Resorts International (1988)

$ Ronald Perelman's acquisition of five failed S&Ls from the FSLIC (1988)

$ Leon Black's purchase of Executive Life Insurance Co.'s junk-bond portfolio (1992)

$ Kohlberg Kravis Roberts & Co.'s acquisition of American Re (1992)

Every father teaches his son three things: Don't play golf for money with someone who carries a one iron; don't get into a public argument with someone who buys ink by the barrel; and don't negotiate with your betters. The last part, actually, originated with Sun-Tzu, who taught military leaders from ancient China to the present day that, when outmanned, the proper response is to retreat.

The lessons of the first nine chapters should make it clear that deal making is a skill. It can be used to varying degrees, and can be decisive in establishing the terms of a deal. As with any skill, some practitioners are very good at it; some might want to consider other work.

It is hard to admit you are outclassed, no matter how skilled the opposition. Particularly in large or complex deals, there is a tendency to think that individual negotiating skills do not account for much; everybody has advisors, and everyone breathing this rarified air has roughly equivalent skills.

Any review of a series of large-scale deals will indicate that there is a significant disparity in negotiating ability, and it accounts for some very lopsided deals. When the government tries to negotiate with experienced financial professionals, it is frequently at a disadvantage. As much as all individuals fear the power of the government—ask any of these corporate bigwigs what they think of the IRS—when the government loses its aura of power and bellies up at the negotiating table, it gets walked on.

When the federal government tried to make the savings and loan crisis disappear by selling ailing S&Ls to private investors, it was taken advantage of. In the worst deal, it offered Ronald Perelman and affiliates securities to shore up the S&Ls' balance sheets, billions in net operating losses, and it also promised to pay all interest not paid by borrowers and to make up deficiencies the value of foreclosed assets. Just before Perelman was getting ready to sell the S&Ls, the successor to the agency Perelman snookered asked to renegotiate. In exchange for the equity the government still owned in the S&Ls, Perelman agreed to take one payment for the rest of the government's guarantees. Of course, when Perelman sold a few months later, the government lost its chance to take 20 percent of the sale, having given up its equity.

When Leon Black, with the backing of Credit Lyonnais, negotiated with the California Department of Insurance for the purchase of the Executive Life junk-bond portfolio, it was at a huge disadvantage. Black, as an advisor to many of the companies whose junk bonds were part of the portfolio, had superior knowledge about the value of the bonds and the expected direction of the junk-bond market. The value of the bonds increased by $800 million in the few months between the agreement and the closing, and Black & Co. made billions, both in appreciation of the bonds' value and in controlling the reorganization of scores of companies.

Whenever outsiders take on financial professionals, there is some likelihood the professionals have the advantage. When KKR bought American Re from Aetna, for example, Aetna could hardly be described as ignorant or naive. Still, responding to a need to increase financial reserves, it sold KKR a company that, two months later, it took public in a transaction that would have made Aetna, if it had just taken American Re public itself, another billion dollars. Compared with KKR's knowledge and access to the public equity markets, the people at Aetna were novices, and the result showed that.

Likewise, when Merv Griffin got involved in the bidding for Resorts International, he took on Donald Trump. Trump had some subsequent problems with the debt he carried on his properties, but Griffin was no match for him. Trump had bid on Resorts primarily to obtain the unfinished Taj Mahal casino. Not only was Trump able to buy it from Griffin when he let Griffin in the bidding, but he got Griffin to assume all the debt in connection with the project. It took less than a year for Griffin to go bankrupt with Resorts.

Whether it was a conflict of interest or lack of skill, Ronald Reagan was no match for the producers' representatives negotiating against him when, as head of the Screen Actors Guild (SAG), he attempted to resolve the issue of TV and movie residuals. In exchange for a relatively nominal payment to start SAG's health and welfare plan, Reagan gave up members' rights to residuals for all films made before 1960. (MCA, the agency representing him, had just bought the film library of Paramount.) He also agreed to residuals being paid for just the first six airings of television episodes. Consequently, stars from shows including *Gilligan's Island, The Beverly Hillbillies,* and *Leave it to Beaver,* are famous, but not rich, their residuals having run out long ago.

# Ronald Reagan's negotiation of residuals for the Screen Actors Guild (1960)

Ronald Reagan owed much of his television- and film-career success (and perhaps his start in politics) to his association with MCA. MCA was the talent agency that represented him and, as a television production company, hired him after it appeared his acting career was over. He may have paid MCA back by his poor job in negotiating on behalf of the Screen Actors Guild (SAG) in resolving its 1960 strike. The impact of that contract still reverberates today, 40 years later.

Reagan liked to present himself as pro-union (without actually being in favor of any of the causes unions espoused) based on his experience as SAG president. Reagan served six one-year terms as Guild president, the last being in 1960. Guild members struck for 42 days over the issue of television residuals.

Residuals are the payments actors (or writers or directors) receive for showings of their work after the initial airing or release. Until 1960, movie actors received nothing for films shown on television. The issue had been a source of dispute since television's early days, and the actors finally went on strike in 1960 until it was resolved.

The producers' representatives agreed to a royalty system, but they wanted to pay only on films produced after the date of the agreement. The Guild's position was that royalties should be paid on films produced after the issue became disputed, in 1948.

The agreement reached, after a 42-day strike, has been referred to as "The Great Giveaway." Reagan agreed to give up the residual rights to pre-1960 films, in perpetuity, for a $2,625,000 payment to establish the Guild's pension, health, and welfare plan. Even though the strike-ravaged Guild ratified the contract, it has been denounced ever since as a pittance compared to the residuals actors have given up for films produced during that period. Residuals currently amount to more than $600 million per year.

It may not be coincidental that MCA, in 1959, had purchased Paramount's film library and was poised to capitalize on the library, now residual-free. This was not the first time Reagan, as Guild president, acted in a way that was at least circumstantially contrary to Guild interests and in favor of MCA. In 1952, he approved a blanket waiver allowing MCA (then a talent agency) to hire Guild members in its television productions. The opportunity for a conflict of interest, when an agent becomes a client's employer, is obvious and, until then, the Guild granted exceptions only on a per-project basis. Although Reagan's popularity had greatly diminished, MCA hired him on one of its productions, General Electric Theater, for $125,000 per year, and later gave him a 25-percent interest in the production. (His status as producer should have precluded him from serving as president in 1959 and 1960, negotiating *against* producers for the Guild.)

Reagan's negotiation of residuals due to television performers for reruns did further and long-lasting damage to SAG clients. TV performers got residuals for the first time, but only for the first six airings. Reagan's successors did only marginally better on this one; it was not until 1977 that TV performers got perpetual residuals. Still, actors on shows such as *Gilligan's Island, The Beverly Hillbillies,* and *Leave It to Beaver* received nothing from the immense popularity of their shows on local television through the 1970s and on cable and satellite television up to the present time.

## What Went Wrong

Reagan should not have been involved in those negotiations against the studios. The negotiation over residuals was too important, and had consequences far ranging, to leave to someone with a conflict of interest.

# Merv Griffin's acquisition of Resorts International (1988)

Merv Griffin might have simply been in the wrong place at the wrong time. Griffin, who had a net worth of between $300 and $400 million as a result of practically inventing the television-syndication business, put in a bid for Resorts International, a pioneer of Atlantic City and Bahamian gaming, at the behest of a dissident shareholder who thought Donald Trump was trying to pull a fast one. Despite the fact that Trump already controlled the company, Griffin won the messy, expensive eight-month battle. On numerous occasions, he almost pulled out of the deal; he should have followed that instinct.

Donald Trump wanted the Taj Mahal. He probably would have liked the original in Agra, India, but in 1987, he had his eye on the imitation, being built as a casino resort in Atlantic City by Resorts International, next to its namesake property on the boardwalk. It was the largest, grandest project in Atlantic City, and it looked like it might be available. Following the death of founder William Crosby in 1986, the Crosby family wanted to sell the public company, whose assets also included Atlantic City and Bahamian land holdings, and the Paradise Island resort outside Nassau.

In March 1987, Trump agreed to pay $79 million for 585,000 shares of class B super-voting stock from the Crosby family and estate. The class B shares represented 93 percent of the voting power of the company, and Trump acquired 80 percent of those shares. The deal, priced at $135 per class B share, looked especially good for Trump, in part because three other groups had offered between $140 and $210 per share. Later in 1987, Trump offered to buy the remaining class B shares for the same price, running his total cost of acquiring control to about $100 million. (Resorts had two classes of stock, A and B. Class A stock, owned by the family of founder William Crosby, possessed 100 votes per share. Class B stock, owned by public shareholders, was worth one vote per share.)

The remaining stock consisted of 5.7 million shares owned by the public. In December 1987, Trump proposed buying all those shares for $15 per share. Explicit in the offer was the threat that the Taj Mahal would never get the estimated $550 million in additional financing needed for completion unless he committed the resources, and he wasn't going to do that if he had to share ownership with the public. Considering that class A shareholders had an equal share of the company with class B shareholders (other than voting power), it was not surprising when they howled with displeasure at the offer. Trump raised his offer in February 1988.

At this unlikely moment, Merv Griffin entered the picture. Griffin was flush from selling his production company to Coca-Cola for $250 million a few years earlier and was investing in hotels and radio stations. A shareholder of Resorts encouraged Griffin to make a competing bid, offering him an option to purchase 160,000 shares of class A stock. In March 1988, Griffin bid $35 per share for the class A shares.

This created the potential for a very bizarre deadlock. Trump already owned voting control, so even if the bid succeeded, Griffin could not control the company. On the other hand, Trump was loath to share his successes with outside investors, which was why he was bent on acquiring the remaining shares to begin with.

In April 1988, Griffin and Trump entered into a truce. Griffin would buy the class A shares for $207 million ($36 per share), as well as Trump's class B shares. He would then sell the Taj Mahal and the Atlantic City land back to Trump.

The next month, the deal fell apart. Both sides claimed the other tried to change the terms. They also fought over ownership of a parking lot between Resorts and the Taj Mahal. Two weeks later, they patched up their differences. Then, in October, Griffin withdrew his tender offer. Reasons variously given were buyer's remorse, difficulty in obtaining financing, problems with the Casino Control Commission, and tax issues with the structure of the transaction. After Griffin reaffirmed his intention to complete the deal, he again appeared to back out in November when he learned his financing costs would be considerably higher than expected.

Finally, on November 16, 1988, Griffin and Trump completed the deal. Amazingly, Griffin obtained control of the company, despite Trump's resistance and backed up by majority voting control. Accomplishing such a feat does not come cheap, though, and Trump, by all accounts, took Griffin to the cleaners.

Griffin's total cost broke down as follows:

▸ $205 million ($36 per share) for the outstanding shares of class A stock;

▸ $100 million to Trump for his class B stock;

▸ $60 million to Trump to buy out the management contract he signed himself to when he first acquired control of Resorts the year before;

▸ assumption of $650 million of Resorts debt (most of which was incurred building the Taj Mahal, which Trump would be buying for a fraction of the construction cost); and

▸ $50-60 million of his own money into the deal (the rest was financed, largely with junk bonds from Drexel).

Trump, in turn, would pay Griffin $273 million for the Taj Mahal, which he would be acquiring debt-free.

Griffin was right to be so reluctant to complete the transaction. The deal was a horrible loser from the start. For more than $700 million (the costs of buying out Trump and other shareholders and assuming all the debt, minus Trump's payment for the Taj Mahal), all Griffin got was two decrepit resorts, not especially well-run, and in dire need of renovation.

Griffin managed to make only one interest payment on $325 million of junk bonds before declaring bankruptcy in November 1989. Presenting a prepackaged plan (that is, already agreed to by a majority of creditors) to the bankruptcy court, the new capital structure valued the company at

$536 million ($400 in debt, $136 million in equity), more than 40 percent less than the $915 million the company was capitalized with a year earlier. Under the plan, Griffin would have to put another $30 million into the company, in exchange for keeping 22 percent of the equity.

This was not the end of Griffin's troubles. He had to take Resorts through a second prepackaged bankruptcy in 1994. Griffin had to give up all equity in the Bahamian property (which South African hotelier Sol Kerzner bought in 1994 and transformed into Atlantis) and contribute another $14 million in equity, plus sign over licensing and service contracts worth $9 million. When Kerzner bought the Atlantic City operation in 1996, Griffin received about $45 million. He lost at least $50 million on his flirtation with casino ownership.

Amazingly, both participants in the deal ended up losers. Despite the giant discount at which Donald Trump bought the Taj Mahal, he still could not make enough money from it to service its gigantic new debt. Freed from the $650 million in Resorts junk-bond debt, Trump immediately raised $650 million in *new* junk-bond debt to pay for his purchase of the Taj Mahal, its future construction costs, and the interest due on all this new debt before the project was finished. Trump made it only about two years with the Taj before bringing his prepackaged bankruptcy to court in November 1990. Trump had to give up 50 percent of the equity in the resort in exchange for relaxing the terms of the bonds.

## What Went Wrong

Although Donald Trump has had numerous problems in the last decade, his skills as a negotiator are substantial. He enjoyed huge negotiating advantages over Merv Griffin in resolving their competitive interest in acquiring Resorts International: He controlled the super-voting stock, he knew the business, and he knew what portion of the company he really wanted. In contrast, Griffin entered the bidding from a position of weakness, never really sure he wanted to acquire the company. Trump was able to obtain the asset he wanted—the Taj Mahal—without having to acquire its huge debt.

# Ronald Perelman's acquisition of 5 failed S&Ls from the FSLIC (1988)

One of the great scandals of the Reagan Administration was the savings and loan (S&L) crisis. Reagan simultaneously lifted regulations on S&Ls—including who could own them, what they could invest in, and how much capital they had to keep available for depositors—while gutting the regulatory agency responsible for monitoring abuses, the Federal Savings and Loan Insurance Corporation (FSLIC). Regardless of the merits of Reagan's philosophy of a hands-off federal government in general, this was one area where regulation was appropriate. The federal government insured all deposits up to $100,000 per account (an amount that increased dramatically during Reagan's presidency), thus giving the government a legitimate interest in assuring sound, conservative practices.

By 1988, the savings and loan industry had come completely unraveled. In Texas, one-third of all S&Ls had been seized by the government. Throughout the South and the West, S&Ls were in danger of defaulting on their depositors, and the government was realizing that the assets—both those owned by the operators and those supporting the S&Ls' lending activities—were flimsy or nonexistent. With few restrictions and a federal guarantee to depositors, S&Ls could jack up interest rates to assure a flow of deposits, then shoot the money out the door to fund crazy or self-dealing transactions. One of the most storied failures was Vernon Saving & Loan, in Dallas, Texas. Operated by Don Dixon, Vernon and its owners bought Rolls Royces, six airplanes, and the sister yacht to the President's Sequoia. It made millions in loans to enterprises controlled by Dixon and his cronies, virtually all of which were fraudulent or at least ill-advised. When the government put it in receivership in early 1988, it discovered that 96 percent of its loans were delinquent or nonperforming.

Political pressure was building for the FSLIC and its chairman, M. Danny Wall, to do something. During the final days of the Reagan administration, the FSLIC embarked on a plan that would obfuscate the costs of the crisis and get the federal government out of the business of running S&Ls.

The FSLIC would package up failing and failed thrifts and sell them to well-heeled investors. Why would wealthy investors buy a hopelessly unprofitable business? The FSLIC would make them an offer they couldn't refuse. First, the FSLIC promised to pay any future losses on loans on the books, as well as any interest lost while those loans were nonperforming.

For example, if investors acquired a thrift with a defaulted $1 million loan on its books, the FSLIC would pay the interest due while the investors sold it and would make up the difference if the security on the loan sold for less than $1 million. Second, the FSLIC would actually give the acquirer money to include as statutory capital. Third, and in many instances most significant, the FSLIC was offering some enormously attractive net operating losses (NOL).

Because of the NOL issue (along with the political expediency of having this problem "solved" before George Bush took office), there was a great rush to complete transactions involving hundreds of failed thrifts by December 31, 1988. The Tax Reform Act of 1986 eliminated the ability to shelter income by acquiring NOLs, but S&Ls were exempt from the change. Even that was being cut back by the end of 1988, though, so the race was on to buy an S&L with a large NOL by December 31. For example, Ford Motor Co., one of the nation's largest taxpayers, was an active bidder for S&Ls with billions in NOLs.

On December 28, 1988, the FSLIC announced one of the largest deals, an acquisition by Gerald J. Ford (not the former president) and MacAndrews and Forbes Holdings, Ronald Perelman's investment company, of five insolvent Texas thrifts, including Vernon Saving & Loan. The five thrifts had assets of $12 billion but liabilities of $12.8 billion. Ford, a bank turnaround specialist, would run the new entity, and Perelman would put up the $315 million contributed by the group.

The FSLIC's press release tried to put a brave face on the transaction, stressing that "no taxpayer funds [we]re involved." All that really meant was that the FSLIC would not be writing out any checks from the treasury *that day*. In exchange for Perelman's group contributing $315 million, the FSLIC gave up the following:

- a 10-year, $866 million note, wiping out the negative net worth of the thrifts;
- a guarantee that the FSLIC would make up the value of any assets sold at a loss; and
- a guarantee that the FSLIC would pay any interest due on those assets while they were nonperforming.

In addition, Perelman's group would get the thrifts' NOL, estimated at worth somewhere between $600 million and $1.8 billion.

The group was also making a bet that the Texas real estate market had bottomed out (most of the nonperforming assets being Texas real estate), making it easier to sell assets at greater prices in the future. Even if it was wrong, however, the FSLIC's guarantees prevented the group from losing money, and it would still get the NOL. Although the FSLIC did not mention the NOL, it claimed the federal assistance had a present value of $5.1 billion.

It was no surprise that some of the wealthiest, most savvy investors around were the ones who took advantage of these last-minute fire-sale type deals. In addition to Perelman, Robert Bass acquired a large failed California S&L. Other beneficiaries were former Treasury Secretary William Simon, former Commerce Secretary Peter Peterson, Ford Motor Co., real estate development company Trammel Crow, the Pritzker family, and former Salomon vice chairman Lewis Ranieri. In the final days of the year, FSLIC sold off 20 S&Ls in this fashion.

After the fact, Congress criticized the sales, focusing attention on the sweet deal accorded the Perelman group. The Resolution Trust Corp. (RTC), created to replace the FSLIC in overseeing S&L asset dispositions, determined in 1990 that First Gibraltar Bank (the new name for the five thrifts) achieved a 45-percent return on investment in the first year of the deal. According to an RTC audit conducted in mid-1990, First Gibraltar would receive $8.7 billion in assistance payments. It received $610 million in 1989 (that amount rose to $921 million by March 31, 1990) and reported a net income of $129 million. A major portion of that income was the result of assistance payments.

The deal was so good that Perelman even let the government renegotiate in February 1992. Under the new agreement, the RTC would pay off the $3.2 billion 10-year tax-advantaged government notes that helped finance the purchase. This would end the government's guarantees of interest payments and making good on bad assets. The RTC estimated that the taxpayers would save $178 to $600 million over six years under the new terms. In exchange for First Gibraltar waiving covenants against such a prepayment, the RTC gave up its right to purchase 20 percent of First Gibraltar's common stock.

It was widely estimated that Perelman, three years into the deal, had more than recouped his original $315 million investment. Later in 1992, Perelman decided to liquidate First Gibraltar, selling most of it to BankAmerica but holding on to some lucrative pieces.

Financial journalist Allan Sloan estimated Perelman's take in the deal at $1.2 billion. The majority of this came from the NOL, valued at about $1 billion. (Perelman's people disputed not the amount but the value because, in 1992, he had not yet made use of the NOL.) The rest came from cash dividends, the proceeds of the sale to BankAmerica, and the small portion of First Gibraltar's assets he kept. Sloan even figured that Perelman made $45 million as a result of the government's renegotiation, because he sold out to BankAmerica without having to give the RTC its 20 percent, and that 20 percent was worth much more than the savings it obtained through the prepayment of its notes.

## What Went Wrong

To sweep the S&L crisis under the rug before George Bush took office in 1998, the FSLIC offered some ridiculously generous deals. The government attracted the kind of buyers it had no business negotiating with: savvy, wealthy, and experienced at complex transactions. Ronald Perelman's group made a great deal and, under the guise of letting the government renegotiate, managed to take back the government's equity stake in the venture.

# Leon Black's purchase of Executive Life Insurance Co.'s junk-bond portfolio (1992)

Executive Life was one of the highest of the high fliers during the junk bond–dominated 1980s. Recruited early as a big junk-bond buyer by Michael Milken, it offered superior returns on whole life policies and structured settlements as a result of the initial returns from the risky bonds Drexel Burnham Lambert was selling it. As the deals got worse and Drexel faltered, however, and the risks of junk bonds caught up with the benefits, it was clear that Executive Life was badly undercapitalized. In April 1991, when it was seized by California Insurance Commissioner John Garamendi, more than $6 billion of its $10 billion in assets were in the form of junk bonds.

In attempting to rehabilitate the company for the benefit of policyholders, the Commissioner sold the junk-bond portfolio. In March 1992, for $3.25 billion, Altus Finance, a 60-percent-owned subsidiary of Credit Lyonnais, France's state-owned bank, purchased $6 billion in face value of junk bonds from Executive Life's portfolio.

A key player in the deal, advising Altus, was Leon Black. In the 1980s, Black was a young investment banker at Drexel, known for being loud, aggressive, and having a huge appetite for deals and food. One of his many nicknames was "Jabba the Hut." Black structured the deal and had decision-making authority over the disposition of the portfolio. He would receive 15 to 20 percent of all profits.

The deck was stacked in Black's favor. First, Garamendi was a Desperate Seller. In a highly politicized climate, Garamendi figured to score points with voters by bringing the Executive Life matter to a quick conclusion. Thus, he was short with other bidders and turned down opportunities to hold the bonds while the market recovered, or sell them piecemeal (probably for more money). Second, Black had more knowledge than anybody (except Milken and, perhaps, John Kissick, one of Black's partners) about the quality of junk bonds and their issuers because of his heavy involvement in most of Drexel's big deals during the 1980s. Third, Black accurately predicted that Garamendi's moves, and similar moves by regulators of S&Ls, had temporarily depressed the prices of junk bonds. These bonds were not particularly liquid, the main market-maker for the bonds (Drexel) was out of business, and the regulators were ordering widespread liquidation of junk-bond portfolios. It has been estimated that the value of the portfolio rose $800 million in just the time between the time Black's offer for the portfolio was accepted in the fall of 1991 and when the money actually changed hands in March 1992.

By doing nothing more than being patient and clipping coupons, Black and Altus could be expected to make a huge profit. Fifteen months after the deal, *Business Week* estimated that the value of the bonds in the portfolio had risen by $1.3 billion.

The group reaped its biggest gains, however, on the reorganizations of bankrupt companies. Most of the big junk-bond defaults had been good companies, with good earnings prospects and/or valuable assets. The defaults were the result of being overleveraged, not a lack of profitability. In transforming himself into the leading vulture investor of the 1990s, Leon Black turned the purchase of the Executive Life portfolio into one of the bonanzas of the decade.

Executive Life was the single largest holder of junk bonds in many of the largest defaults of the decade. Adding to it some acumen on when to purchase additional bonds (at very depressed prices), Black put the group into a controlling position in nearly all the junk-bond bankruptcy reorganizations in the 1990s.

*Forbes* has spent much of the 1990s trying to estimate Black's take on this deal. It figured that Altus and related entities made between two and three billion dollars in profits, and Black made between $300 and $500 million. The portfolio contained 424 companies' bonds, with significant stakes in 100 companies. For the companies that defaulted, Black was usually the largest senior debt holder. By controlling the most senior class of junk bonds, Black could block any unfavorable reorganization and frequently take control of the entire company.

For example, Gillett Holdings, a former Drexel client, owned several mid-market television stations and a Vail, Colorado ski resort. The company had been in deals valued at a billion dollars, but the capitalization consisted almost entirely of debt, and it was forced to default. Part of the Executive Life portfolio was $120 million of senior junk debt. Black and Altus probably paid less than half of face value for it. With this position and a promise to put $40 million into the company, Black emerged from the bankruptcy as a 54-percent shareholder of a company that had $500 million less in debt than when it commenced bankruptcy proceedings. This scenario was replayed scores of times, with Black receiving significant transaction fees and a cut of the profits. Although Credit Lyonnais has subsequently reorganized, and many of the deals in which it participated were tainted and lost huge sums, in this deal, it made billions. A few years ago, John Garamendi joined in a partnership with Leon Black.

## What Went Right

The California Department of Insurance was no match for Leon Black in negotiations. Apart from being desperate to unload Executive Life's junk-bond portfolio in a hurry, Black had far greater knowledge than the Department's negotiators of the conditions of the hundreds of companies that issued the bonds. He was able to make a very favorable deal and significantly enrich himself and his investors. Although the total gain is difficult to figure, some commentators have called this the best business deal of the decade.

# Kohlberg Kravis Roberts & Co.'s acquisition of American Re (1992)

After completing the buyout of RJR Nabisco in 1989, Kohlberg Kravis Roberts & Co. (KKR) did not complete another transaction for more than a year. Although it was busy managing the huge deal, there was widespread speculation that its buyout days were over: too much bad publicity, wary fund investors, no more affordable targets, the loss of Drexel's junk bonds, etc. In fact, KKR was managing RJR Nabisco and several other 1980s buyouts, such as Safeway and Duracell. (See Chapters 3 and 6, respectively, for profiles of these deals.) It was also evaluating how to adapt to changes in circumstances relating to Drexel's demise and the public attitude against highly leveraged transactions.

One of its first deals of the 1990s was the phenomenally profitable acquisition of reinsurance company American Re from Aetna for $1.4 billion in 1992. KKR put up $300 million in equity and financed the rest through a combination of bank loans and junk-bond debt. In an unusual move, Aetna also agreed to protect American Re from certain losses. American Re maintained a loss reserve of $2.1 billion. In certain circumstances, if losses required American Re to increase reserves, Aetna would contribute 80 percent of the increase.

Analysts concluded that KKR got a great deal. It paid only 10 times the 1991 earnings, and the reinsurance market was considered to be slumping. Aetna was concerned about the nearly $2.5 billion in bad loans in its investment portfolio and about the prospect that that amount might grow to $3.5 billion by the end of 1992. A cash sale would allow Aetna to boost its cash reserves.

The deal closed in September 1992. Hurricane Andrew followed, which, ironically, significantly boosted the value of American Re. Insurance companies took huge losses as a result of the catastrophe, sending them rushing to increase the amount of insured risk they would pass off on reinsurers.

In November, only two months after closing the deal, KKR announced that it was taking American Re public. Seizing on the spike in value, plus the operating cushion some additional capital would provide—KKR would not be selling any stock—KKR sold approximately one-third of the company to the public (11.6 million shares) at $31 per share in an offering that concluded in January 1993.

The response to the offering was enthusiastic. The size of the offering had been increased from 10.75 million shares to 11.8 million shares, and the price rose from $28 to $31 per share. (KKR's initial equity stake translated into a purchase price of $9 per share.) The offering was oversubscribed and, within two weeks, the stock was trading at $37, 20 percent higher than the IPO price. At $37 per share, the market valued the equity at $1.5 billion. Considering that American Re had $1.1 billion more in debt than when Aetna sold it several months earlier, it seems the insurer cost itself about a billion dollars by not doing a similar transaction without KKR. KKR's equity stake, as of February 1993, had a market value of $1.1 billion.

In August 1996, German reinsurance giant Munich Re agreed to acquire all the outstanding shares of American Re for $3.3 billion, allowing KKR to cash out its 64-percent ownership. After deducting for the shares of public stockholders and management, KKR and its partners received approximately $2 billion, a nearly sevenfold return in less than four years.

## What Went Right

KKR followed its time-tested formula: Management participated in the buyout and held equity in the new company, and KKR stayed out of corporate affairs, except for certain financial and strategic decisions. Aetna felt pressured to sell some assets, so it placed itself in a position of weakness in negotiations compared to KKR. By holding on to American Re for just a few months, KKR was able to recognize a significant paper profit. American Re continued to thrive, and it was an extremely profitable four-year investment for KKR.

# CHAPTER 11

Another Nifty 50

When it comes to picking the winners and losers in big business deals, opinions can differ dramatically. I am including, in chronological order, an additional 50 noteworthy deals. Someone else could evaluate some of these deals and determine that they should have made the list of the 50 best and worst. Others are merely large and very interesting.

## The creation of U.S. Steel (1901)

J.P. Morgan created this trust by combining the assets of the 10 leading steel companies. Morgan acquired the largest, Carnegie Steel, for $480 million, in what was the largest transaction ever at that time. U.S. Steel at one time controlled 70 percent of all steel produced in the United States.

## The breakup of Standard Oil (1911)

John Rockefeller entered the oil business in 1863. By 1871, be began buying out competitors; at the end of the decade he controlled 90 percent of the industry. The Justice Department, upon approval by the United States Supreme Court, finally broke up the trust as an illegal monopoly in 1911. When shares of the individual Standard components went public, Rockefeller's net worth tripled (to $900 million).

# Henry Ford's repurchase of Ford Motor stock (1919)

Clashing with investors over dividends and expansion plans, Ford borrowed $75 million as part of a $106 million deal to buy out the other shareholders of Ford Motor Co. When the company went public in 1956, the market value of that stock (mostly transferred for tax purposes to the Ford Foundation) was approximately $5 billion.

# Samuel Insull's utilities trust (1920s)

Samuel Insull, a one-time assistant to Thomas Edison, attempted to offer electricity to rural areas. To finance this enterprise, he created a web of interlocking holding companies, the lowest level of which were electric utilities. At one time, he controlled more than 200 companies in 39 states and took in more than 10 percent of all money spent on electricity. Insull and his corporate structure were ruined in the 1929 stock market crash, but he had a role in the creation and growth of many of the utility companies still serving their markets today.

# The breakup of Alcoa (1945)

Alcoa had 80 percent of the aluminum producing capacity in the United States before World War II. The government subsidized competitors, and Alcoa's loss in an antitrust case in 1945 required that it sell some plants and provide proprietary information to competitors. By 1960, even though competitors had taken over half the market, Alcoa's sales had tripled.

# The Dodgers' Chavez Ravine deal (1957)

Walter O'Malley bought the Brooklyn Dodgers in 1950 for between $700,000 and $1 million. His son Peter sold it in 1957 to Rupert Murdoch for between $300 and $350 million, the most ever for a sports franchise. The defining event in creating this value was O'Malley's decision to move the Dodgers from Brooklyn to Los Angeles. Stymied in his attempt to get a favorable deal on Brooklyn land to build a stadium to replace

Ebbets Field, O'Malley grasped the possibilities of having the Los Angeles market to himself. Starved for big-league sports, Los Angeles agreed to pay millions of dollars in improvements and, to get O'Malley to build a state-of-the-art stadium, give O'Malley 300 acres of extremely valuable land in Chavez Ravine. The deal made it possible for O'Malley to build one of baseball's best facilities, Dodger Stadium, and one of its best franchises. It also paved the way for numerous land-grabbing, city-hopping sports deals.

# Howard Hughes' purchase of the Desert Inn (1967)

In 1966, Hughes, by then a recluse, arranged to take over the top floor of the Desert Inn for 10 days. When he refused to leave, management complained that he was costing the hotel significant revenue because it could not honor its commitments to lodge high rollers in the suites on the top floor. Hughes, flush from the recent sale of his TWA stock for $550 million, responded by buying the hotel for $13 million. Upon learning of certain tax benefits in connection with the purchase, he sent his lieutenant, Robert Maheu, on a buying spree, eventually purchasing the Sands, the Castaways, the Silver Slipper, the Frontier, and the Landmark, most of which had huge parcels of vacant land. He recognized that he was, indeed, costing the Desert Inn gaming revenue by taking up the whole top floor, so he moved to a hotel in the Bahamas—in 1970, nearly four years later. His purchases changed the Las Vegas landscape and were considered instrumental in the transition from mob ownership to corporate ownership of casinos.

# Xerox acquisition of Scientific Data Systems (1969)

Xerox paid $920 million, a huge price at the time, for Scientific Data Systems (SDS), an obscure computer company in an attempt to get into the computer business. SDS proved worthless, and Xerox wrote off the entire investment by 1975. In response, however, Xerox created the Palo Alto Research Center (PARC) to develop computer technology internally. Although Xerox failed to capitalize on PARC's achievements, it can claim credit for developing the first laser printer, the first desktop computer, the first user-friendly operating system, and programming that paved the way for networking and JAVA.

# Berkshire Hathaway's purchase of Washington Post Co. stock (1973)

During the market downturn of 1973 and 1974, Warren Buffett picked up $11 million in Washington Post Co. stock, eventually a 16-percent stake. Even though the stock has been stagnant the last few years, Berkshire's stake is now worth nearly $1 billion.

# International Nickel's hostile takeover of ESB (1974)

International Nickel (INCO) gave ESB three-hours' notice before launching the tender offer of $28 per share, a 44-percent premium to the stock's prior close. United Aircraft responded with a friendly bid of $34. INCO replied with bids of $36, $38, and then $41. ESB agreed to be taken over; this was the first instance of a hostile takeover. Shareholders received a 110-percent premium to the trading price prior to the takeover activity.

# Atlantic Richfield's acquisition of Anaconda Copper (1978)

Atlantic Richfield (ARCO) bought Anaconda during the oil industry's diversification kick in the 1970s. ARCO spent millions to modernize operations and open new mines, increasing its bet on the cyclical, capital-intensive mining industry. The company lost $315 million on the division in 1982 and, upon unloading Anaconda's operations in 1985, took a write-off of $785 million.

## American Express' investment in Warner Amex Cable (1979)

Strapped for cash to expand, Warner Communications sold American Express a half-interest in its cable system for $150 million. The enterprise, although trying to expand rapidly, was poorly managed and still under-financed. American Express sold its share back to Warner in 1985 for $385 million, actually managing a profit. With sales, spin-offs, and public offerings, however, Warner's cable assets were valued within a year at $1.6 billion.

## Exxon's acquisition of Reliance Electric (1979)

Exxon bought Reliance Electric for $1.4 billion in order, it claimed, to provide the manufacturing capability for an energy-saving motor it claimed would save one million barrels of oil per day when mass produced. It abandoned the device after two years, upon discovering it was too expensive to build on a large scale. After spending a lot of money to develop Reliance's operations, it sold the company to a management group in 1986 for $1.35 billion.

## United Artists' production of *Heaven's Gate* (1980)

United Artists, reeling from the loss of key executives to form Orion Pictures, had to do anything necessary to lock up Michael Cimino's—director of Academy Award–winning *The Deer Hunter*—next picture. It ceded complete control of the film to Cimino, who spent nearly four times the $11 million budgeted for the film. *The New York Times* called the indulgent, unwatchable film a "total disaster." With marketing costs, United Artists lost about $50 million. Corporate parent Transamerica dumped the company, which has never really recovered.

## Bendix-Martin Marietta-United Technologies-Allied Corp. (1982)

This was the first juicy news story of the deal-hungry 1980s. It introduced a new breed of young hotshot investment bankers, who reveled in creating complex maneuvers with names such as "Pac Man," "dead man's trigger," and "poison pill." It also introduced romantic intrigue into big deals; William Agee, Bendix's wunderkind CEO, was being advised by his former assistant and wife, Mary Cunningham. The deal began when Bendix made a hostile $43 per share (later increased to $45 per share) offer to Martin Marietta. Martin Marietta responded by enlisting United Technologies to assist it in buying Bendix, for $75 per share. Bendix later brought in Allied Corp., which bought Bendix for $85 per share.

## Quaker Oats' acquisition of Stokely-Van Camp (1983)

Quaker paid $220 million to acquire the owner of Gatorade and other brands. Gatorade became Quaker's growth engine and now has annual sales of $1.5 billion and an 80-percent share of the sports drink market. The creator of Gatorade, Dr. Michael Cade, originally developed the drink for University of Florida (the Gators) football players. He sold it to Stokely-Van Camp in a royalty deal that pays him and the University of Florida about $25 million a year.

## Texaco's acquisition of Getty Oil (1984)

This $10 billion deal was one of the largest takeovers of the 1980s and was complicated by Getty's prior agreement to be acquired by Pennzoil. Pennzoil's suit against Texaco in a Texas state court for interference with contract resulted in the largest-ever jury verdict, punitive damage award, and bankruptcy. The deal-making community regarded the proceedings as a circus that ignored how deals of this magnitude involving public companies were negotiated. Victorious plaintiff's attorney Joe Jamail supposedly made $300 million for representing Pennzoil.

# The Bass brothers' purchase and sale of Texaco stock (1984)

While Texaco was taking over Getty, the Bass brothers bought nearly 10 percent of Texaco's stock. To keep them from taking over Texaco, the company paid them a premium for their stock. They made $450 million on the short-term investment.

# Forstmann Little's LBO of Topps (1984)

Forstmann Little has avoided higher-profile hostile deals and thus never acquired the notoriety of KKR. The company is virtually unknown to the public but, in deal-making circles, is admired for its acumen. It arranged the LBO of Topps using $10 million in cash and $90 million in debt. It took Topps public again in 1987, paid all shareholders (including itself) a $140 million special dividend, and exited in 1991, having made about $700 million.

# The attempted takeover of Disney (1984)

Roy Disney, son of one of the founders of the company (referred to by Walt Disney as "my idiot nephew"), determined either to increase the value of Disney's dwindling stock or sell out. Raiders Saul Steinberg and the Bass brothers threatened takeovers, causing the stock price to rise. Although Steinberg was paid greenmail (a premium price, not offered to other shareholders, to sell out and abandon its takeover), Disney remained independent, but brought in a new management team, headed by Michael Eisner (who brought in former Paramount colleague Jeffrey Katzenberg to revive the Disney studio) and Frank Wells. (Steinberg and Disney later had to pay $45 million in damages to investors.) They expanded the theme parks and aggressively increased prices, developed the Disney brand name and sold huge amounts of Disney merchandise, restored Disney's animation department to the forefront of the movie industry, turned the studio into a big money maker, and developed numerous ingenious financing techniques to limit risk in all these steps. Even with missteps in the late 1990s and a slumping stock price, the market value of the company increased from $2 billion in 1984 to $70 billion in 2000.

# Jeffrey Katzenberg's employment contract with Disney (1984)

Katzenberg joined Michael Eisner when he left Paramount Studios to become Disney CEO. Katzenberg became Disney's studio chief. Denied a stock-option deal like the one that later enriched Eisner, he agreed to compensation including 2 percent of all profits from projects made during his tenure. Movie accounting being what it is, the deal was not especially lucrative for several years. By 1994, it began paying off. Katzenberg left Disney when he realized he would not succeed Eisner as CEO. He had to sue Disney to collect the remainder of his contract—it was one of those "perpetuity" deals, which always seem to be bonanzas. (See the deal profiles on the Spirits of St. Louis and Reagan and SAG in Chapters 7 and 10, respectively.) Disney paid Katzenberg $117 million in 1997 and settled for the rest, estimated to be an additional $150 million, in 1999.

# General Electric's acquisition of RCA (1985)

General Electric (GE) paid $6.3 billion for RCA, which had electronics, communications, and entertainment operations, most notably the NBC network. GE essentially got NBC for free. It combined its consumer electronics and defense businesses with RCA's, and sold them to Thomson and Martin Marietta, respectively, for a total of $3.8 billion in cash plus Thomson's medical equipment business. NBC's profits have fluctuated tremendously, but it could be worth several times what GE paid for the entire transaction.

# Capital Cities Communication's acquisition of ABC (1986)

Capital Cities Communication (Cap Cities), a profitable but relatively unknown collection of local television stations and newspapers, shocked the investment community when it acquired ABC, four times its size, for $3.5 billion. Cap Cities' top officers, Thomas Murphy and David Burke, along with shareholder Warren Buffett, knew what they were doing. Cap Cities imposed financial discipline and rode the wave of media-merger activity in the late 1980s and 1990s, finally selling out to Disney for $19 billion in 1996.

## Burroughs' merger with Sperry to create Unisys (1986)

Burroughs merged with Sperry in a $4.8 billion deal, with the goal of creating a computer giant to compete with IBM and DEC. After forming Unisys, the merger merely magnified the weaknesses of both companies. After two good years of earnings, the results and Unisys' stock price fell apart. It took more than a decade for the stock price to return to 1987 levels, and Unisys had to take more than $2 billion in write-offs in connection with the merger.

## LBO of Macy's (1986)

Macy's' CEO Edward Finkelstein led this $3.6 billion LBO. The deal was based on overly optimistic projections, and the company choked on its huge debt-servicing costs. Finkelstein even added debt after the buyout, buying some assets from Robert Campeau–led Federated (after previously trying to acquire the whole company). Macy's filed for bankruptcy in January 1992 and was purchased by Federated (after it completed its own bankruptcy) in 1994.

## General Electric's acquisition of Kidder Peabody (1986)

GE purchased brokerage-firm Kidder Peabody for $600 million. The purchase quickly turned sour when Kidder's head of mergers and acquisitions, Martin Siegel, pled guilty to charges of insider trading, and Kidder paid a large civil fine. Kidder was repeatedly linked with securities scandals and lost $300 million in 1994. GE sold most of Kidder to Paine Webber that same year. GE lost between $1.5 and $2 billion on the firm during its eight years of ownership.

## Ivan Boesky's plea bargain (1986)

Boesky pled guilty to insider trading and agreed in November 1986 to disgorge $50 million in profits and pay a $50 million fine. Before announcing the deal, however, the government allowed Boesky time to liquidate much of his investment portfolio, free of the panic selling that occurred—and to which other investors were exposed—when his guilty plea was announced. The government has also taken its lumps for soft plea deals given to Dennis Levine (who paid no fine and had to repay only the profits the government was able to find in one Bahamian bank) and Michael Milken (although Milken paid $650 million, he was still left with a substantial fortune; the government never figured out the amount of equity he had stashed away for himself, his family, and his foundation from hundreds of LBOs, many of which later became valuable public companies).

## General Motors' buyout of Ross Perot's stock (1986)

In 1984, General Motors (GM) bought Ross Perot's company, EDS, and issued a tracking stock, GM class E, that paid dividends based on EDS's performance. Perot, from his seat on GM's board of directors, became a vocal critic of the company, which was squandering its leadership in the auto industry. To shut Perot up, GM bought out Perot for $750 million, roughly twice the trading value of his class E stock. In exchange, Perot had to resign his board seat and refrain from making negative comments about GM; failure to obey would require that Perot pay a $7.5 million "fine" to GM.

## ZZZZ Best's defrauding of financial professionals (1987)

For a few years, Barry Minkow and his carpet cleaning company, ZZZZ Best, appeared to be a Great American Success Story. At 20 years old, Minkow was worth more than $100 million and his company was growing by leaps and bounds. Drexel Burnham Lambert was preparing to underwrite a $40 million offering so the company could acquire a larger, established carpet cleaning company. The whole thing, however, was made up. Minkow and his buddies defrauded Drexel, the lawyers, the accountants, and public investors by faking an entry into the building-restoration business. They made up tens of thousands of pages of invoices and permits, bribed third parties to vouch for their abilities, and even rented and paid for the restoration of buildings to show the professionals their "work." Two days before the debt offering closed, reports of a minor, unrelated credit card fraud caused ZZZZ Best stock to plummet and brought out fringe players who disclosed the fraud. Minkow and his associates went to prison and gave a big black eye to the financial community.

# Chrysler's acquisition
# of American Motors Corporation (1987)

Chrysler bought American Motors Corporation (AMC) for $1.5 billion, a price that was a bargain for acquiring the Jeep platform. Developing a new vehicle from scratch would have cost several times the purchase price, and Jeep immediately became one of Chrysler's best-selling and highest margin lines. Especially with its 1992 redesign, the Jeep Cherokee remains one of the best-selling sport utility vehicles.

# Vanango River's LBO of the Chicago,
# Missouri & Western Railroad (1987)

This was one of the most over-leveraged and unsuccessful deals ever, escaping the radar screen of most deal aficionados because of its size. Illinois Gulf Central sold this short-line railroad to Vanango River Corp. for $85 million. Of that, only $50,000 was equity (and that amount was borrowed as well). It went bankrupt in a year, and the assets were auctioned off for a fraction of the purchase price.

## KKR's LBO of Jim Walter Industries (1987)

To assure that financing of the acquisition could be completed, some of the debt had a floating interest rate, to assure that it would trade at par (that is, face value). As the asbestos lawsuits against Jim Walters Industries and some of its subsidiaries rose following the deal, it became impossible to set a rate that would get the bonds to trade at par. KKR got legal opinions prior to the deal that it could limit the exposure of the entire company to asbestos liability, but no one seemed to count on the Texas courts' interpretation of the law. Asset sales became impossible and the company had to file for bankruptcy.

## The LBO of Southland Corp. (1987)

Southland, 7-Eleven's parent company, was one of the first high profile junk bond–financed LBOs to topple from the weight of its debt. The Thompson family, which originally founded the company, offered $4.9 billion, a huge premium to the stock price, to discourage competing offers and maintain control. To raise $2 billion in unsecured debt, the Thompsons had to offer 17-percent interest. In three years, they were forced to sell 70 percent of the company for $430 million to Japanese licensees to avoid bankruptcy.

## Shearson Lehman's acquisition of E.F. Hutton (1987)

Shearson, majority-owned by American Express at the time, bought Hutton for $1 billion after the 1987 stock market crash, expecting to pay a bargain price for adding a network of retail brokers to sell Shearson products. The price was at a low, however, because Hutton was emerging from an embarrassing check-kiting scandal. (Hutton persistently—over an 18-month period and for hundreds of millions of dollars—wrote checks for larger sums than it had in its checking accounts, shuffling the funds from one bank to another. This enabled it, in effect, to overdraw its accounts, thus basically getting interest-free loans.) It also turned out Hutton was thinly capitalized, had monstrous overhead, and had little in the way of financial controls. American Express eventually spun off the profitable Lehman Brothers segment of Shearson, and tried to throw money and Shearson Hutton to stem the losses ($750 million in 1990 alone). In 1994, Sandy Weill's Primerica bought all the Shearson Hutton assets for $1 billion.

# Donald Trump's purchase of the Plaza Hotel (1988)

Donald Trump's fortunes can be neatly summarized by his transactions in tony New York hotel properties. In 1985, he bought the St. Moritz for $72 million; he sold it for $180 million in 1988. That same year, he bought the Plaza Hotel for $400 million. (He installed his then-wife, Ivana, as president of the hotel, for "one dollar a year and all the dresses she can buy.") Trump put up no equity, borrowing more than $400 million, $125 million of which he personally guaranteed. Between $50 and $150 million were spent on renovations. Although he later claimed he could sell the hotel for $800 million, he gave up 49 percent in 1992 to creditors in exchange for their canceling his personal guarantee. The creditors sold the hotel in 1995 for $325 million.

# Kodak's acquisition of Sterling Drug (1988)

Kodak bought Sterling for $5.1 billion, claiming some kind of synergies no one could figure out and which never materialized. As with the much-derided Mobil acquisition of Montgomery Ward (and Container Corp.), it was part of a diversification strategy that never worked, yet still made a profit. Kodak sold Sterling piecemeal for more than $6 billion in 1994. The debt servicing ate up the profits, but barrels of ink were spent complaining about Kodak's folly, even after it essentially broke even.

# Robert Maxwell's acquisition of Macmillan Publishing (1988)

Maxwell and his corporate entity, Maxwell Communications, won a contested takeover fight for Macmillan by offering $2.6 billion, a half billion more than the competing bidder. Maxwell, during the next couple years, struggled under the huge debt load of this and other acquisitions. Maxwell died mysteriously, by drowning, in November 1991. It turned out that he had entered into numerous fraudulent transactions to hide the financial condition of his assets: pledging assets as collateral in multiple deals, raiding pension funds, altering records to give an appearance of profitability. Maxwell's empire went bankrupt a month after his death. Paramount bought Macmillan in 1993 for $553 million.

# KKR's LBO of RJR Nabisco (1989)

This $25 billion deal was the largest takeover ever for a number of years and is still the largest leveraged acquisition. The 1989 $5 billion junk-bond offering to finance the deal was Drexel Burnham Lambert's last hurrah. The deal itself has been immortalized in countless magazine cover stories, several books, and a movie. In the end, KKR did little better for its investors than break even.

# Mitsubishi Estate's purchase of Rockefeller Center (1989)

Comprised of 12 Art Deco buildings in Manhattan built by John D. Rockefeller, Jr. at the height of the Depression, Rockefeller Center was probably the most famous of the "trophy properties" acquired by Japanese interests in the late 1980s—and the biggest failure. Mitsubishi bought an 80-percent interest from a public real estate investment trust (REIT) for $1.4 billion. A fall in real estate values doomed Mitsubishi's highly leveraged structure (it owed $1.3 billion on a mortgage held by the REIT). Mitsubishi simply stopped paying on the mortgage when rents went down, walking away from a billion dollar investment.

# Berkshire Hathaway's purchase of USAir preferred stock (1989)

Warren Buffett *almost* lost money with this deal. Warren Buffett, as previously described, has become one of the world's richest individuals by following a careful, rigorous analysis of all his investments. During the 1980s, he made several deals to buy stock in companies threatened with takeovers. In 1989, he bought $358 million in USAir preferred stock. He almost immediately realized the investment was a mistake. Although his company, Berkshire Hathaway, had some protection as a result of its senior security status, Buffett made a serious mistake in his analysis: He did not account for the fact that USAir's historical results would not likely continue because, in the then-recently deregulated environment, airlines with higher costs, such as USAir, would suffer competitively. USAir lost market share, and then its profit margins shrank. At the end of 1994, Berkshire wrote down the investment to $89 million. Results improved in 1995, however, and Berkshire marked it back up to 60 percent of par. Buffett tried to sell the preferred stock at 50 percent of what Berkshire paid but received no takers. That was lucky for Berkshire, because USAir continued its recover, and actually profited on the investment.

# Time, Inc.'s acquisition of Warner Communications (1989)

This deal was the crowning achievement of Warner CEO Steven Ross, capping a career in which he built a chain of funeral homes into the world's leading entertainment company. Although Time acquired Warner, Ross outmaneuvered the Time executives and maintained control of the larger enterprise. He also landed a compensation package worth more than $200 million.

# The failed LBO of UAL Corp. (1989)

Some top managers of UAL, the parent company of United Airlines, offered a giant premium to acquire the company. Bankers and advisors signed on because of the possibility of huge fees, but no one would actually put up money at the insane price proposed of $300 per share. Announcement of the deal's cancellation caused the whole stock market to plummet and helped usher in the bear market of 1989 and 1990.

## The Herschel Walker trade (1989)

This trade ranks as one of the great giveaways in sports history. The Dallas Cowboys traded Walker, a star running back, to the Minnesota Vikings in exchange for five players and eight draft choices. The Cowboys used those choices to pick up Emmitt Smith, along with other players who formed the core of the team that won three Super Bowls between 1992 and 1995. By the end of Walker's three-year contract with the Vikings, he was playing only part-time and failed to gain 1,000 yards. Minnesota, finishing 0-1 in the playoffs in those three seasons, cut Walker after the 1991 season.

## The Kansas City Royals' free-agent signing of Mark Davis (1989)

The free-agency era in professional sports has spawned countless deals where star players received long-term contracts, only to turn out to be busts. Mark Davis is one of the most storied examples. A mediocre pitcher for several years with the San Francisco Giants, Davis had two great years as a relief pitcher San Diego in 1988 and 1989. In 1989, he saved 44 games and won the National League Cy Young Award. The Kansas City Royals won a bidding war for Davis, agreeing to pay $13 million for four years, a huge amount at the time for a relief pitcher. Davis never regained his form from the 1988–89 season. He saved only seven games in nearly three years with the Royals. The Atlanta Braves picked him up in 1992. (Their general manager, John Schuelholz, was responsible for originally signing Davis to the Royals.) After a few undistinguished games, the Braves released Davis, who pitched ineffectively for three more teams before retiring after the 1997 season.

# Barry Diller's purchase of QVC (1992)

In early 1992, Barry Diller resigned as chairman of Fox, Inc. to find a media property he could own as well as run. In December, he was invited to QVC, the home-shopping channel. He purchased 3 percent for $25 million. After significantly increasing the profile of the company—making a highly publicized but unsuccessful attempt to buy Paramount, which he once ran, and in the midst of reaching a deal to buy CBS—the men who brought Diller in (John Malone of TCI and Brian Roberts of Comcast) bought him out. Comcast and TCI bought the rest of QVC in 1994 in a deal valuing the company at $2.5 billion. Diller made $100 million in less than two years, but he lost the opportunity to realize his goal of owning a network.

# Paul Allen's sale of AOL stock (1994)

Paul Allen, a cofounder of Microsoft, was an early investor in AOL and held a 25-percent stake. When AOL turned down his offer in 1994 to buy more, he sold his shares for a profit of $100 million. By doing that, he missed out on a phenomenal five-year run-up. At the end of 1999, that stake would be worth $33 billion.

# Viacom's acquisition of Blockbuster Entertainment (1994)

In another of Sumner Redstone's moves to build Viacom into an entertainment conglomerate, it acquired Blockbuster Entertainment for $8.4 billion. Cash flow dried up, inventory had to be written down, and the executive suite became a revolving door. Losing $300 million per year, the public reaction to a partial spin-off of the company to shareholders in 1999 was, understandably, lukewarm. After six months as a public company, Blockbuster's market capitalization was a puny $2.5 billion.

# Banc One's acquisition
# of First USA (1997)

Banc One grew into a banking powerhouse through acquisitions. Its last several moves—along with those of other acquisitive banks—appear to have been blunders. Banc One acquired First USA for $9.7 billion, more than five times book value and a 43-percent premium to its stock price. Banc One promised First USA would grow by 20 percent per year for the next several years, an impossible feat given its size and the competitiveness of its credit card business. In 1999, the First Card division enticed holders with teaser rates, hiking rates as soon as possible or if holders were even one day late with a payment. These tactics lowered margins and increased attrition, leading to a negative earnings report from Bank One (renamed after its $30 billion merger with First Chicago), which caused its stock to plummet.

# NationsBank's acquisition
# of Barnet Banks (1997)

In 1997, NationsBank agreed to acquire Barnet Banks for $15.5 billion. This was, at the time, the biggest bank merger ever. (Merger mania in banking has since produced three larger mergers, including NationsBank's $60 billion merger with BankAmerica less than a year after this deal.) Based on the rich price—four times book value—and NationsBank's slumping stock price, the prognosis for the deal, especially in the short-term, does not look good. Especially telling is NationsBank CEO Hugh McColl's response to a question about whether prices for banks had become too high: "Let me ask the question another way: What is the price of not making an acquisition?"

# The proposed merger
# of AOL and Time Warner (2000)

Announced as the biggest deal ever, this merger would combine the largest entertainment company with the largest Internet company. The combined market value of the two companies would be more than $250 billion, though the initial investor reaction was so negative that it knocked $20 billion off AOL's market capitalization. Although there are still numerous regulatory issues to be addressed as of August 2000, and AOL's stock has fallen an additional 20 percent, the parties continue to move forward to close the deal.

# AFTERWORD

It would be cliché to say that we are at a critical juncture in the history of corporate transactions. We are *always* at a critical juncture, as these highlights illustrate:

- In 1965, it seemed that the inevitable trend of business was to conglomerate.
- In 1970, following the demise of LTV and similar trouble with other conglomerates, the deal business was supposedly dead.
- In 1985, new, aggressive operators dominated the corporate landscape—leveraged buyout artists, investment bankers—and every established enterprise quaked in fear of being taken over or threatened with a takeover by these upstarts.
- In 1989, the purchase of trophy properties such as Rockefeller Center and Pebble Beach by groups of Japanese investors was viewed as a trend toward domination by foreign investors.
- In 1990, the demise of Drexel Burnham and Michael Milken, along with the negative publicity from the RJR Nabisco LBO and the failure of such takeover operators as Robert Campeau and William Farley, killed the market for leveraged transactions, and a revised history of the 1980s was quickly being written, focusing on greed, excess, and illegal acts. (The Japanese "invasion" was over, due to economic collapse in Japan and poor judgment in acquisitions in the U.S.)
- In 1995, the wave of media mergers signaled a communications revolution, where only the largest and most diversified companies could survive. Such thinking immediately followed in the banking industry.

▸   In 1999, the Internet Revolution had shifted all deal making focus on bringing nascent Web companies public, regardless of the quality of the companies, their management, their business plans, or their likelihood of achieving profitability. The market eagerly bought up these stocks in their IPOs and in the aftermarket, turning these companies—often little more than a concept and a Web site—into multibillion dollar enterprises.

Right now, most of those big bank mergers have failed to deliver to shareholders the expected returns. It would be premature, however, to declare such mergers "dead"; AT&T is being punished by the stock market for failing to deliver from its acquisition binge, but that has not stopped a wave of mergers in the telecommunications business. The current industry thinking, despite AT&T's struggles, is that your future is bleak unless you own a piece of everything:  business long-distance, cable, Internet, wireless, and so on.

The wave of Internet IPOs and outrageously valued mergers has slowed to a trickle. The inability of most of these new public enterprises to demonstrate profitability has soured the public on these issues. The next wave of deal making activity may occur as established "old economy" companies pick up the carcasses of these unprofitable Web companies at bargain prices.

In the end, the principles described in this book, rather than the Bright Idea of the Moment, ordain the success or failure of these deals. Smart people with good ideas will prosper, and everyone else will eventually fail. The market is very efficient that way, at least in the long term. (In the short run, any fool can buy a ticket and take a ride.)

The latest developing example of this is the proposed merger of Vivendi and Seagram. The participants in this deal, and much of the popular press, are hailing this deal as the creation of a media powerhouse. If you give any credence to the principles in this book, you have to be skeptical. Vivendi is a conglomerate of French media properties and other wildly disparate businesses (such as a water utility) and completely unknown in the U.S. Seagram has taken some very successful, unglamorous, cash-generating businesses (spirits, stock ownership in DuPont) and tried to transform itself into a media company. By spending enough, it has succeeded in becoming a force in the music business; $15 or $20 billion will get you that much. The price it paid—in cash and in stock, giving up stakes in DuPont and Time Warner, supporting many money-losing assets that came with the music acquisitions—has been far too high.

Edgar Bronfman, Jr. is lucky to have found someone to bail himself out of this situation. That he could build Seagram this way over the past decade and get his shareholders out at a premium can only be proof of the continued validity of the Greater Fool Theory. But if he overpaid and is in turn overpaid for his company, how can the enterprise offering this bounty survive? Jean-Marie Messier, Vivendi's CEO, is strutting about these days like a global media titan, but it seems unlikely he can succeed. It is likely, to complete the deal, that Vivendi will sell Seagram's spirits business, the only really profitable part of the company.

Of course, for sheer size, Vivendi-Seagram pales in comparison to the biggest deal of 2000, the proposed merger of America Online and Time Warner. Although the combined enterprise will be a dominant player in the Internet (AOL) and cable (Time Warner owns several cable networks and has access to millions of homes), not to mention have Time Warner's substantial assets in movies, publishing, and music, there is also reason to be skeptical about the ultimate success of this venture.

Neither Steve Case, CEO of AOL, or Gerald Levin, CEO of Time Warner, could ever be said to be strongly in control of these already far-flung enterprises. AOL periodically suffers the growing pangs of a leading, aggressive player in a hot new industry; missteps are to be expected. The company has only recently started showing a profit. Time Warner, a major player in so many aspects of the capricious entertainment business, would almost by its nature have internecine power struggles, political and regulatory issues, and some high-profile failures. Neither company has a grasp of its subsidiary operations like Jack Welch, CEO of General Electric, does. Nearly all of GE's business segments are business leaders and each seems headed by an executive who, if necessary, could run the whole company.

It seems inevitable that whatever problems AOL and Time Warner periodically have will increase, rather than decrease, as the enterprise doubles in size. It has never really been proven—and the exceptions tend to prove the rule—that vertical integration benefits the modern corporation. Most of those big bank mergers of a few years back haven't proven it. Disney has yet to demonstrate any great benefits from its acquisition of Capital Cities Communications and has been criticized for spreading its management too thin and taking on a television network, in an era where the power of networks is waning. Viacom's acquisition binge—Blockbuster and Paramount—has not brought about any great synergies, and the stock market has been unimpressed by the results of the larger enterprise.

Of course, AOL Time Warner may succeed. GE acquired NBC as part of its RCA acquisition in 1985 and, despite some problems along the way, that has worked.

Deal making does not—other than the fees to advisors and bonuses to executives—create value. At best, it reveals value. Jack Welch, for example, has defended the purchase of NBC because GE's smart deal making allowed it, in effect, to get NBC for free. He told *Fortune*, "We combined RCA's consumer electronics business with ours and traded them off to Thomson in exchange for its medical equipment business—that fit right into our stuff—and $800 million in cash. Then we put RCA's defense business with ours and sold that to Martin Marietta for $3 billion. And we essentially ended up owning what was left—NBC—for free."

There will always be someone with a new financing technique or a new theory of corporate combinations. There will always be people who flock to the newest toy and declare it to be revolutionary. But, in the end, it's an evolution, not a revolution. The intelligent people who work in the corporate world will always have new ideas for deal making. The keys to success, however, never change: brains, tenacity, flexibility, foresight.

And that's the way it should be.

*September 2000*
*Scottsdale, AZ*

# BIBLIOGRAPHY

This book relies heavily on hundreds of articles from business and financial publications, especially *Forbes, Fortune,* and *Business Week*. The daily reporting of big business deals by the financial press, including *The New York Times, The Wall Street Journal,* and the *Los Angeles Times*, likewise, provided contemporaneous accounts from which many of the profiles are drawn.

Akst, Daniel. *Wonder Boy: The Kid Who Swindled Wall Street.* Charles Scribner & Sons, 1990.

Allen, Michael Patrick. *The Founding Fortunes: The New Anatomy of the Super-Rich Families in America.* Truman Talley Books, 1987.

Anders, George. *Merchants of Debt: KKR and the Mortgaging of American Business.* Basic Books, 1992.

Bach, Steven. *Final Cut: Dreams and Disaster in the Making of* Heaven's Gate. Outpost Productions, 1985.

Baker, George and George Smith. *The New Financial Capitalists: Kohlberg Kravis Roberts and the Creation of Corporate Value.* Cambridge University Press, 1998.

Bianco, Anthony. *The Reichmanns: Family, Faith, Fortune, and the Empire of Olympia & York.* Times Books, 1997.

Bronson, Po. *The Nudist on the Late Shift and Other True Tales of Silicon Valley.* Random House, 1999.

Bruck, Connie. *The Predators' Ball: The Inside Story of Drexel Burnham and the Rise of the Junk Bond Raiders.* Penguin USA, 1989.

Chancellor, Edward. *Devil Take the Hindmost: A History of Financial Speculation.* Farrar, Straus and Giroux, 1999.

Cringely, Robert. *Accidental Empires: How the Boys of Silicon Valley Make Their Millions, Battle Foreign Competition, and Still Can't Get a Date.* Addison-Wesley Publishing Co., 1992.

Creamer, Robert. *Babe: The Legend Comes to Life.* Simon & Schuster, 1974.

Griffin, Nancy and Kim Masters. *Hit & Run: How Jon Peters and Peter Guber Took Sony for a Ride in Hollywood.* Simon & Schuster, 1996.

Gross, Daniel (Ed.). *Forbes: Greatest Business Stories of All Time.* John Wiley & Sons, 1996.

Johnston, Moira. *Takeover: The New Wall Street Warriors: the Men, the Money, the Impact.* Arbor House, 1986.

Kilpatrick, Andrew. *Of Permanent Value: The Story of Warren Buffett.* McGraw-Hill, 1998.

Love, John. *McDonald's: Behind the Arches.* Bantam Books, 1986.

Lowenstein, Roger. *Buffett: The Making of an American Capitalist.* Random House, 1995.

Madsen, Axel. *The Deal Maker: How William C. Durant Made General Motors.* John Wiley & Sons, 1999.

Pickens, T. Boone. *Boone.* Random House, 1988.

Pluto, Terry. *Loose Balls: The Short, Wild Life of the American Basketball Association—As Told by the Players, Coaches, and Movers and Shakers Who Made it Happen.* Simon & Schuster, 1990.

Strouse, Jean. *Morgan: American Financier.* Random House, 1999.

Ritter, Lawrence. *The Glory of Their Times: The Story of the Early Days of Baseball Told by the Men Who Played It.* Vintage Books, 1985.

Rothschild, John. *Going for Broke: How Robert Campeau Bankrupted the Retail Industry, Jolted the Junk Bond Market, and Brought the Booming Eighties to a Crashing Halt.* Simon & Schuster, 1991.

Sirower, Mark. *The Synergy Trap: How Companies Lose the Acquisition Game.* The Free Press, 1997.

Sobel, Robert. *When Giants Stumble: Classic Business Blunders and How to Avoid Them.* Prentice Hall, 1999.

Sloan, Allan. *Three Plus One Equals Billions: The Bendix-Martin Marietta War.* Arbor House, 1983.

*Sun Tzu: The Art of War.* Translation of Samuel Griffith. Oxford University Press, 1963.

Taylor, John. *Storming the Magic Kingdom: Wall Street, the Raiders, and the Battle for Disney.* Knopf, 1987.

Wasserstein, Bruce. *Big Deal: The Battle for Control of America's Leading Corporations.* Warner Books, 1998.

# GLOSSARY

**Bridge loan**—In the takeover business, the temporary financing necessary to complete a deal promptly, while the acquirer obtains permanent financing. (See **Debt**.)

**Class action**—A legal action in which a few members of a group with common issues seek the court's permission to represent all members of the group, with the results of the case binding on all parties involved, whether or not actually named in the suit.

**Clayton Act**—The shorthand name for federal antitrust law designed primarily to prevent certain ownership or management interrelationships between companies. (See also **Sherman Act**.)

**Debt**—In the debt-driven deals of the 1980s, buyers typically employed numerous levels of debt to pay for their acquisitions. There were "bridge loans," short-term, high-interest loans designed to be replaced by permanent financing or, in some cases, from cash received from immediate asset sales. (The lender was typically the investment bank advising on the transaction and underwriting the financing. The high rate was to justify it putting its own money on the line, though the investment banks offering bridge loans often had more to win or lose—fees, bragging rights, future business—than the buyer.) The most controversial of the debt was the unsecured debt, sometimes called "junior" or "subordinated." This debt left the creditor little protection in the event of a bankruptcy, so it paid a high rate of interest or offered an "equity kicker" (see the following entry) to make it worth the creditor's while to lend the money.

*Equity kicker*—A portion of the equity given to a lender, in addition to repayment of principal, with interest, to induce the lender to make a loan.

*Equity sliver*—Many of the big 1980s takeovers were accomplished almost completely with debt, with the owners contributing very nominal equity. The standard LBO of the era had 10 percent equity and 90 percent debt, but many deal makers pushed the envelope, either putting up less than 10 percent equity or including in equity some funds borrowed from other sources. During that time, the amount of equity was usually the minimum required by the lenders, and lending to leveraged transactions was such lucrative business that it ended up being a race to the bottom.

*ESOP*—Employee stock ownership plan; ESOPs have certain tax advantages to promote employee ownership of company stock. In particular, banks lending to ESOPs get a tax break on the interest they collect on loaning money to ESOPs, which encourages the use of ESOPs in leveraged transactions.

*Greater Fool Theory*—An almost inevitable aspect of every new phase of American finance is that a good idea will be carried to an extreme so that the activity's profitability depends on finding new suckers. (The overheated market for new Internet companies during 1999 is the most recent example.)

*Greenmail*—A particularly odious takeover defense in which the target buys back the prospective acquirer's stock for a premium.

*IPO*—Initial public offering; the first sale of a company's stock to public stockholders.

*Junk bond*—A shorthand term for debt rated below "investment grade." Rating agencies such as Standard & Poors and Moody's provide widely followed ratings of the creditworthiness of corporate debtors. Once the debt reaches a certain level of risk, rating agencies deem it below "investment grade."

*LBO*—Leveraged buyout; the acquisition of a company paid for primarily with debt.

*Leaseback*—The process of selling an asset and then leasing back its use from the new owner. This was used as a technique to finance acquisitions in the 1980s when the target company had substantial hard assets (such as factories and other real estate).

***Lockup***—A takeover defense designed to discourage competitive bidding. After the target company makes a deal with a potential acquirer, it gives the acquirer some benefit, either money or assets. The lockup makes it more expensive for the competing bidder to make a topping bid, because it also has to pay the price of the lockup.

***M&A***—Mergers and acquisitions.

***Pac Man defense***—A rarely used takeover defense from the 1980s in which the target company tries to acquire the prospective buyer.

***Paid-in-kind equity***—A form of debt where the interest would be paid in shares of the company rather than cash, offered by the acquirer when the price of a deal became so high that financing for a portion of it became completely unavailable. Although in some 1980s takeovers this form of payment turned out to be valuable, its presence in the financing scheme signaled that debt coverage was very thin.

***Poison pill***—A takeover defense now in place in nearly all large publicly traded companies. The actual name is a "shareholder rights plan." A poison pill takes effect when anyone who acquires more than a set percentage of the company's stock (15 or 20 percent). The remaining shareholders acquire the right to sell their stock back to the company for an enormous premium. Presumably, this would wreck the company, so a prospective acquirer would not try to acquire that much of the company's stock without the company's cooperation.

***Private***—As in "going private"; purchasing all the outstanding shares of a public company's stock.

***Proxy contest***—A dispute between a public company and a third party, in which the third party attempts to obtain representation on the company's board of directors (or influence the shareholder vote on some other matter). The "proxy" is the card sent to shareholders allowing them to vote on corporate matters (mostly the election of directors) without personally attending the shareholders' meeting.

***REIT***—Real estate investment trust.

***Run up***—A description of a short-term increase in a stock's price. When there are rumors that a company is going to be the subject of a takeover offer (or a merger where it will not be the surviving entity), the stock's price may rise quickly, as acquiring control of a corporation typically involves paying a control premium to its prior owners.

*S&L*—Savings and loan. Savings and loan associations chartered by the federal government are subject to federal regulation. The deregulation of the industry in the early 1980s allowed S&Ls to invest in virtually any risky venture, yet still retain federal deposit insurance.

*Sherman Act*—Federal antitrust laws whose best-known provisions prohibit certain behavior by monopolies and collusive behavior by competitors.

*Speculator*—Someone risking money on some short-term proposition in which the value of the object of the investment can fluctuate significantly. The difference between "investors" and "speculators" is never described in contemporary fashion. It seems that only hindsight can nominate a speculator.

*Vulture capitalist*—An investor who specializes in acquiring the assets (at a large discount) of troubled companies.

*White knight*—A friendly acquirer brought in by a target to buy the company (rather than a hostile acquirer).

*Write down*—Corporate financial statements include a balance sheet listing the company's assets and liabilities. When the value of an asset becomes impaired, accounting and regulatory rules require that its value be restated.

# INDEX

# ABOUT THE
# AUTHOR

In 15 years as a class-action lawyer, Michael Craig participated in many large business deals, as well as numerous large securities and consumer class actions. He now writes about big business and high finance for *Online Investor* and other magazines.